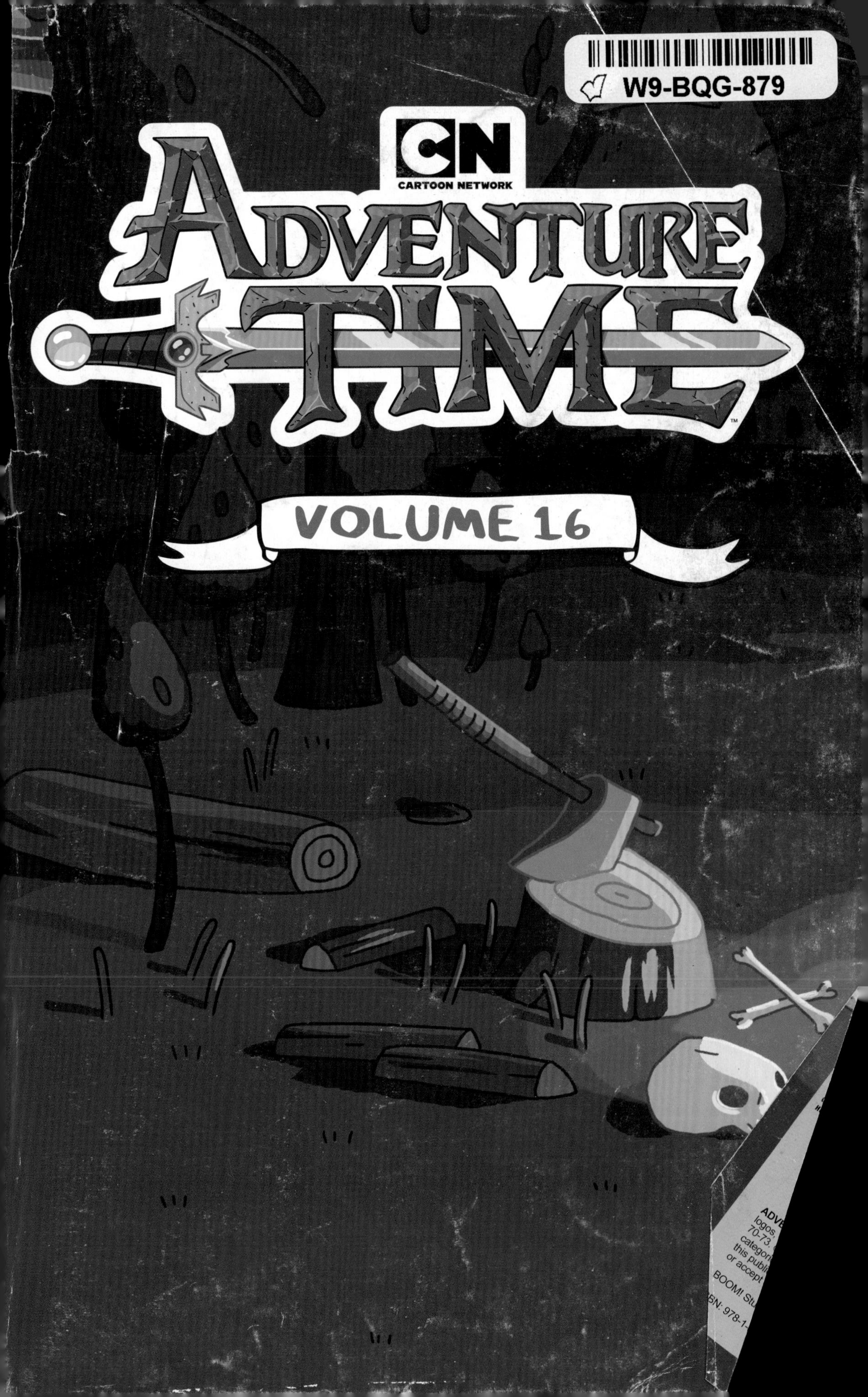
CN
CARTOON NETWORK
ADVENTURE TIME
VOLUME 16

ROSS RICHIE CEO & Founder • MATT GAGNON Editor-in-Chief • FILIP SABLIK President, Publishing & Marketing • STEPHEN CHRISTY President, Development • LANCE KREITER Vice President, Licensing & Merchandising
PHIL BARBARO Vice President, Finance & Human Resources • ARUNE SINGH Vice President, Marketing • BRYCE CARLSON Vice President, Editorial & Creative Strategy • SCOTT NEWMAN Manager, Production Design • KATE HENNING Manager, Operations
SPENCER SIMPSON Manager, Sales • SIERRA HAHN Executive Editor • JEANINE SCHAEFER Executive Editor • DAFNA PLEBAN Senior Editor • SHANNON WATTERS Senior Editor • ERIC HARBURN Senior Editor • WHITNEY LEOPARD Editor
CAMERON CHITTOCK Editor • CHRIS ROSA Editor • MATTHEW LEVINE Editor • SOPHIE PHILIPS-ROBERTS Assistant Editor • GAVIN GRONENTHAL Assistant Editor • MICHAEL MOCCIO Assistant Editor
AMANDA LaFRANCO Executive Assistant • KATALINA HOLLAND Editorial Administrative Assistant • JILLIAN CRAB Design Coordinator • MICHELLE ANKLEY Design Coordinator • KARA LEOPARD Production Designer • MARIE KRUPINA Production Designer
GRACE PARK Production Design Assistant • CHELSEA ROBERTS Production Design Assistant • ELIZABETH LOUGHRIDGE Accounting Coordinator • STEPHANIE HOCUTT Social Media Coordinator • JOSÉ MEZA Event Coordinator
HOLLY AITCHISON Operations Coordinator • MEGAN CHRISTOPHER Operations Assistant • RODRIGO HERNANDEZ Mailroom Assistant • MORGAN PERRY Direct Market Representative • CAT O'GRADY Marketing Assistant • CORNELIA TZANA Publicity Assistant

ADVENTURE TIME Volume Sixteen, December 2018. Published by KaBOOM!, a division of Boom Entertainment, Inc. ADVENTURE TIME, CARTOON NETWORK, the logos, and all related characters and elements are trademarks of and © Cartoon Network. (S18) Originally published in single magazine form as ADVENTURE TIME No. ™ & © Cartoon Network. (S17) All rights reserved. KaBOOM!™ and the KaBOOM! logo are trademarks of Boom Entertainment, Inc., registered in various countries and categories. All characters, events, and institutions depicted herein are fictional. Any similarity between any of the names, characters, persons, events, and/or institutions in this publication to actual names, characters, and persons, whether living or dead, events, and/or institutions is unintended and purely coincidental. KaBOOM! does not read or accept unsolicited submissions of ideas, stories, or artwork.

BOOM! Studios, 5670 Wilshire Boulevard, Suite 400, Los Angeles, CA 90036-5679. Printed in China. First Printing.

ISBN: 978-1-68415-272-8, eISBN: 978-1-64144-134-6

CREATED BY
# Pendleton Ward

WRITTEN BY
## Kevin Cannon

ILLUSTRATED BY
## Joey McCormick

COLORS BY
## Maarta Laiho

LETTERS BY
## Mike Fiorentino

COVER BY
# Shelli Paroline & Braden Lamb

SERIES DESIGNER
**Grace Park**

ASSISTANT EDITOR
**Michael Moccio**

COLLECTION DESIGNER
**Chelsea Roberts**

EDITOR
**Whitney Leopard**

With Special Thanks to Marisa Marionakis, Janet No, Curtis Lelash, Conrad Montgomery, Kelly Crews, Scott Malchus, Adam Muto and the wonderful folks at Cartoon Network.

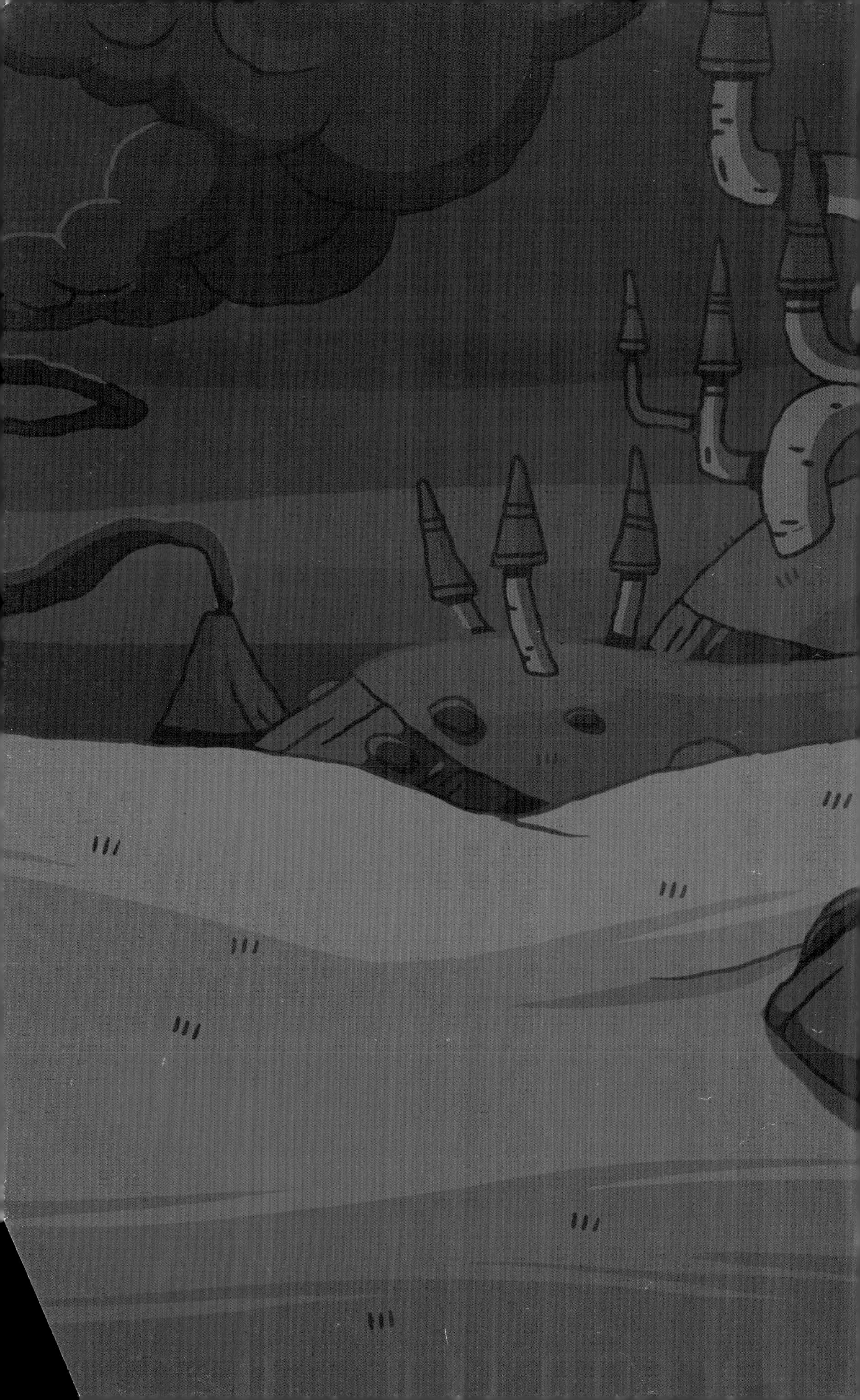

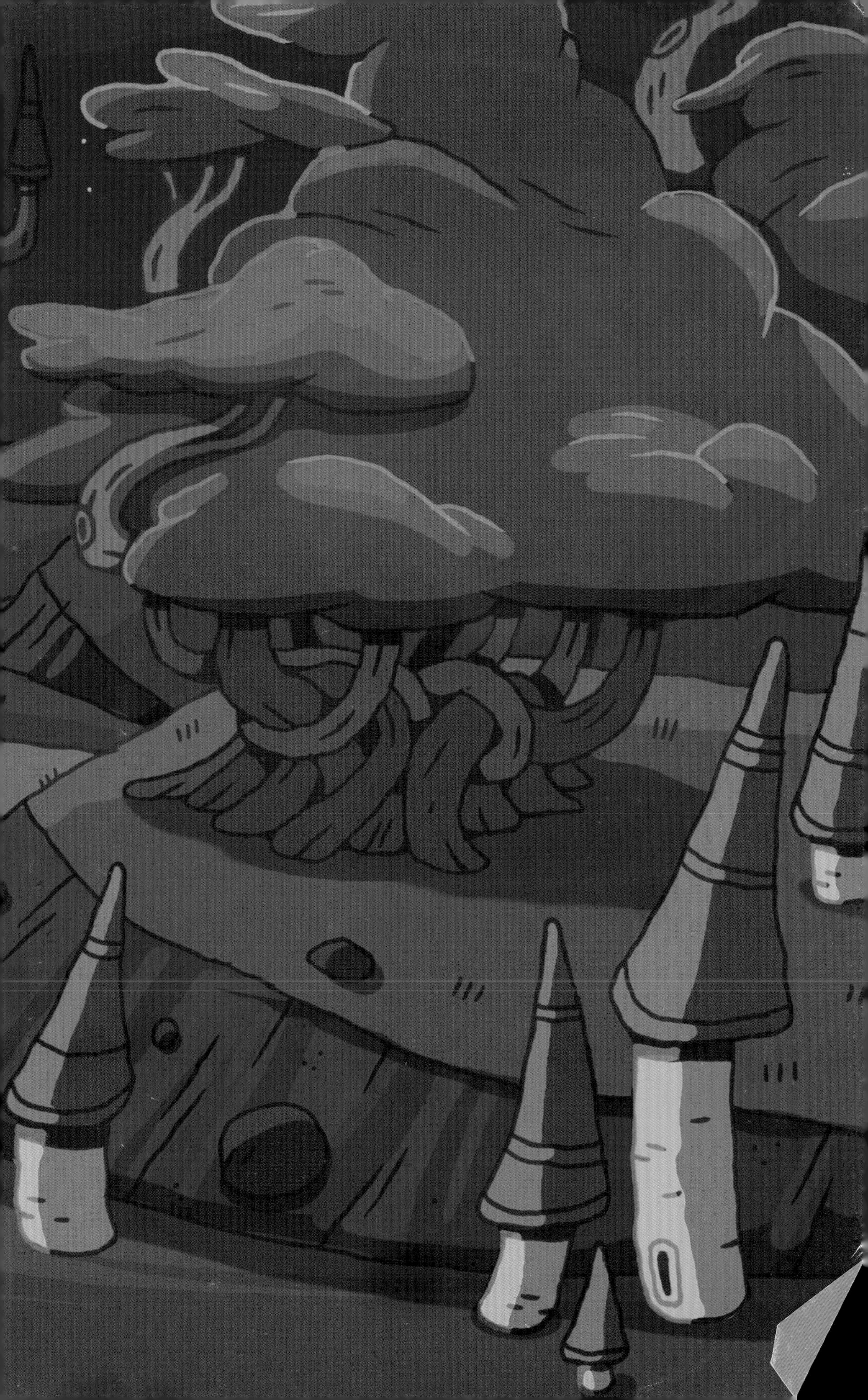

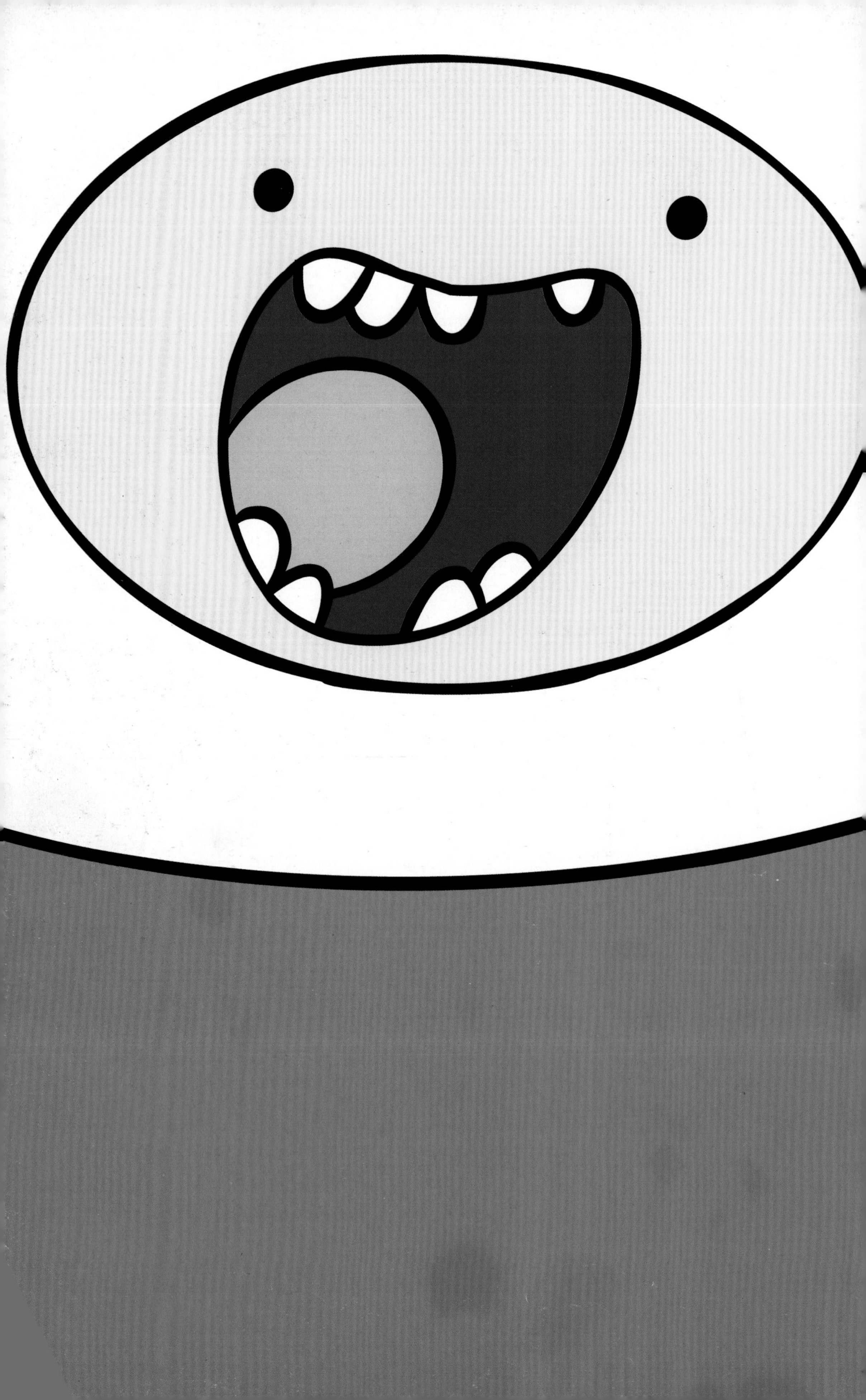

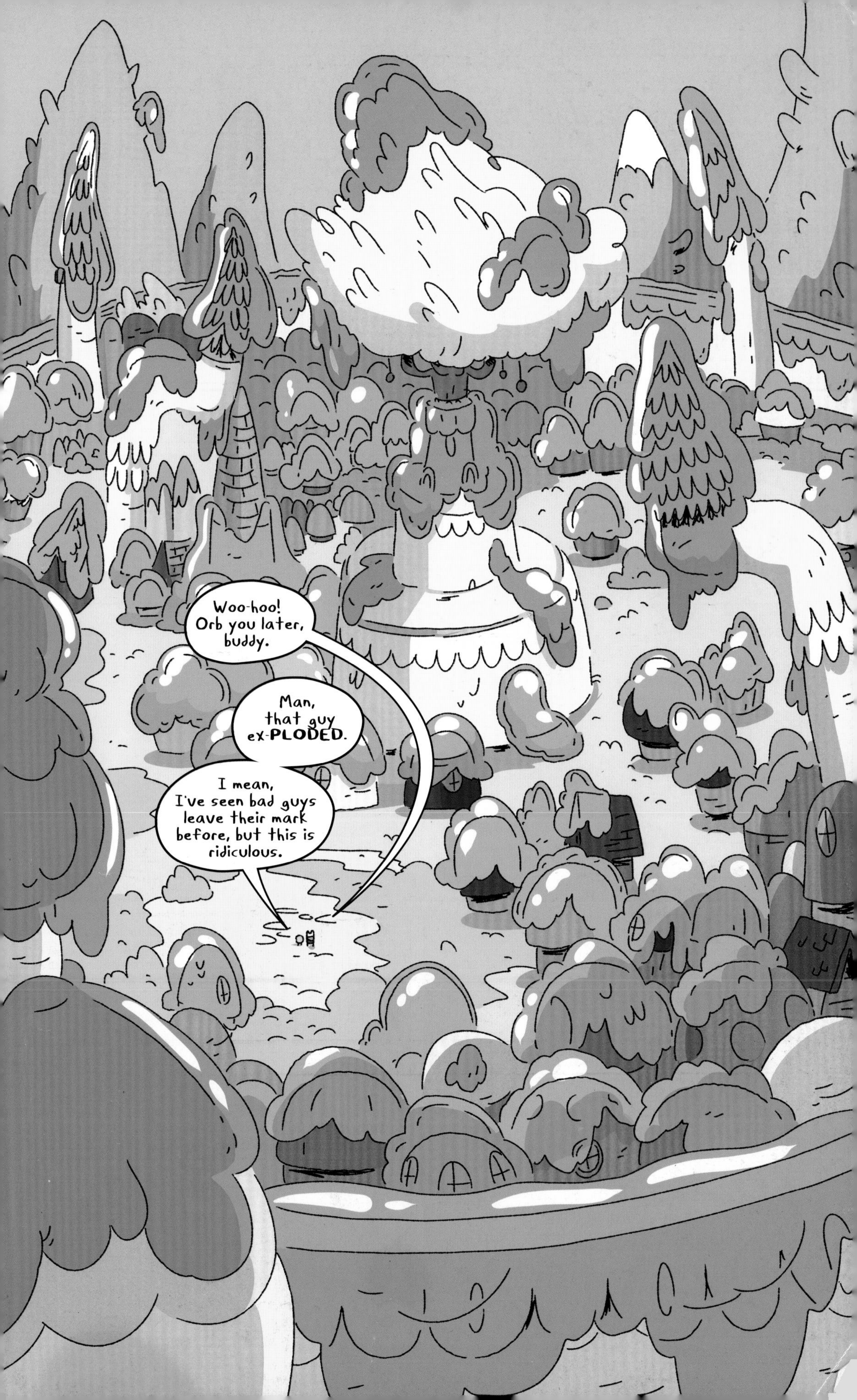
Woo-hoo! Orb you later, buddy.
Man, that guy ex-**PLODED**.
I mean, I've seen bad guys leave their mark before, but this is ridiculous.

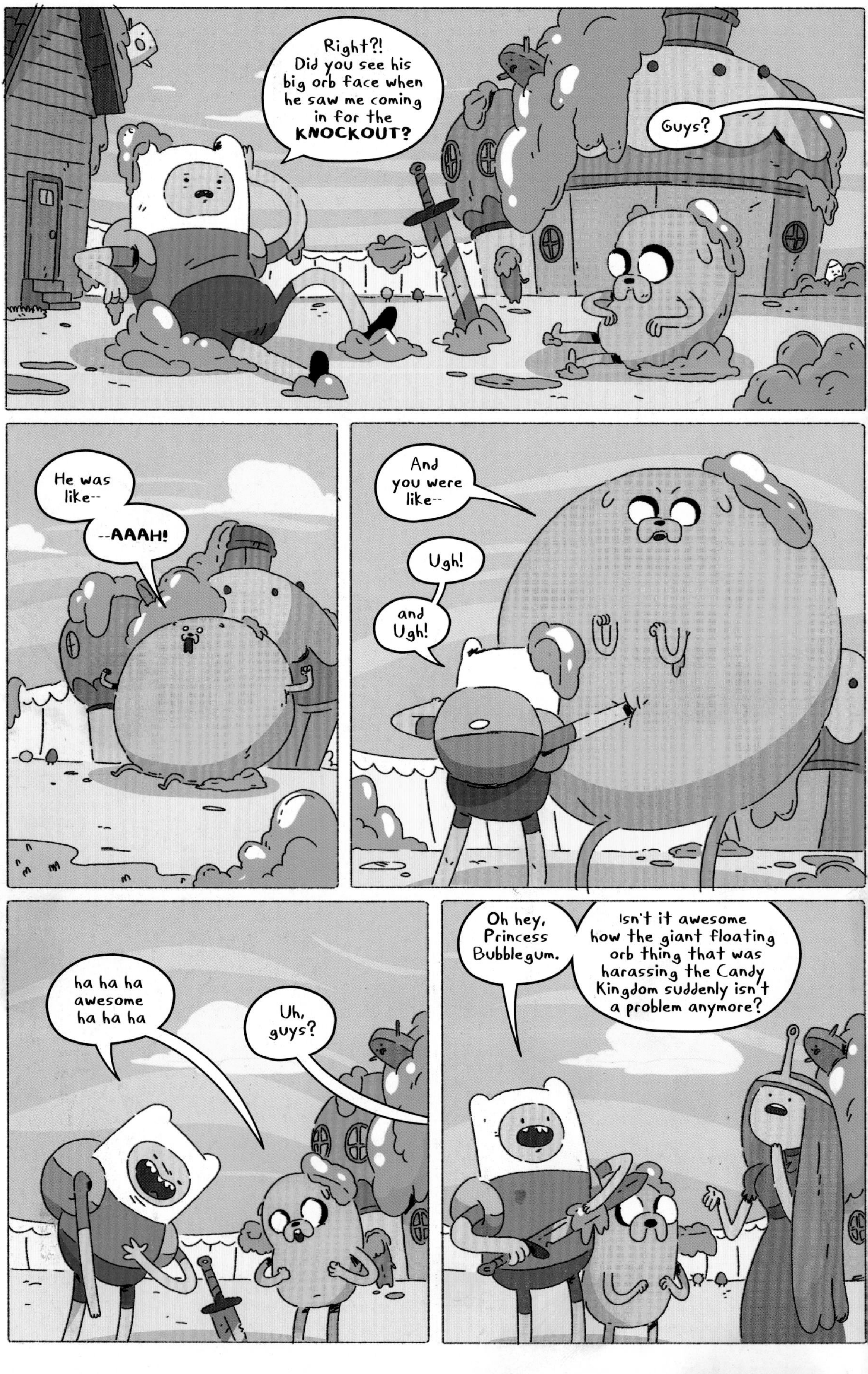
Right?! Did you see his big orb face when he saw me coming in for the **KNOCKOUT?**
Guys?
He was like--
--**AAAH!**
And you were like--
Ugh!
and Ugh!
ha ha ha awesome ha ha ha
Uh, guys?
Oh hey, Princess Bubblegum.
Isn't it awesome how the giant floating orb thing that was harassing the Candy Kingdom suddenly isn't a problem anymore?

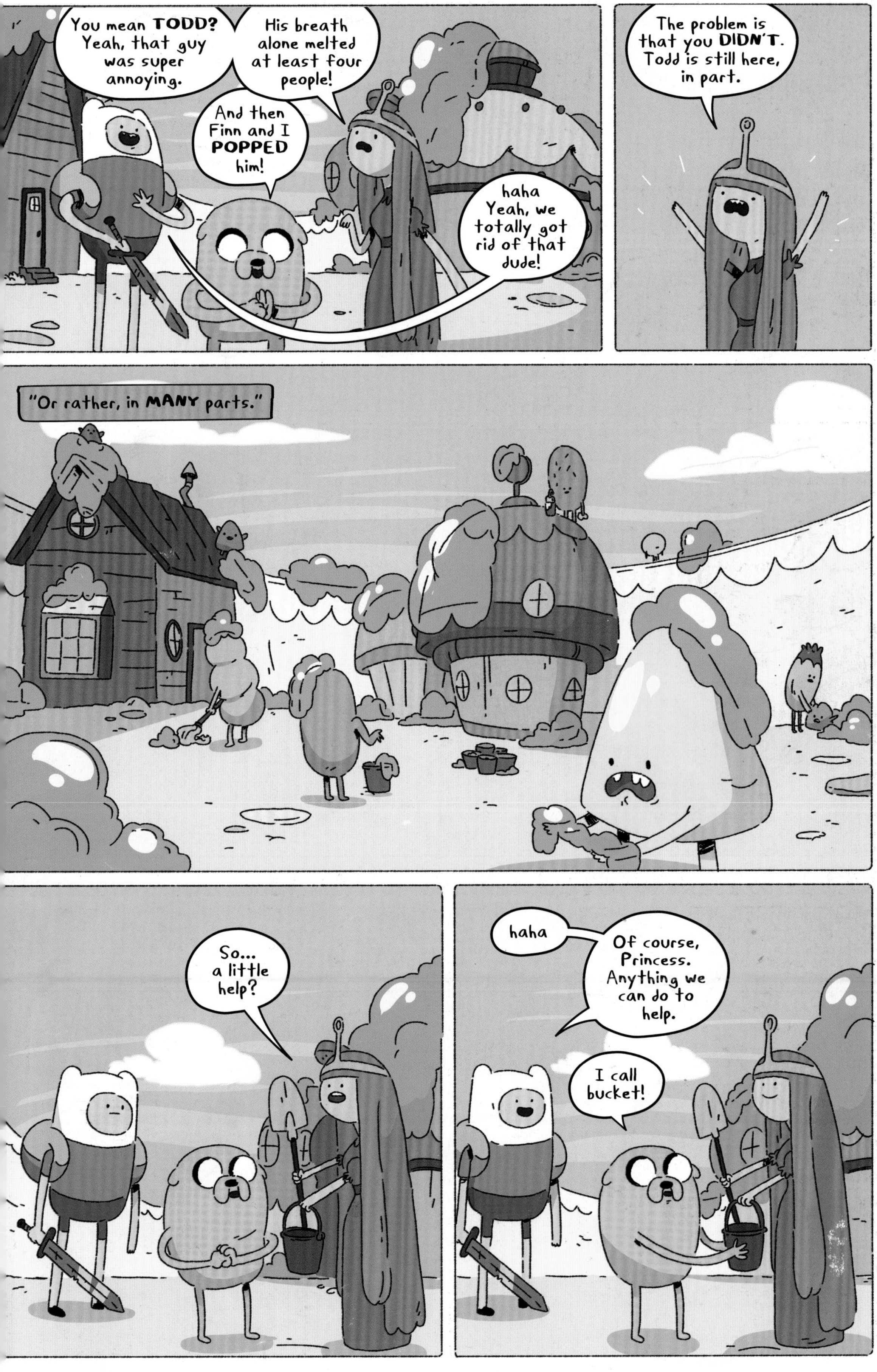
You mean TODD? Yeah, that guy was super annoying.
His breath alone melted at least four people!
And then Finn and I POPPED him!
haha Yeah, we totally got rid of that dude!
The problem is that you DIDN'T. Todd is still here, in part.
"Or rather, in MANY parts."
So... a little help?
haha
Of course, Princess. Anything we can do to help.
I call bucket!

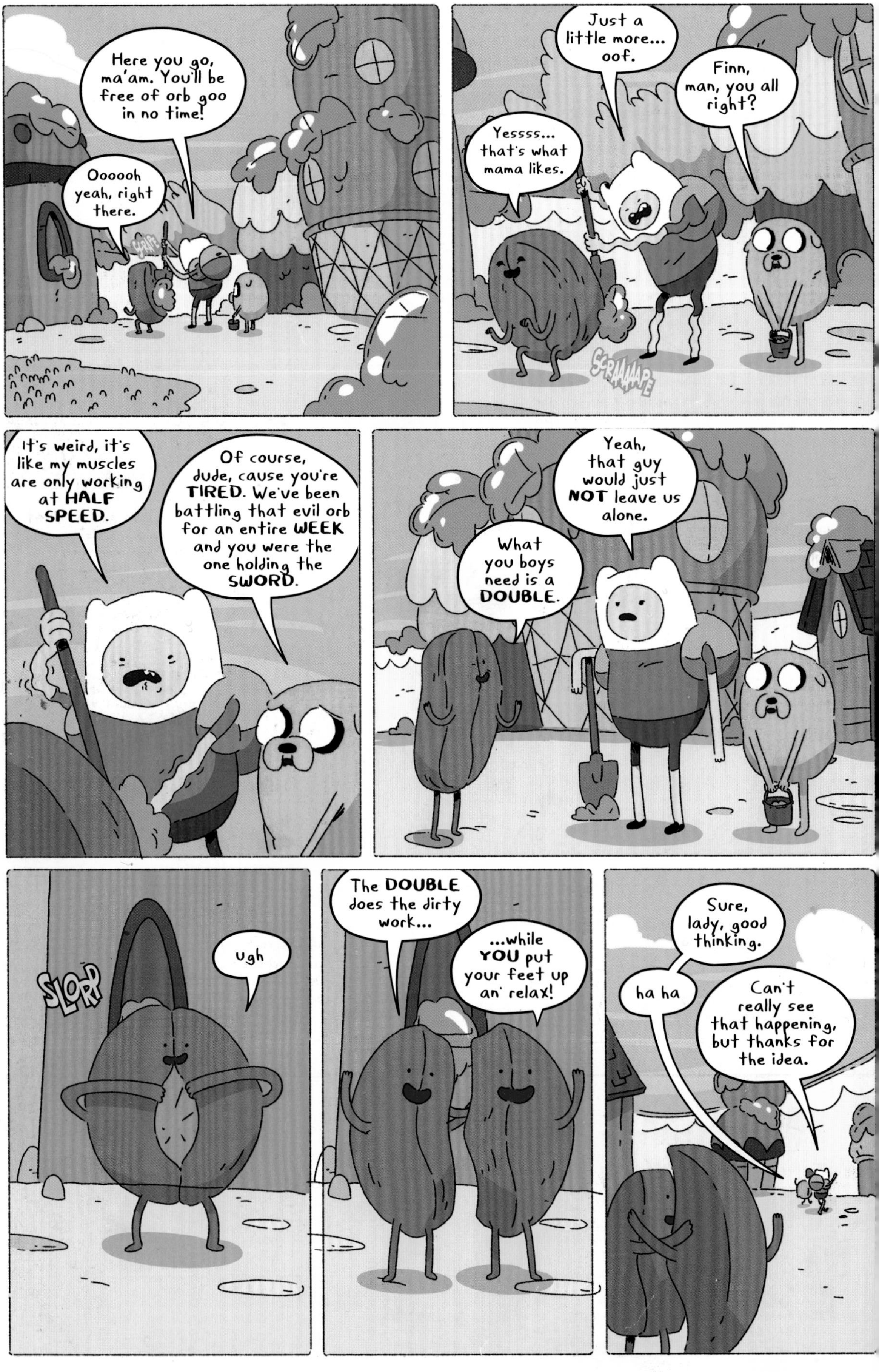
Here you go, ma'am. You'll be free of orb goo in no time!
Oooooh yeah, right there.
Just a little more... oof.
Yessss... that's what mama likes.
Finn, man, you all right?
It's weird, it's like my muscles are only working at **HALF SPEED**.
Of course, dude, cause you're **TIRED**. We've been battling that evil orb for an entire **WEEK** and you were the one holding the **SWORD**.
Yeah, that guy would just **NOT** leave us alone.
What you boys need is a **DOUBLE**.
SLORP
Ugh
The **DOUBLE** does the dirty work...
...while **YOU** put your feet up an' relax!
Sure, lady, good thinking.
ha ha
Can't really see that happening, but thanks for the idea.

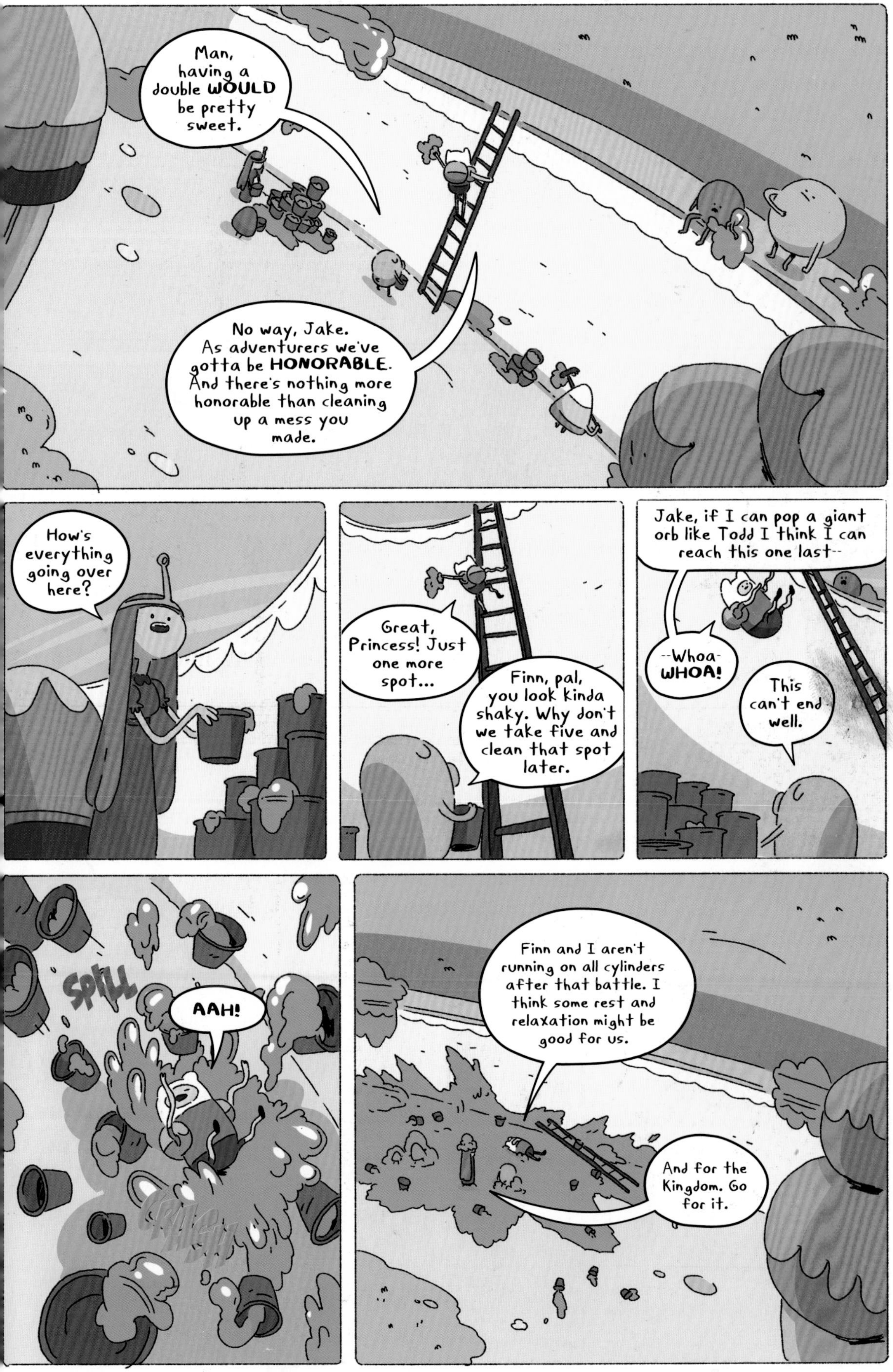
Man, having a double WOULD be pretty sweet.
No way, Jake. As adventurers we've gotta be HONORABLE. And there's nothing more honorable than cleaning up a mess you made.
How's everything going over here?
Great, Princess! Just one more spot...
Finn, pal, you look kinda shaky. Why don't we take five and clean that spot later.
Jake, if I can pop a giant orb like Todd I think I can reach this one last--
--Whoa-WHOA!
This can't end well.
SPILL
AAH!
Finn and I aren't running on all cylinders after that battle. I think some rest and relaxation might be good for us.
And for the Kingdom. Go for it.

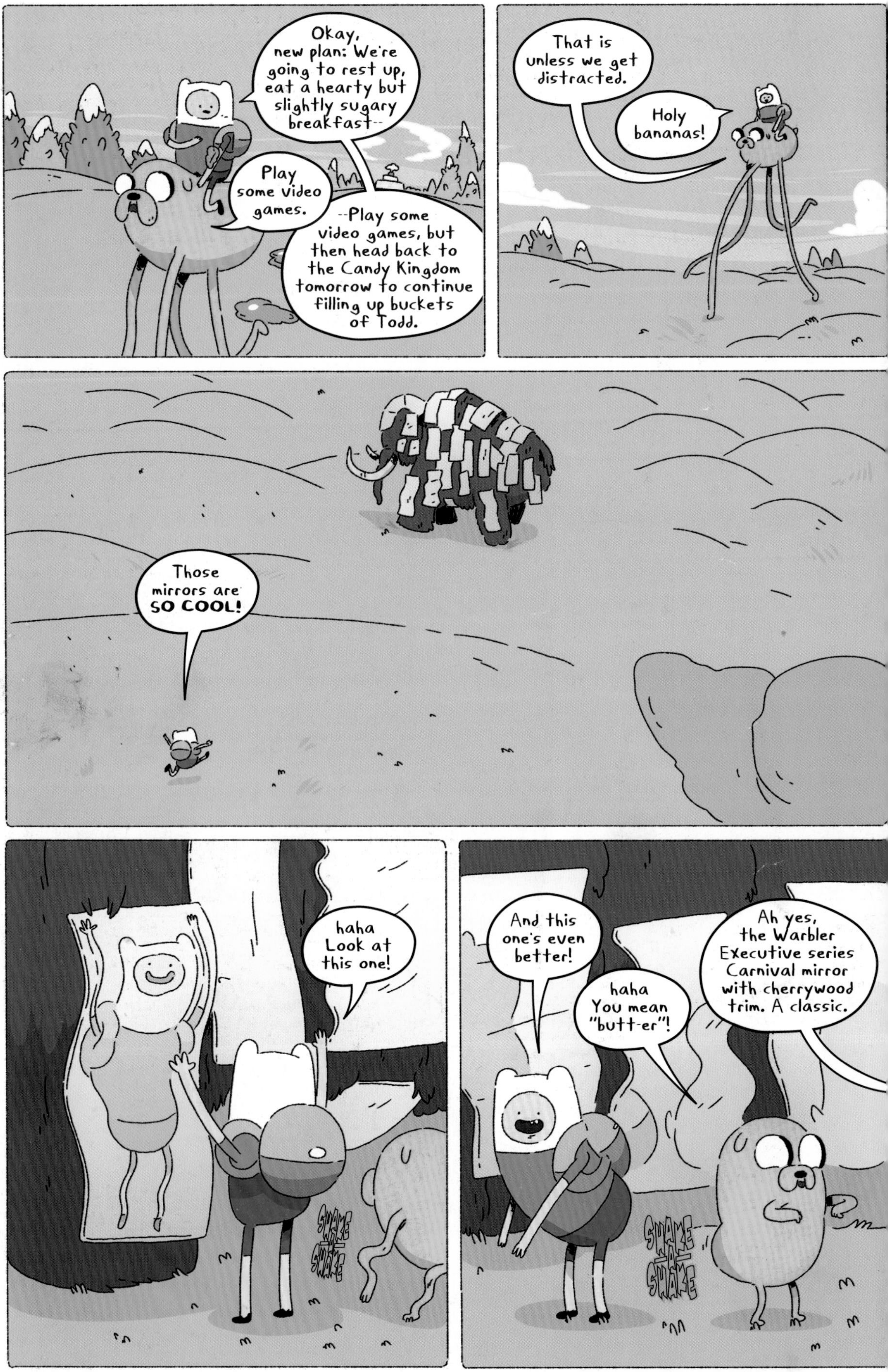
Okay, new plan: We're going to rest up, eat a hearty but slightly sugary breakfast--
Play some video games.
--Play some video games, but then head back to the Candy Kingdom tomorrow to continue filling up buckets of Todd.
That is unless we get distracted.
Holy bananas!
Those mirrors are **SO COOL!**
haha Look at this one!
SHAKE-A-SHAKE
And this one's even better!
haha You mean "butt-er"!
Ah yes, the Warbler Executive series Carnival mirror with cherrywood trim. A classic.
SHAKE-A-SHAKE

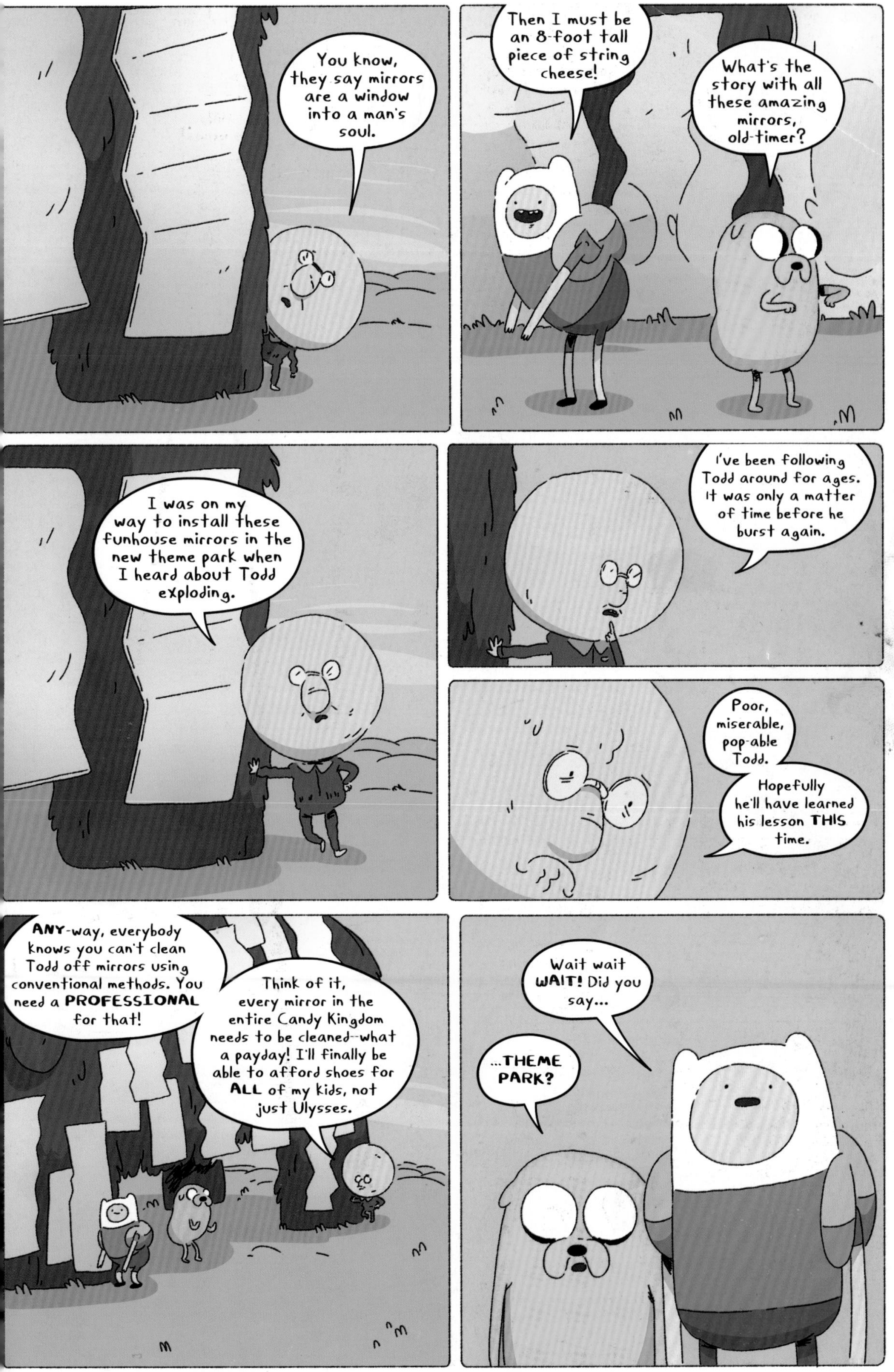

You know, they say mirrors are a window into a man's soul.
Then I must be an 8-foot tall piece of string cheese!
What's the story with all these amazing mirrors, old-timer?
I was on my way to install these funhouse mirrors in the new theme park when I heard about Todd exploding.
I've been following Todd around for ages. It was only a matter of time before he burst again.
Poor, miserable, pop-able Todd.
Hopefully he'll have learned his lesson THIS time.
ANY-way, everybody knows you can't clean Todd off mirrors using conventional methods. You need a PROFESSIONAL for that!
Think of it, every mirror in the entire Candy Kingdom needs to be cleaned--what a payday! I'll finally be able to afford shoes for ALL of my kids, not just Ulysses.
Wait wait WAIT! Did you say...
...THEME PARK?

Well, sure. Adventure Town. It's opening tomorrow morning, a few towns over.

Hang on a sec.

Here.

...

Holy math, Jake--an **ADVENTURE** themed **THEME PARK?**

A little detour never hurt anybody, right?

**WE.**

**HAVE.**

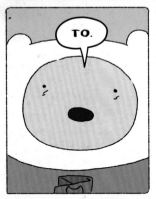

**TO.**

**GO.**

**RIGHT.**

**NOW.**

Wait! If you go, you must stay away from the **WISH WITCH!** She's nothing but **TROUBLE!**

Thanks for the advice, but I'm **PRETTY SURE** we'll be too busy riding the rollercoasters to talk to some **WITCH.**

Don't be so sure.

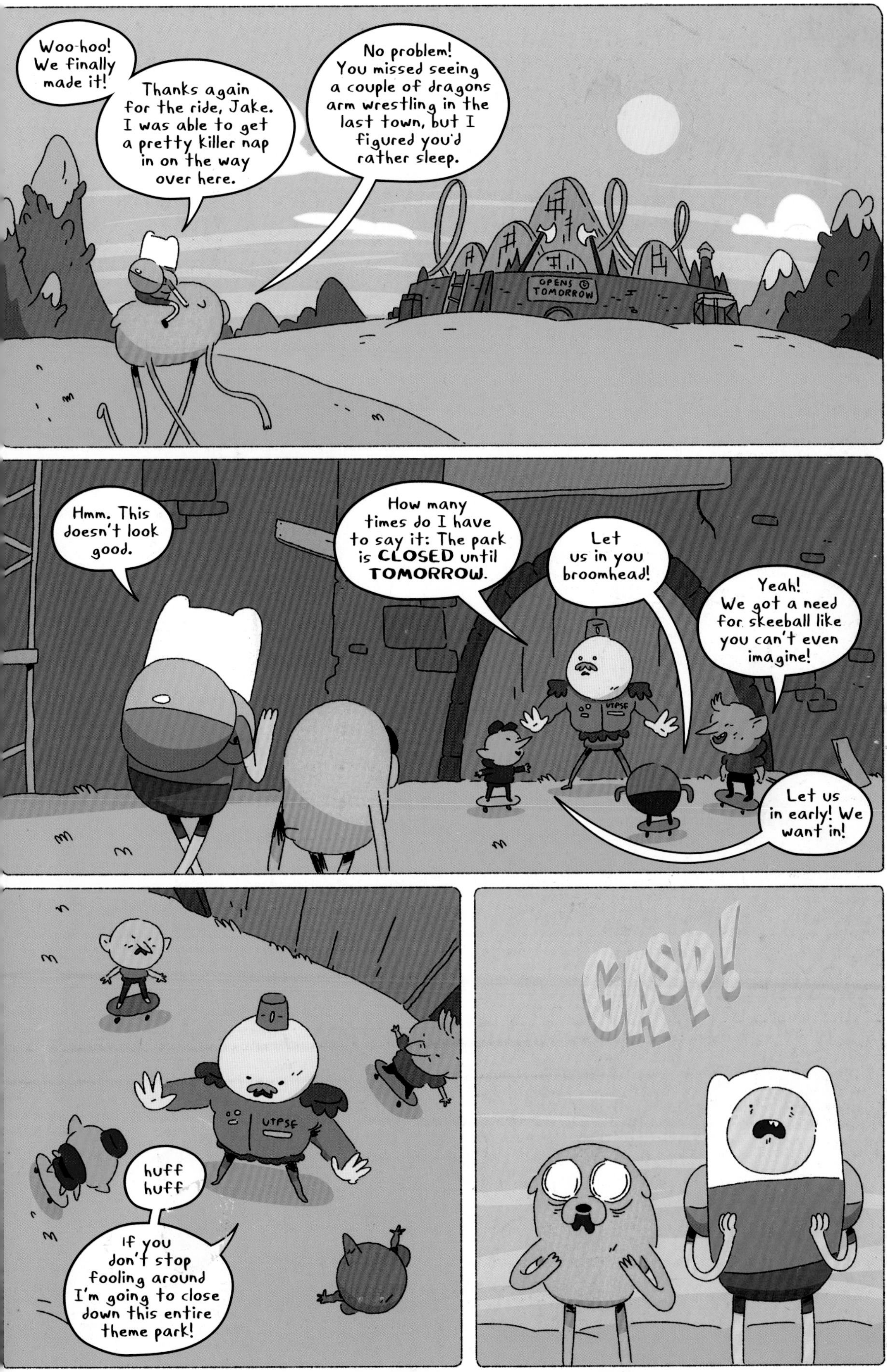
Woo-hoo! We finally made it!
Thanks again for the ride, Jake. I was able to get a pretty killer nap in on the way over here.
No problem! You missed seeing a couple of dragons arm wrestling in the last town, but I figured you'd rather sleep.
OPENS TOMORROW
Hmm. This doesn't look good.
How many times do I have to say it: The park is **CLOSED** until **TOMORROW**.
Let us in you broomhead!
Yeah! We got a need for skeeball like you can't even imagine!
Let us in early! We want in!
UTPSF
huff huff
If you don't stop fooling around I'm going to close down this entire theme park!
GASP!

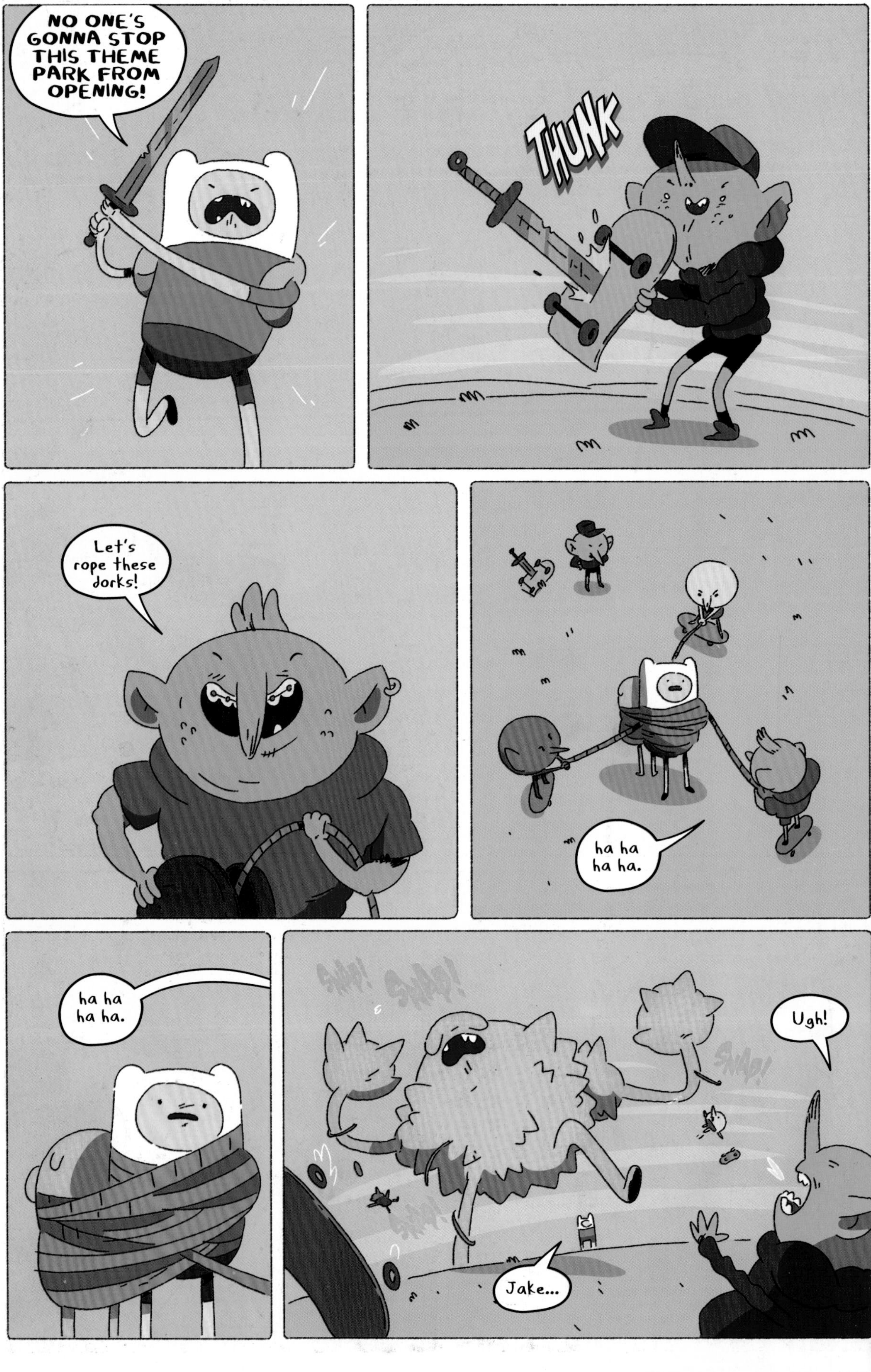
NO ONE'S GONNA STOP THIS THEME PARK FROM OPENING!
THUNK
Let's rope these dorks!
ha ha ha ha.
ha ha ha ha.
SNAP!
SNAP!
SNAP!
Ugh!
Jake...

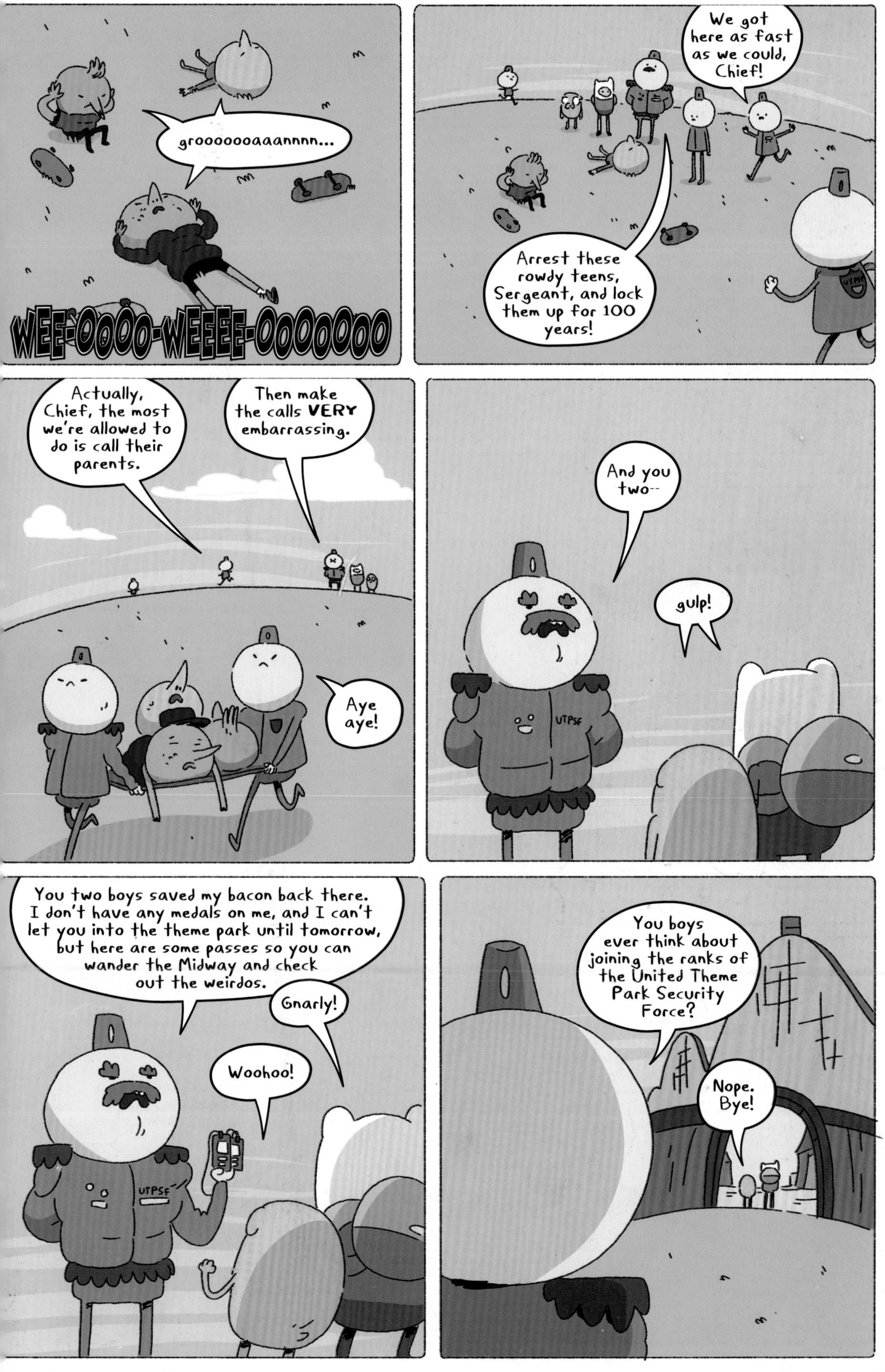
grooooooaaannnn...
WEE-OOOO-WEEEE-OOOOOOO
We got here as fast as we could, Chief!
Arrest these rowdy teens, Sergeant, and lock them up for 100 years!
Actually, Chief, the most we're allowed to do is call their parents.
Then make the calls **VERY** embarrassing.
Aye aye!
And you two--
gulp!
You two boys saved my bacon back there. I don't have any medals on me, and I can't let you into the theme park until tomorrow, but here are some passes so you can wander the Midway and check out the weirdos.
Gnarly!
Woohoo!
You boys ever think about joining the ranks of the United Theme Park Security Force?
Nope. Bye!

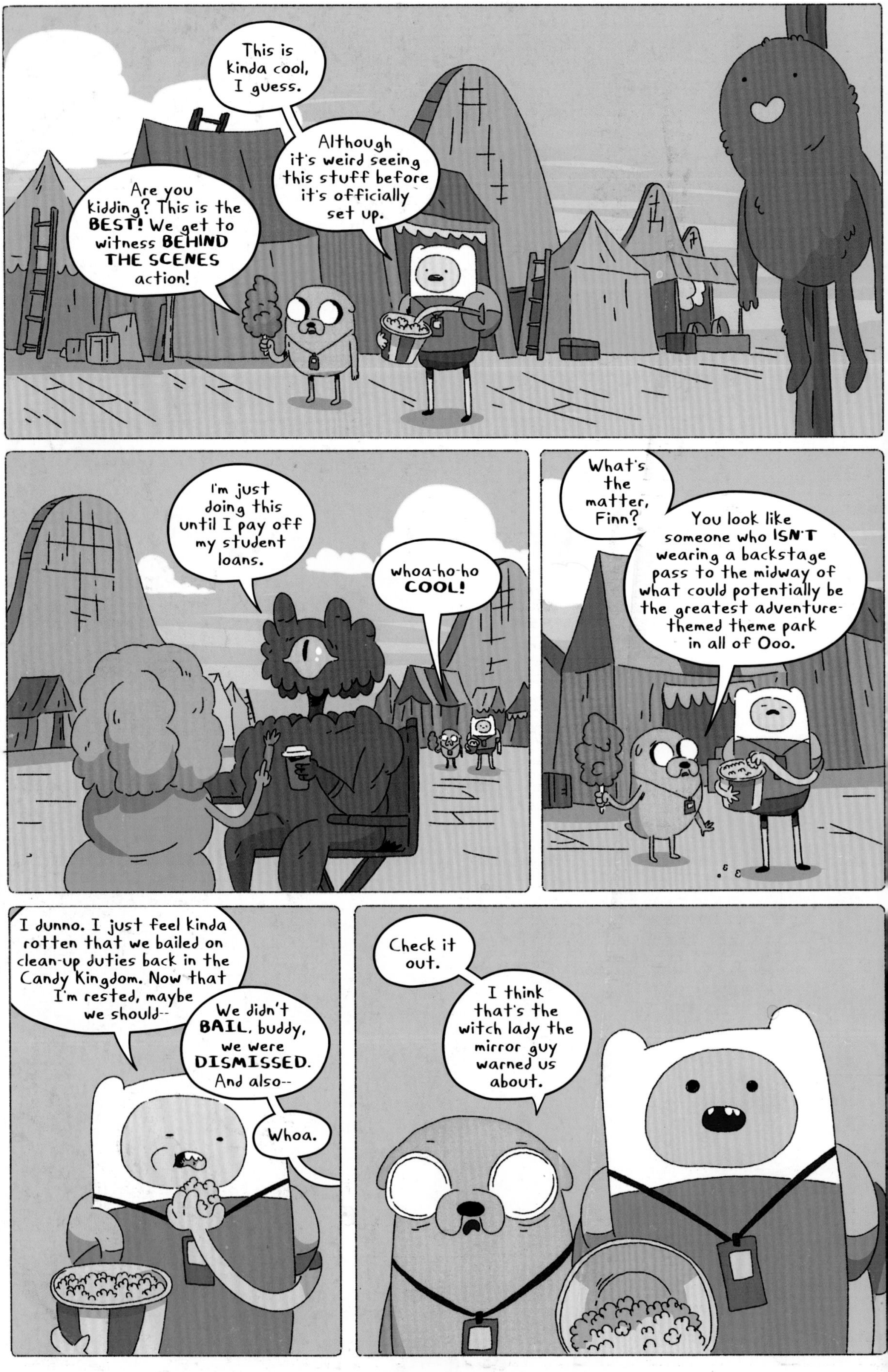
This is kinda cool, I guess.
Although it's weird seeing this stuff before it's officially set up.
Are you kidding? This is the BEST! We get to witness BEHIND THE SCENES action!
I'm just doing this until I pay off my student loans.
whoa-ho-ho COOL!
What's the matter, Finn?
You look like someone who ISN'T wearing a backstage pass to the midway of what could potentially be the greatest adventure-themed theme park in all of Ooo.
I dunno. I just feel kinda rotten that we bailed on clean-up duties back in the Candy Kingdom. Now that I'm rested, maybe we should--
We didn't BAIL, buddy, we were DISMISSED. And also--
Whoa.
Check it out.
I think that's the witch lady the mirror guy warned us about.

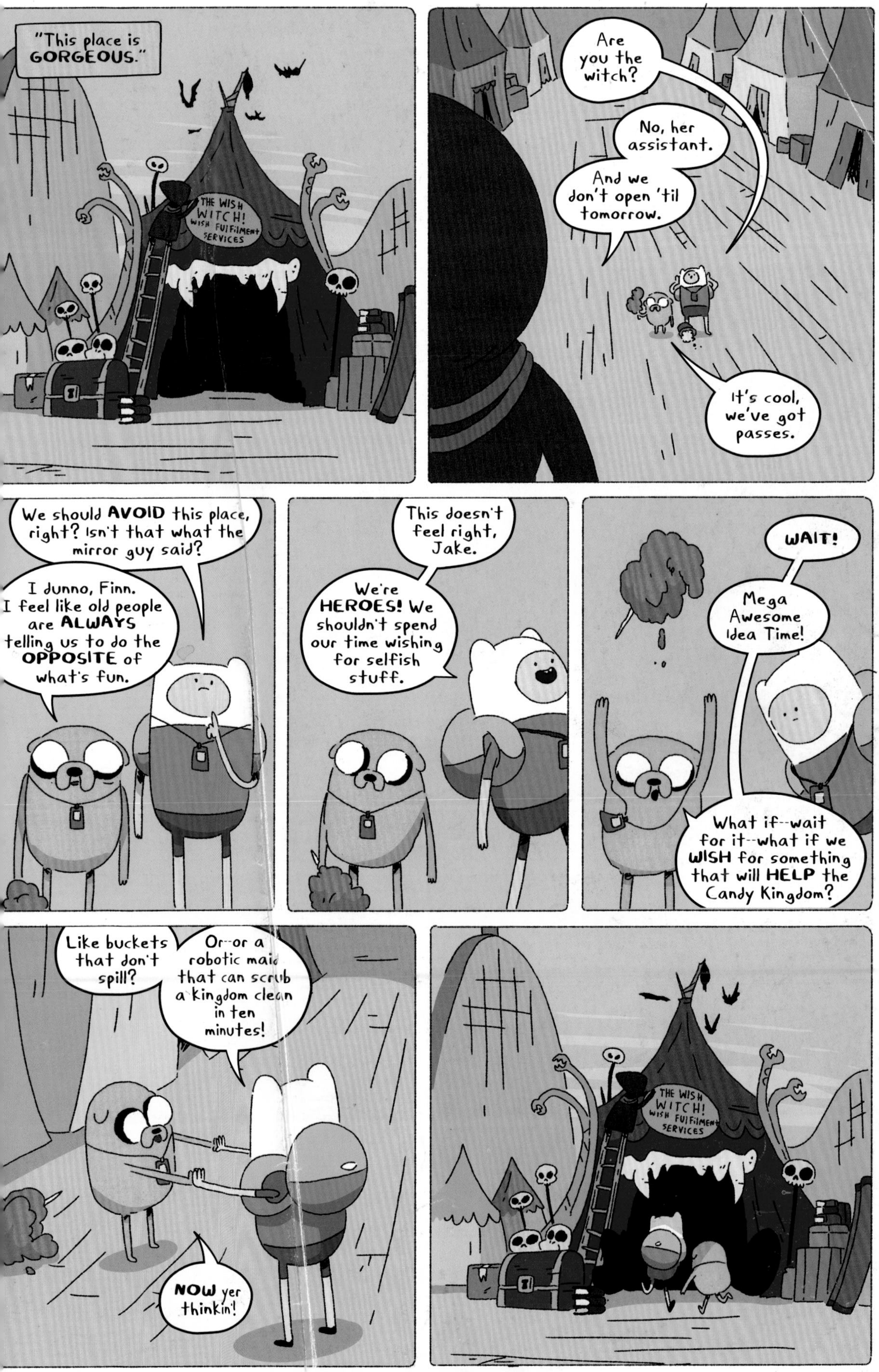
"This place is GORGEOUS."
THE WISH WITCH! WISH FULFILMENT SERVICES
Are you the witch?
No, her assistant.
And we don't open 'til tomorrow.
It's cool, we've got passes.
We should AVOID this place, right? Isn't that what the mirror guy said?
I dunno, Finn. I feel like old people are ALWAYS telling us to do the OPPOSITE of what's fun.
This doesn't feel right, Jake.
We're HEROES! We shouldn't spend our time wishing for selfish stuff.
WAIT!
Mega Awesome Idea Time!
What if--wait for it--what if we WISH for something that will HELP the Candy Kingdom?
Like buckets that don't spill?
Or--or a robotic maid that can scrub a kingdom clean in ten minutes!
NOW yer thinkin'!
THE WISH WITCH! WISH FULFILMENT SERVICES

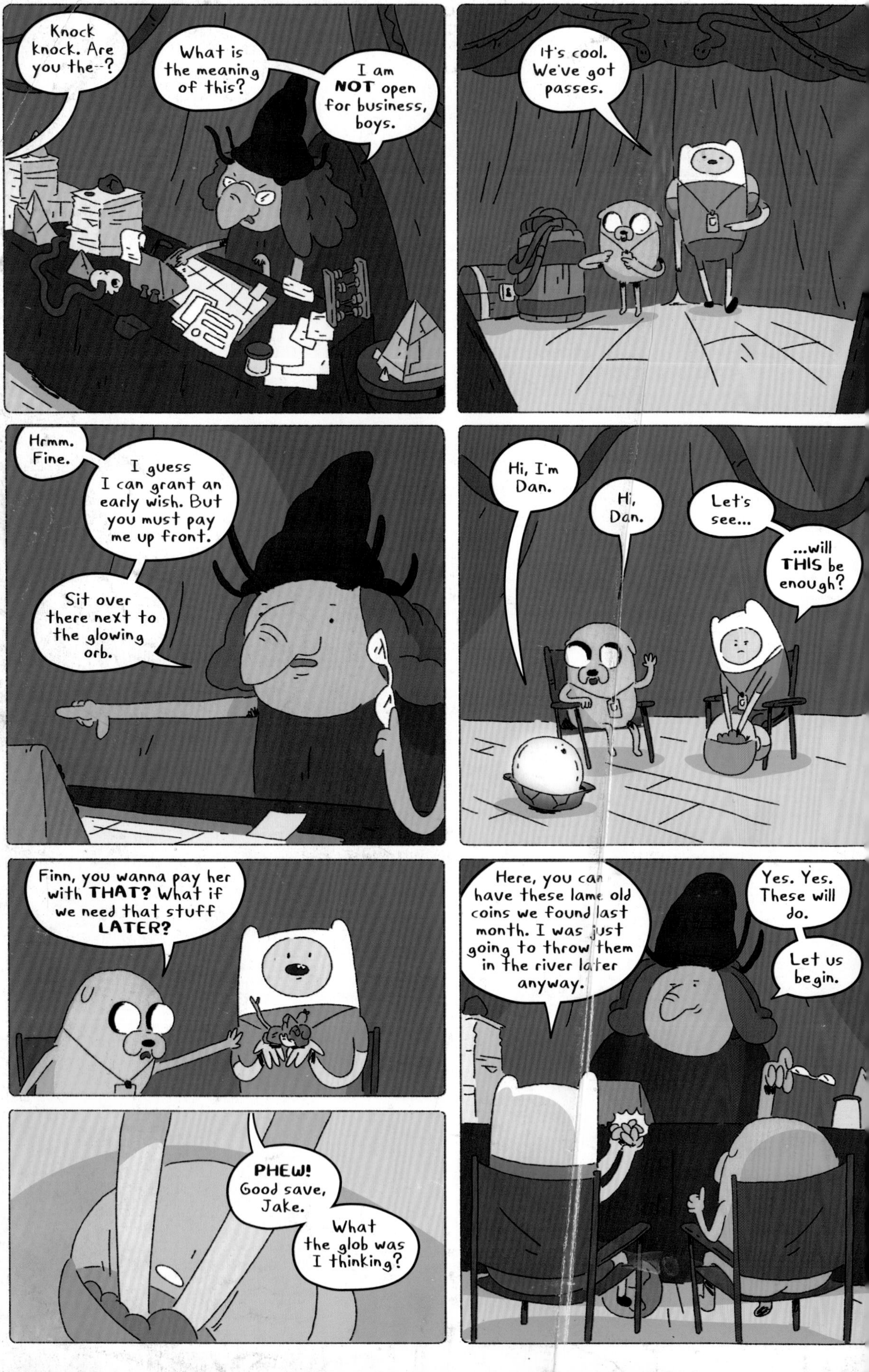
Knock knock. Are you the--?
What is the meaning of this?
I am NOT open for business, boys.
It's cool. We've got passes.
Hrmm. Fine.
I guess I can grant an early wish. But you must pay me up front.
Sit over there next to the glowing orb.
Hi, I'm Dan.
Hi, Dan.
Let's see...
...will THIS be enough?
Finn, you wanna pay her with THAT? What if we need that stuff LATER?
PHEW! Good save, Jake.
What the glob was I thinking?
Here, you can have these lame old coins we found last month. I was just going to throw them in the river later anyway.
Yes. Yes. These will do.
Let us begin.

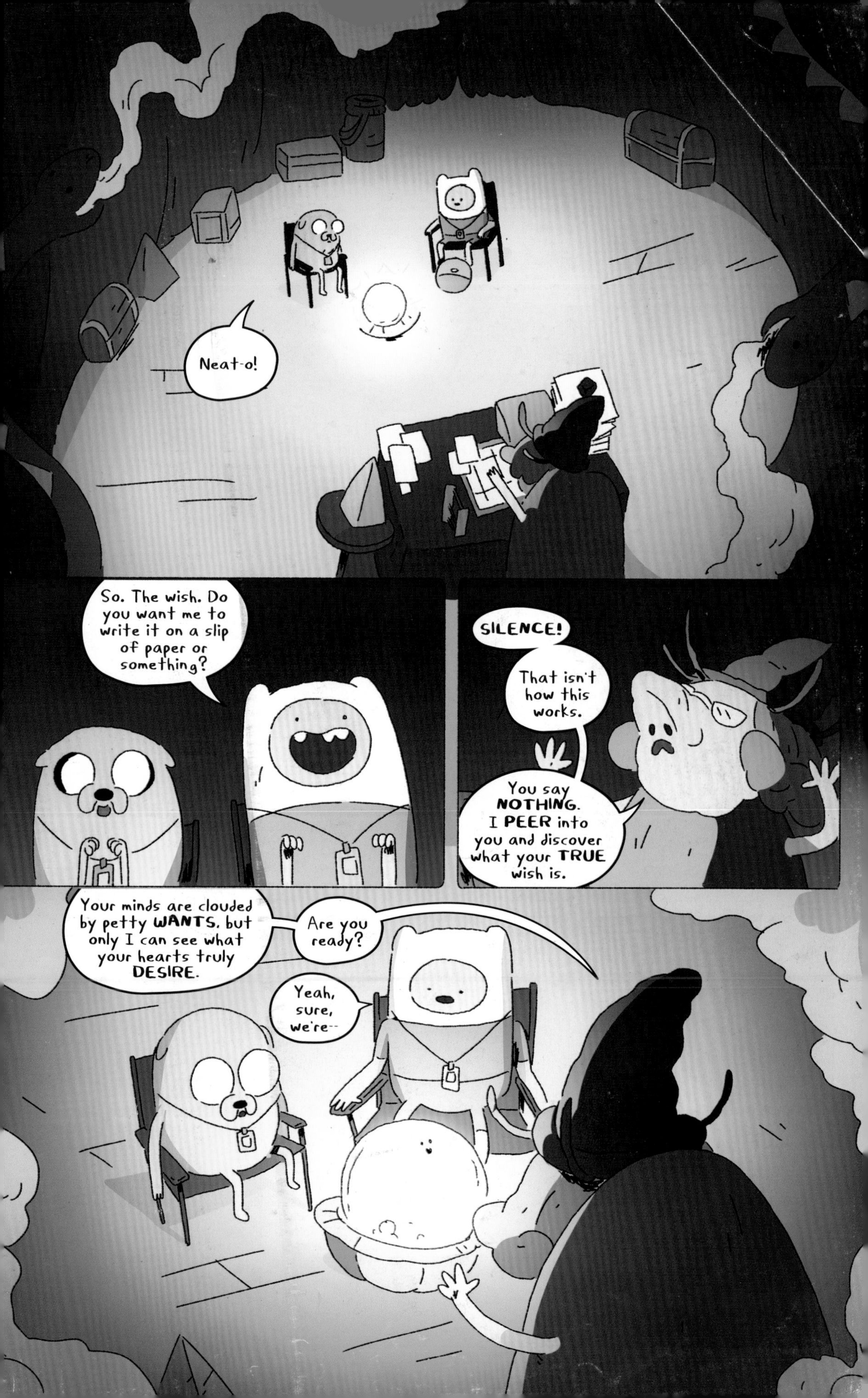
Neat-o!
So. The wish. Do you want me to write it on a slip of paper or something?
SILENCE!
That isn't how this works.
You say NOTHING. I PEER into you and discover what your TRUE wish is.
Your minds are clouded by petty WANTS, but only I can see what your hearts truly DESIRE.
Are you ready?
Yeah, sure, we're--

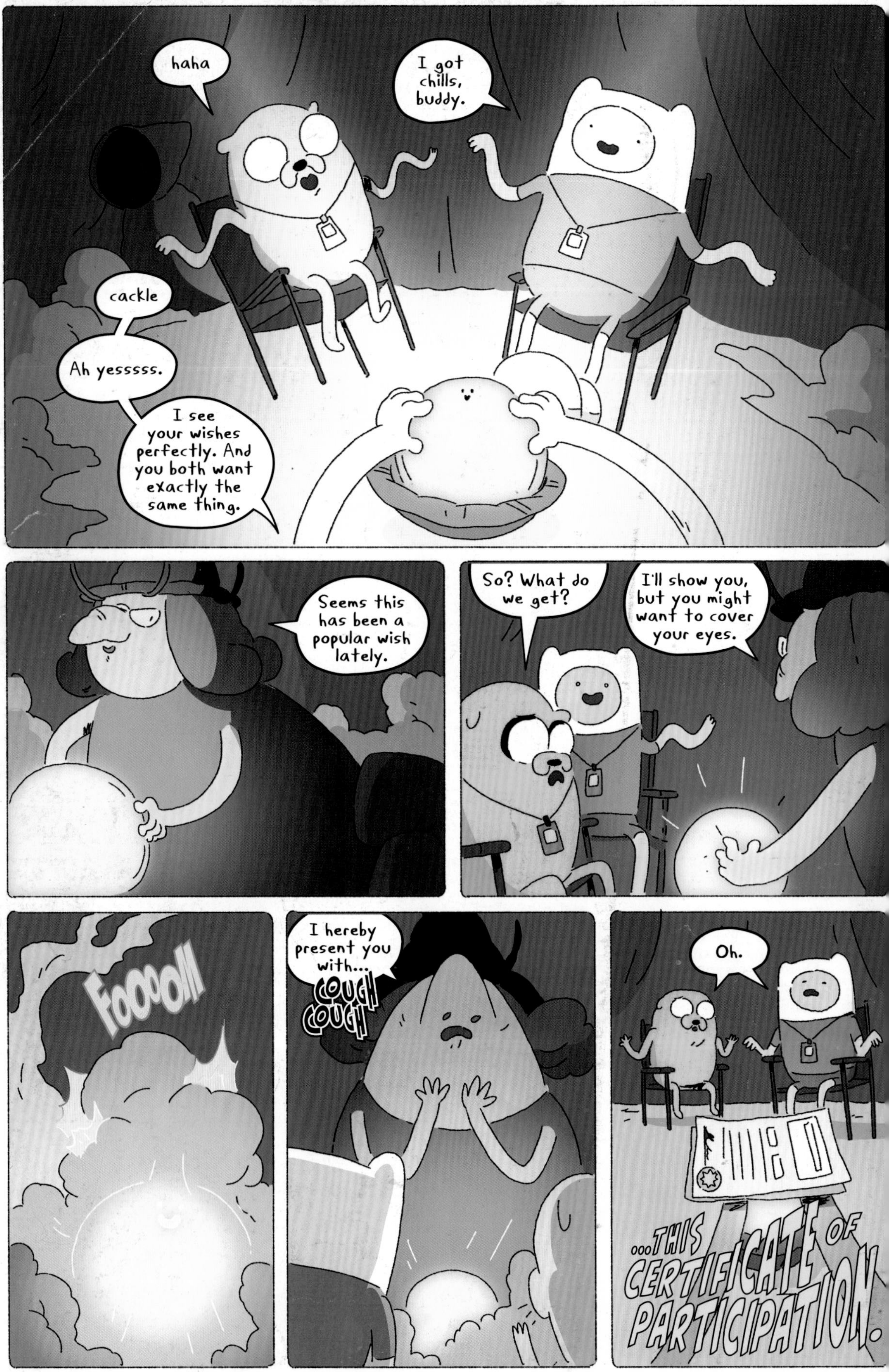
haha
I got chills, buddy.
cackle
Ah yessssss.
I see your wishes perfectly. And you both want exactly the same thing.
Seems this has been a popular wish lately.
So? What do we get?
I'll show you, but you might want to cover your eyes.
FOOOOM
I hereby present you with...
COUGH COUGH
Oh.
...THIS CERTIFICATE OF PARTICIPATION.

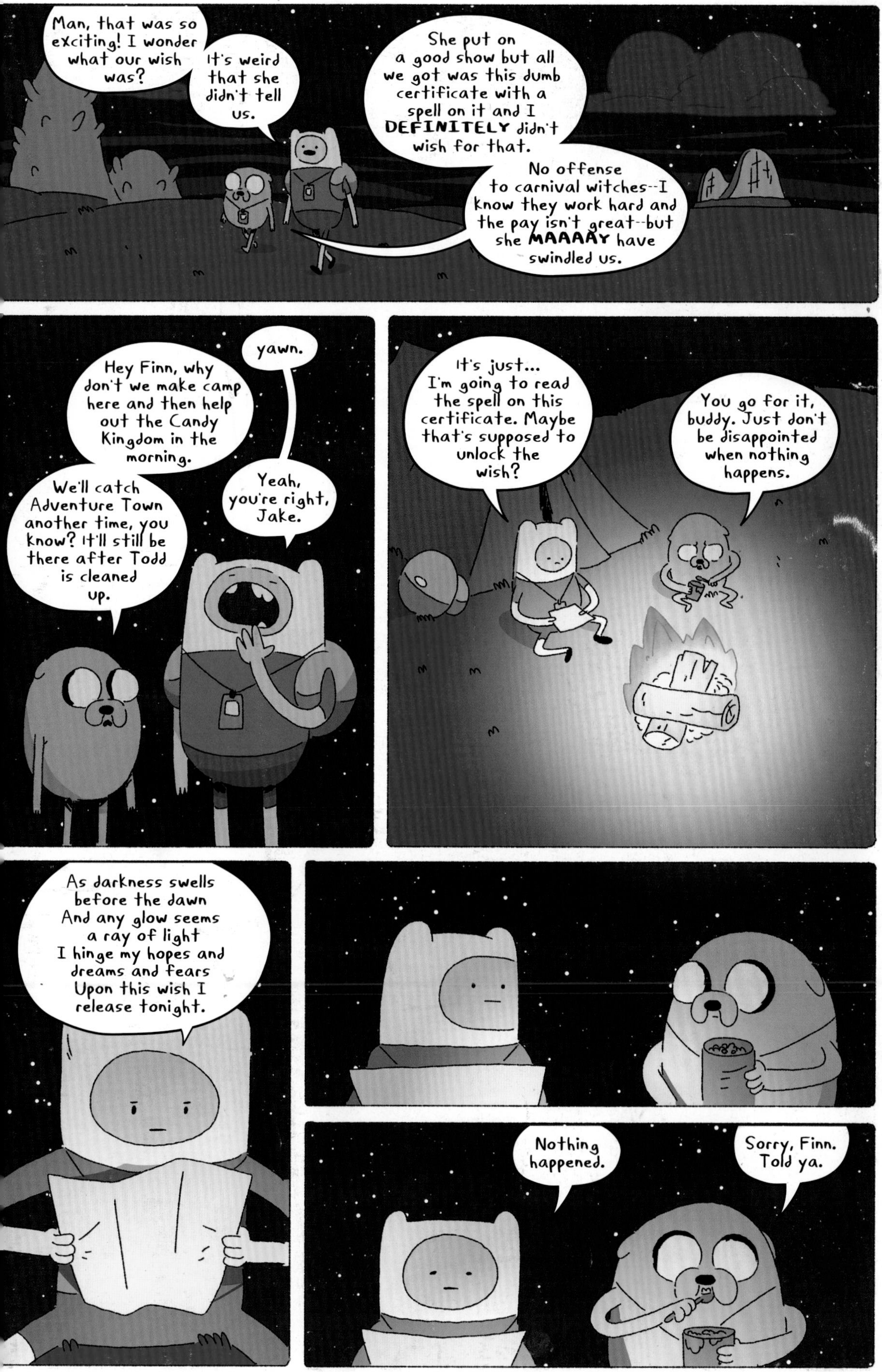
Man, that was so exciting! I wonder what our wish was?
It's weird that she didn't tell us.
She put on a good show but all we got was this dumb certificate with a spell on it and I DEFINITELY didn't wish for that.
No offense to carnival witches--I know they work hard and the pay isn't great--but she MAAAAY have swindled us.
Hey Finn, why don't we make camp here and then help out the Candy Kingdom in the morning.
yawn.
We'll catch Adventure Town another time, you know? It'll still be there after Todd is cleaned up.
Yeah, you're right, Jake.
It's just... I'm going to read the spell on this certificate. Maybe that's supposed to unlock the wish?
You go for it, buddy. Just don't be disappointed when nothing happens.
As darkness swells before the dawn And any glow seems a ray of light I hinge my hopes and dreams and fears Upon this wish I release tonight.
Nothing happened.
Sorry, Finn. Told ya.

SNIFF SNIFF

Mmmm... Thanks for making breakfast, Jake.

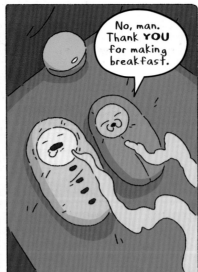

No, man. Thank **YOU** for making breakfast.

!!!

!!!

♪♫

This must be the wish the Wish Witch saw inside of us--To have doubles!

We can totally have these guys replace us inside the Candy Kingdom until Todd is cleaned up!

Meanwhile, we can go to the adventure-themed theme park!

Woot!

Okay, now I seriously need to get some of that breakfast.

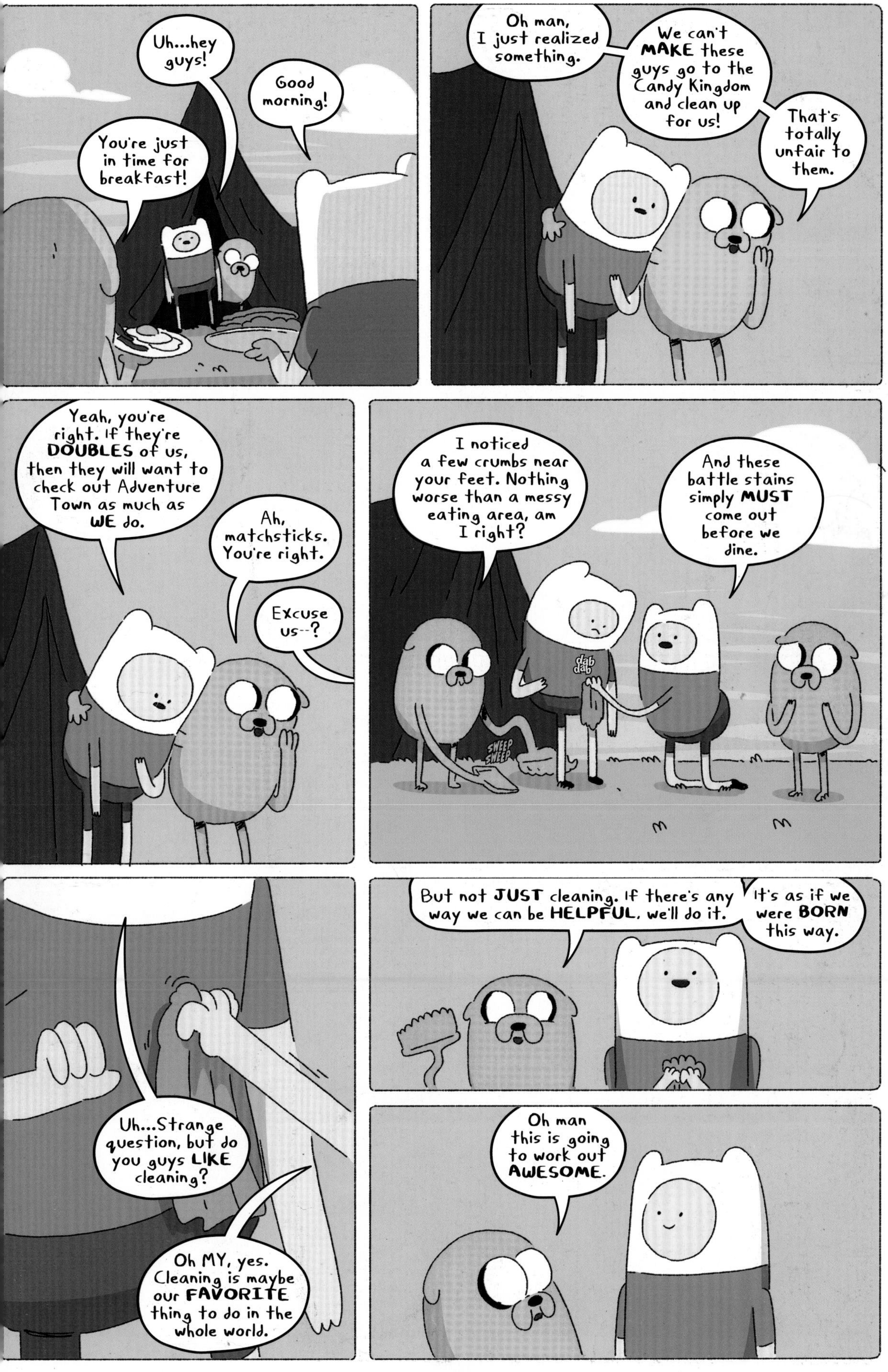
Uh...hey guys!
Good morning!
You're just in time for breakfast!
Oh man, I just realized something.
We can't MAKE these guys go to the Candy Kingdom and clean up for us!
That's totally unfair to them.
Yeah, you're right. If they're DOUBLES of us, then they will want to check out Adventure Town as much as WE do.
Ah, matchsticks. You're right.
Excuse us--?
I noticed a few crumbs near your feet. Nothing worse than a messy eating area, am I right?
And these battle stains simply MUST come out before we dine.
dab dab
SWEEP SWEEP
Uh...Strange question, but do you guys LIKE cleaning?
Oh MY, yes. Cleaning is maybe our FAVORITE thing to do in the whole world.
But not JUST cleaning. If there's any way we can be HELPFUL, we'll do it.
It's as if we were BORN this way.
Oh man this is going to work out AWESOME.

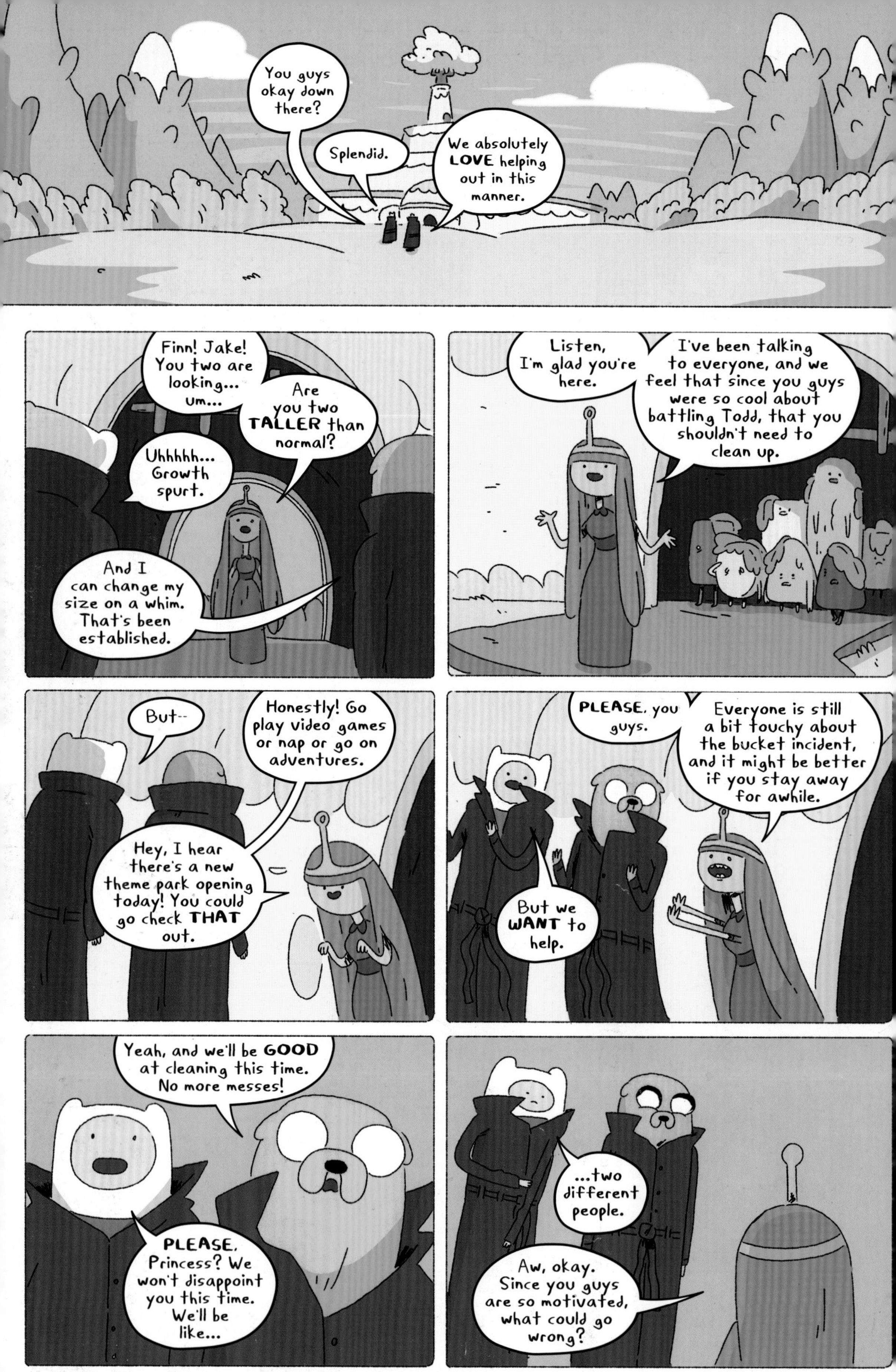
You guys okay down there?
Splendid.
We absolutely LOVE helping out in this manner.
Finn! Jake! You two are looking... um...
Are you two TALLER than normal?
Uhhhhh... Growth spurt.
And I can change my size on a whim. That's been established.
Listen, I'm glad you're here.
I've been talking to everyone, and we feel that since you guys were so cool about battling Todd, that you shouldn't need to clean up.
But--
Honestly! Go play video games or nap or go on adventures.
Hey, I hear there's a new theme park opening today! You could go check THAT out.
PLEASE, you guys.
Everyone is still a bit touchy about the bucket incident, and it might be better if you stay away for awhile.
But we WANT to help.
Yeah, and we'll be GOOD at cleaning this time. No more messes!
PLEASE, Princess? We won't disappoint you this time. We'll be like...
...two different people.
Aw, okay. Since you guys are so motivated, what could go wrong?

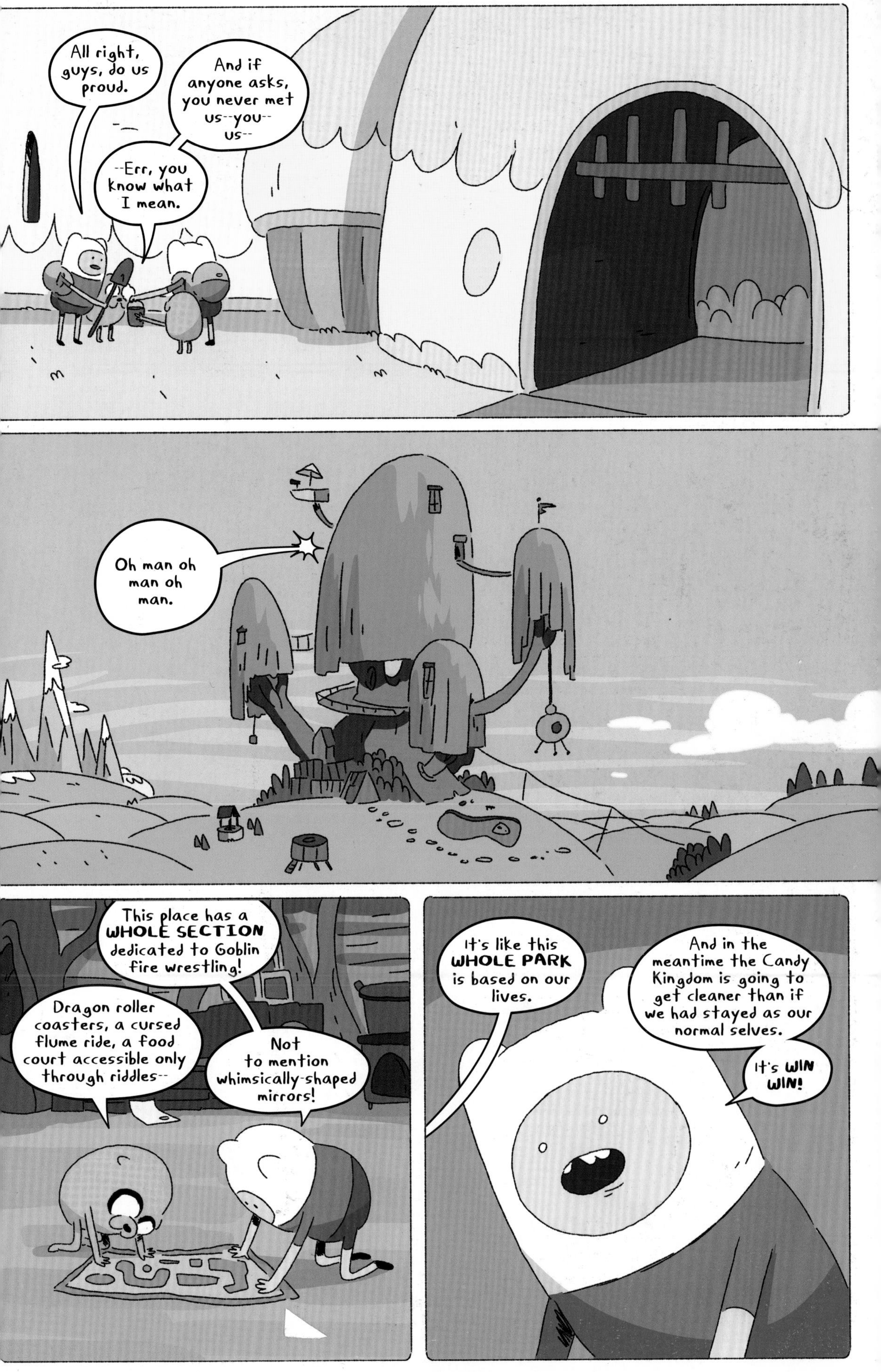
All right, guys, do us proud.
And if anyone asks, you never met us--you-- us--
--Err, you know what I mean.
Oh man oh man oh man.
This place has a WHOLE SECTION dedicated to Goblin fire wrestling!
Dragon roller coasters, a cursed flume ride, a food court accessible only through riddles--
Not to mention whimsically-shaped mirrors!
It's like this WHOLE PARK is based on our lives.
And in the meantime the Candy Kingdom is going to get cleaner than if we had stayed as our normal selves.
It's WIN WIN!

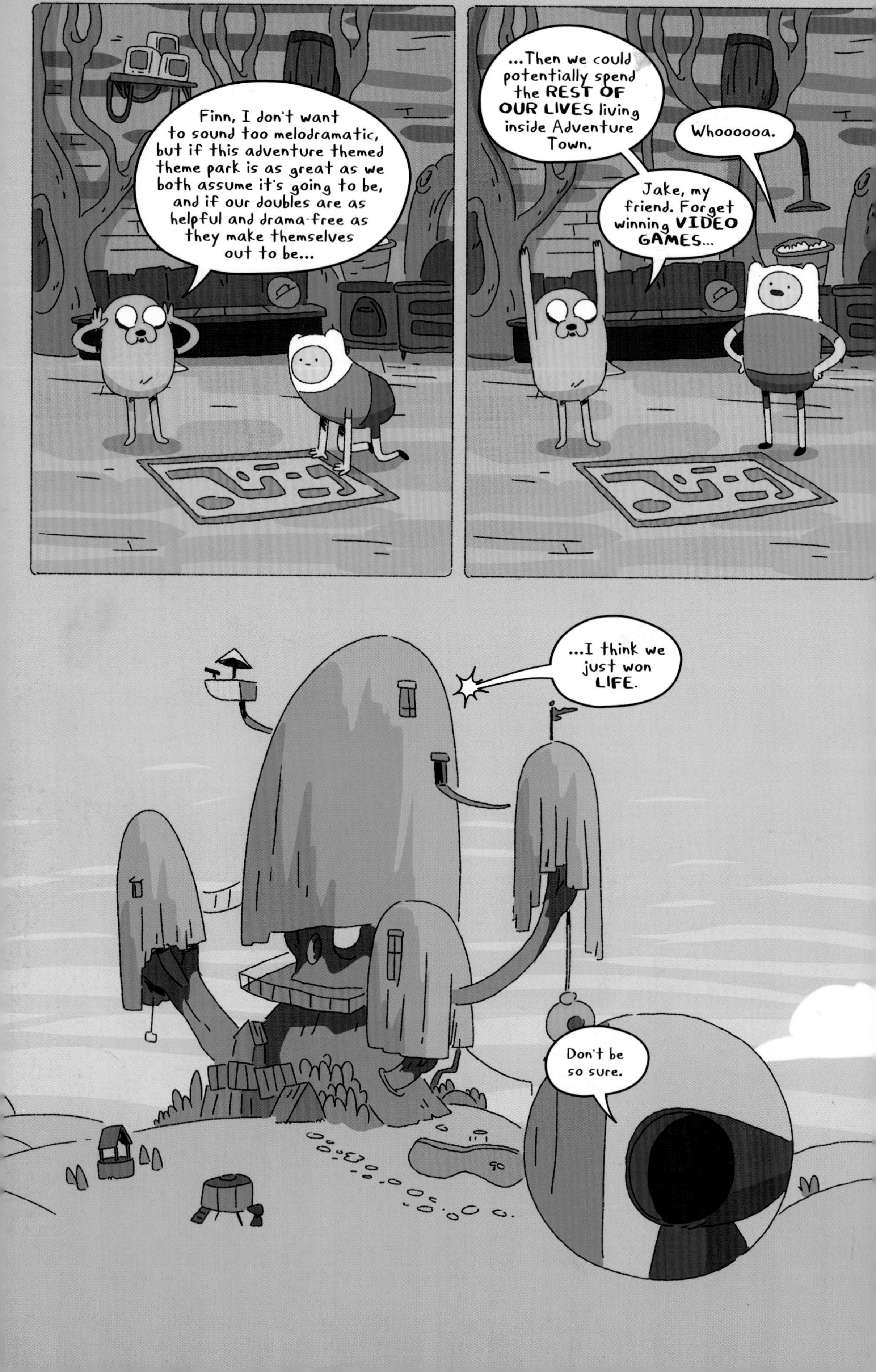
Finn, I don't want to sound too melodramatic, but if this adventure themed theme park is as great as we both assume it's going to be, and if our doubles are as helpful and drama-free as they make themselves out to be...
...Then we could potentially spend the REST OF OUR LIVES living inside Adventure Town.
Whoooooa.
Jake, my friend. Forget winning VIDEO GAMES...
...I think we just won LIFE.
Don't be so sure.

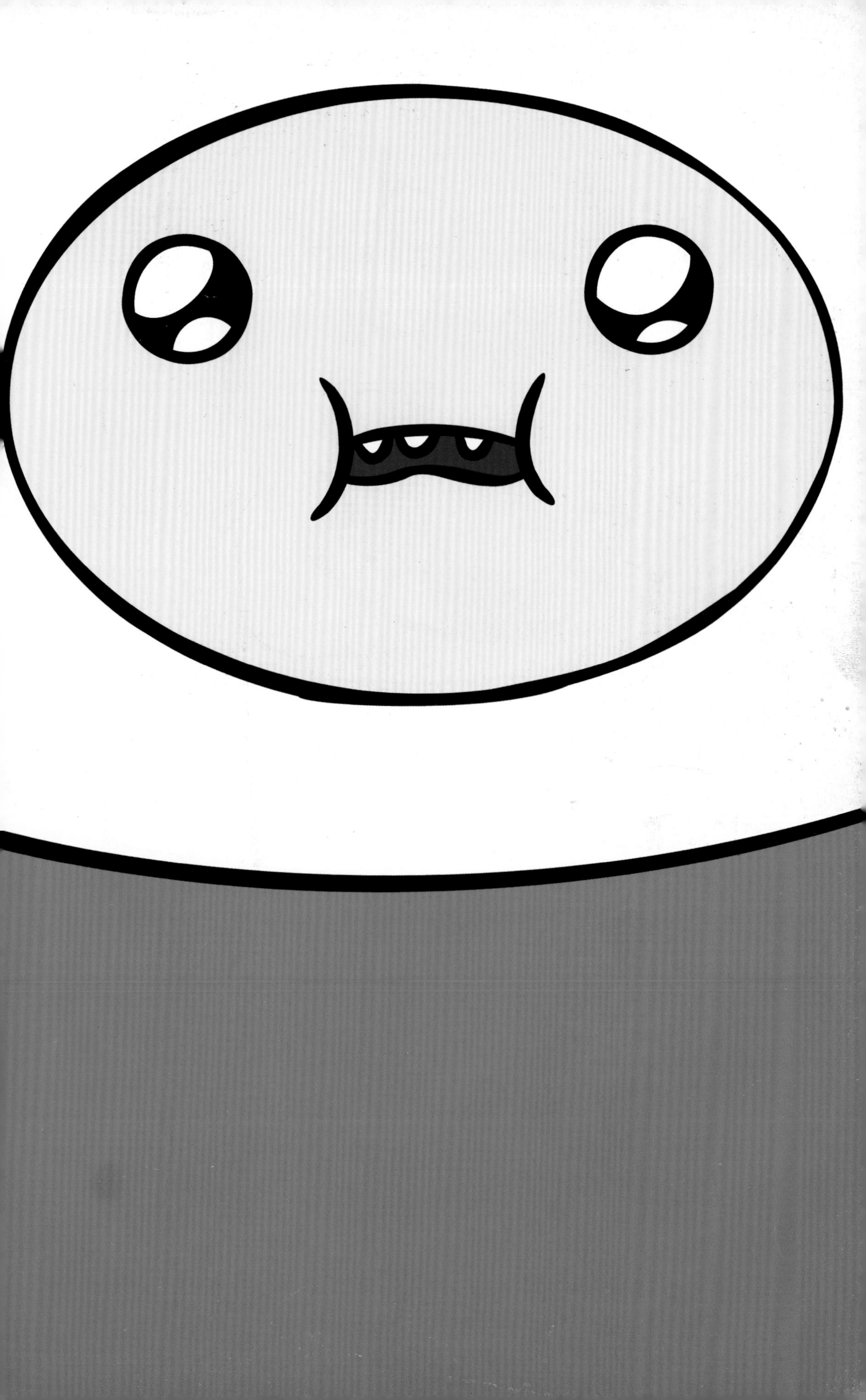

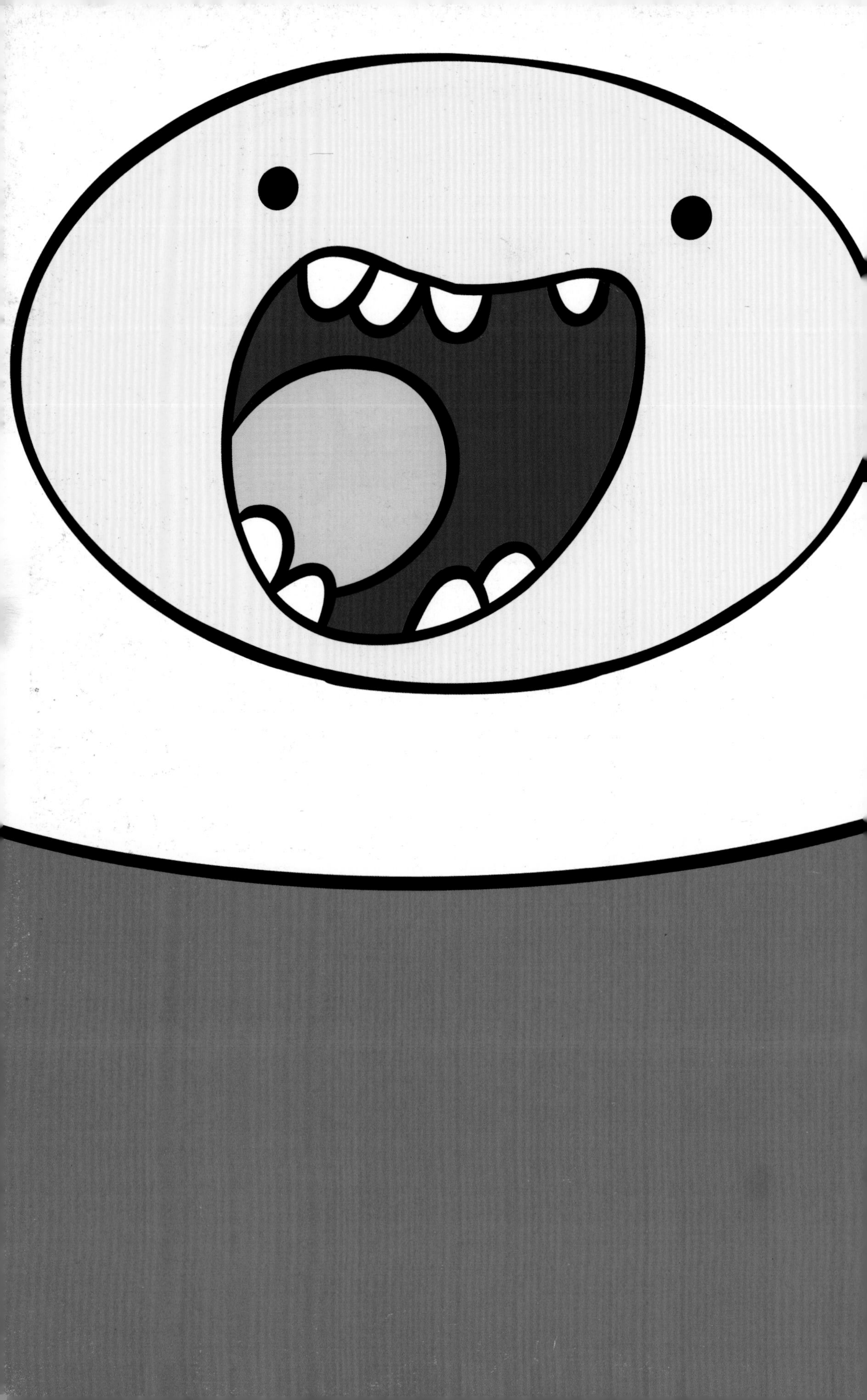

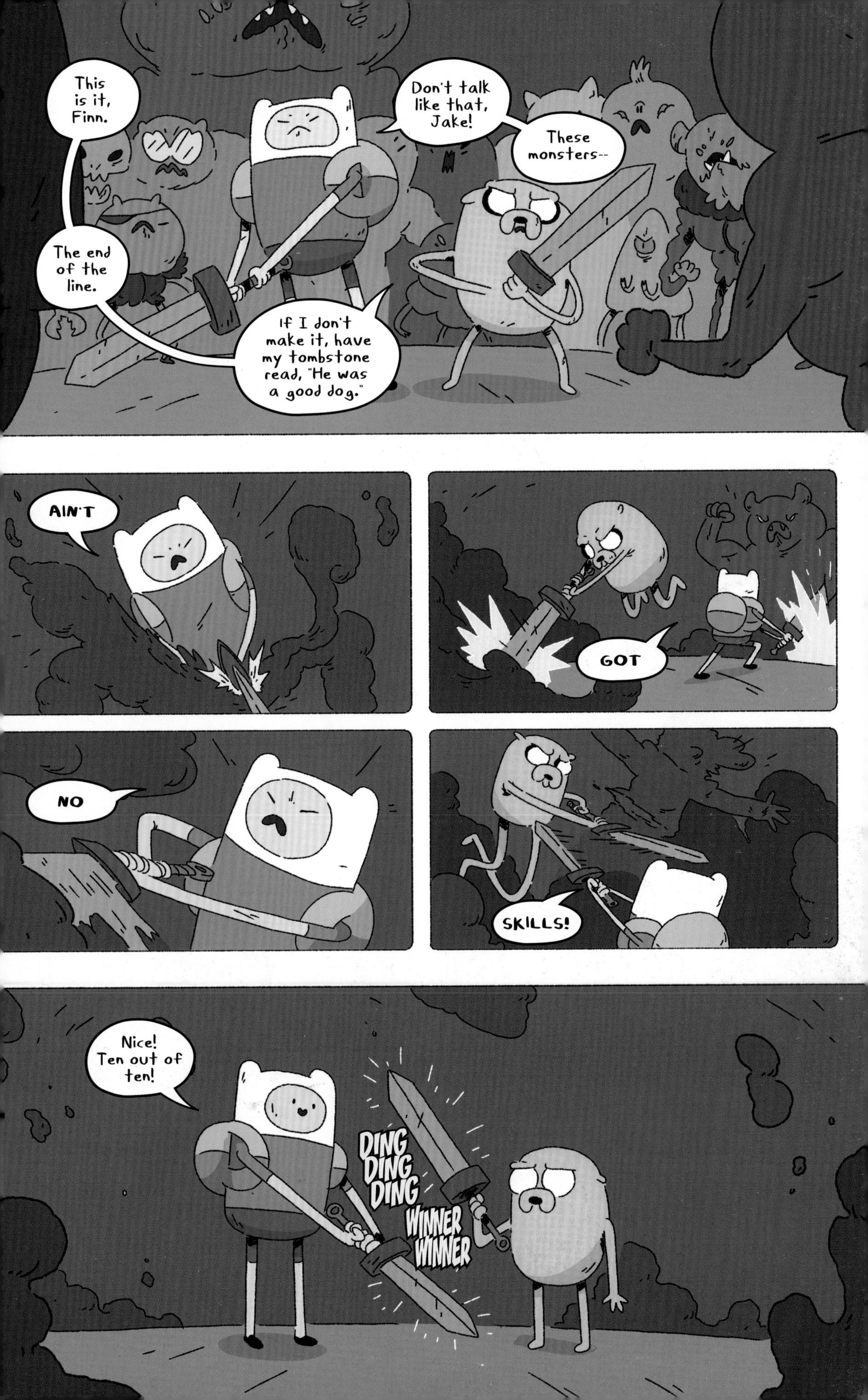
This is it, Finn.
The end of the line.
If I don't make it, have my tombstone read, "He was a good dog."
Don't talk like that, Jake!
These monsters--
AIN'T
GOT
NO
SKILLS!
Nice! Ten out of ten!
DING DING DING
WINNER WINNER

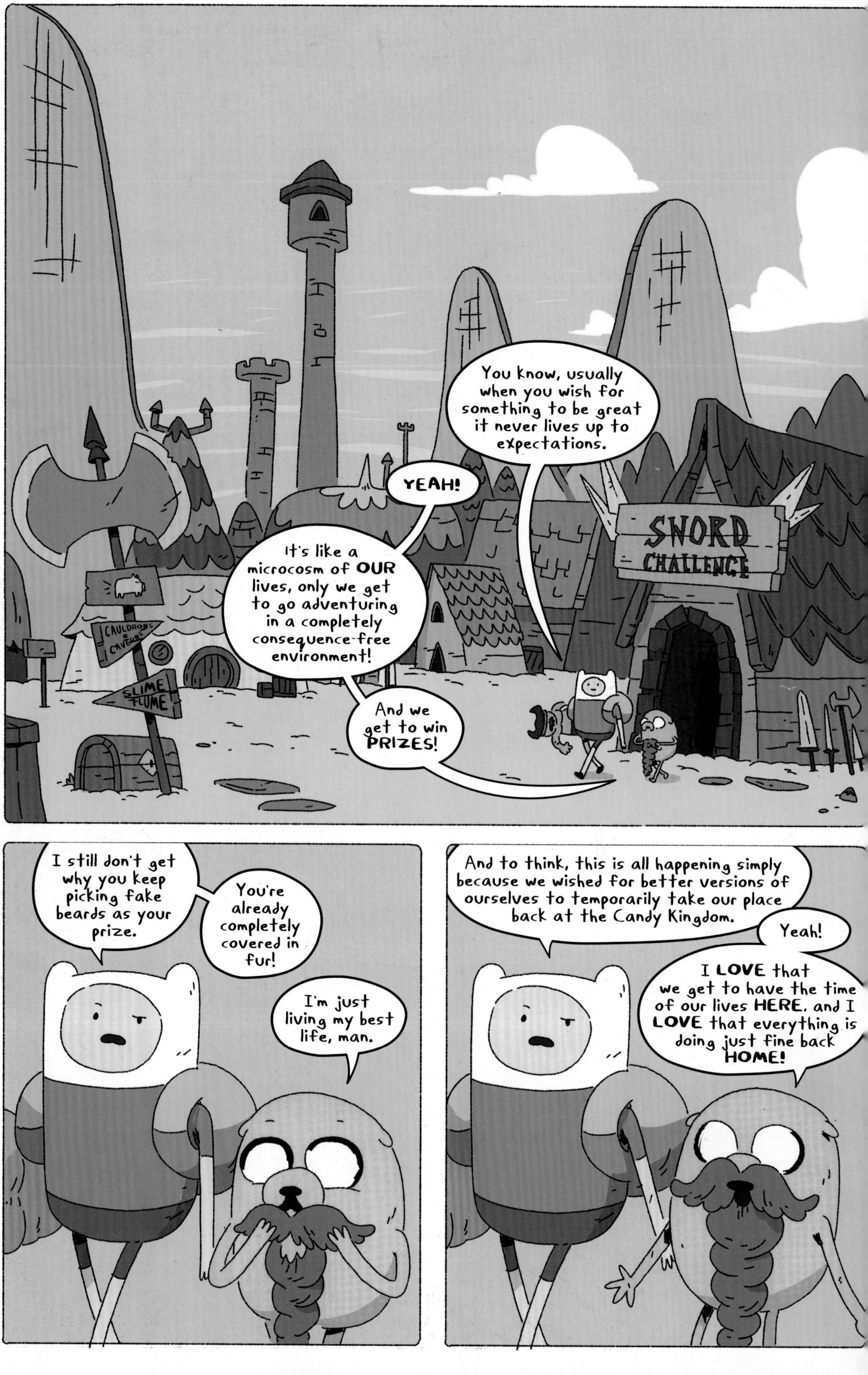
You know, usually when you wish for something to be great it never lives up to expectations.
YEAH!
It's like a microcosm of OUR lives, only we get to go adventuring in a completely consequence-free environment!
And we get to win PRIZES!
SWORD CHALLENGE
CAULDRONS CAVERNS
SLIME FLUME
I still don't get why you keep picking fake beards as your prize.
You're already completely covered in fur!
I'm just living my best life, man.
And to think, this is all happening simply because we wished for better versions of ourselves to temporarily take our place back at the Candy Kingdom.
Yeah!
I LOVE that we get to have the time of our lives HERE, and I LOVE that everything is doing just fine back HOME!

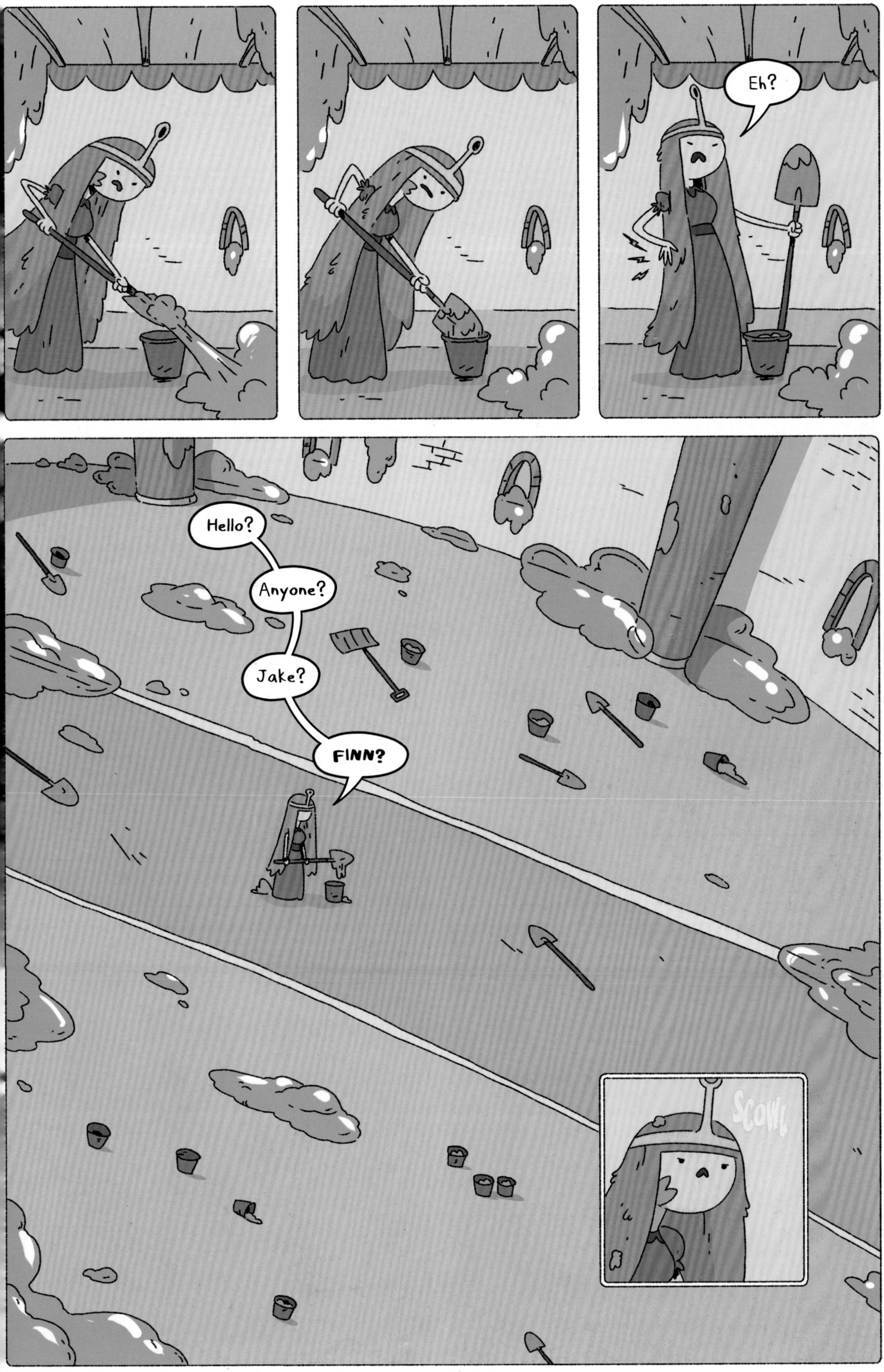
Eh?
Hello?
Anyone?
Jake?
FINN?
SCOWL

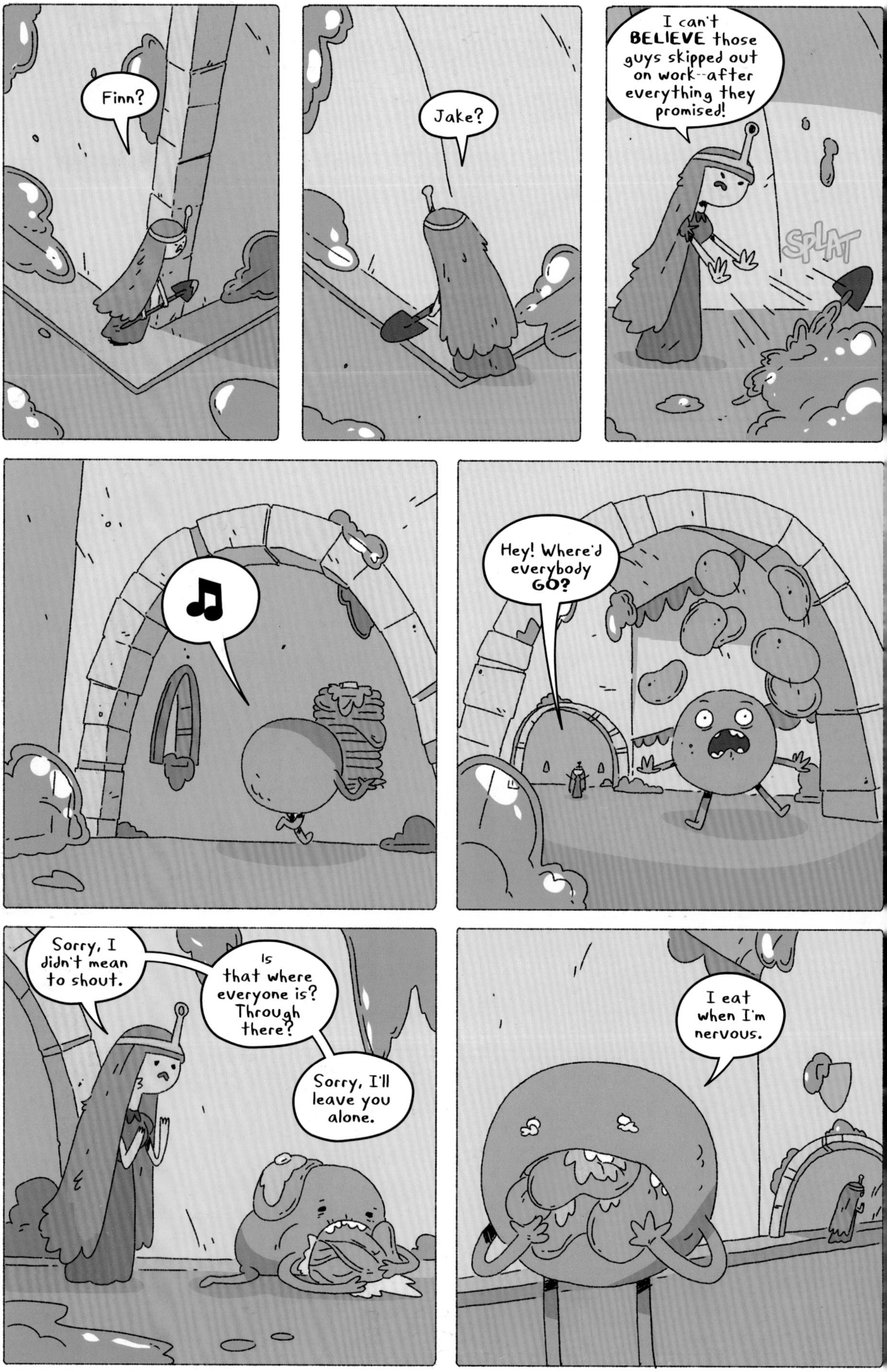
Finn?
Jake?
I can't BELIEVE those guys skipped out on work--after everything they promised!
SPLAT
♫
Hey! Where'd everybody GO?
Sorry, I didn't mean to shout.
Is that where everyone is? Through there?
Sorry, I'll leave you alone.
I eat when I'm nervous.

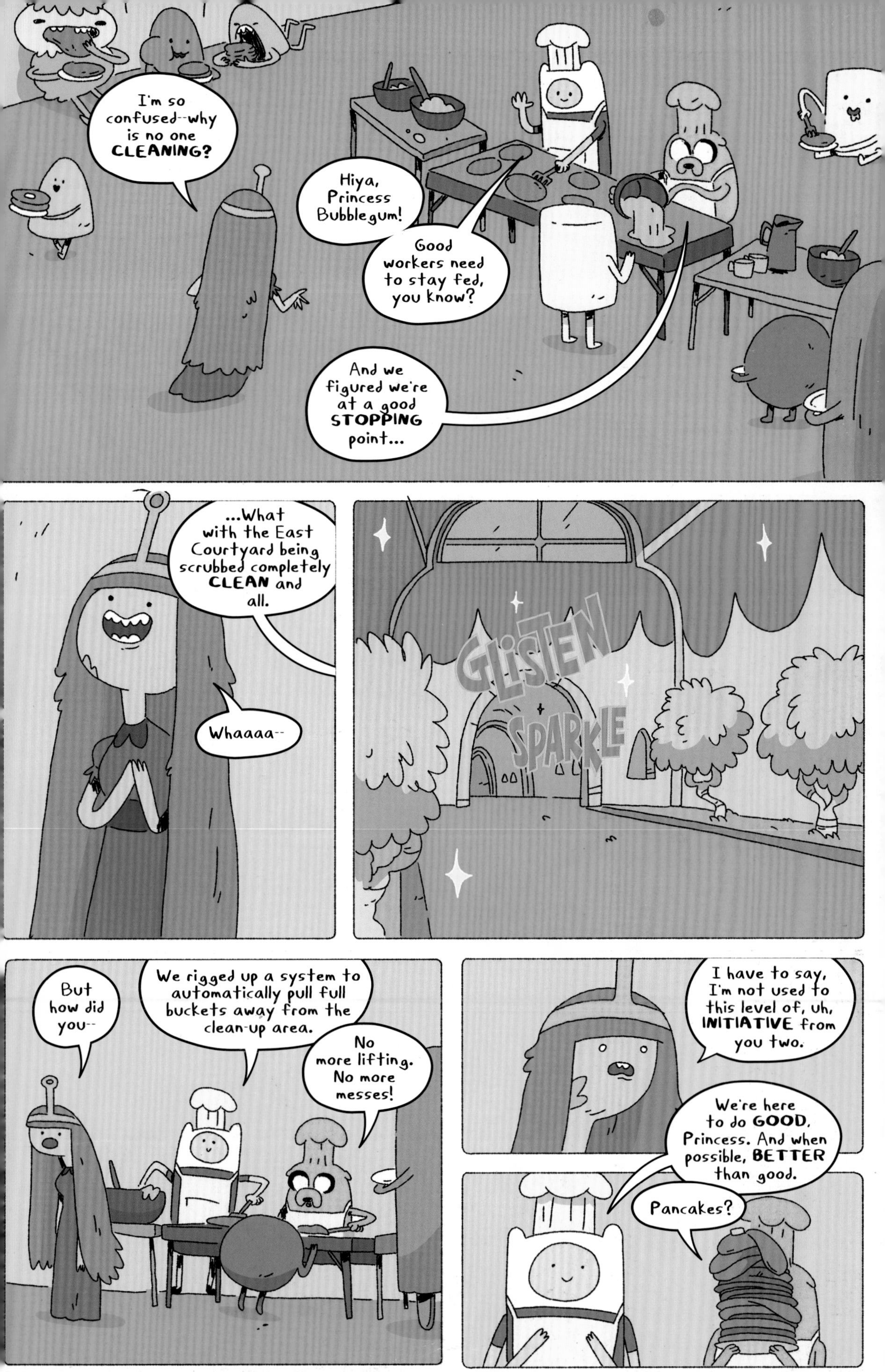

I'm so confused--why is no one **CLEANING?**
Hiya, Princess Bubblegum!
Good workers need to stay fed, you know?
And we figured we're at a good **STOPPING** point...
...What with the East Courtyard being scrubbed completely **CLEAN** and all.
Whaaaa--
GLISTEN
SPARKLE
But how did you--
We rigged up a system to automatically pull full buckets away from the clean-up area.
No more lifting. No more messes!
I have to say, I'm not used to this level of, uh, **INITIATIVE** from you two.
We're here to do **GOOD**, Princess. And when possible, **BETTER** than good.
Pancakes?

CREEAA AAAK

OH NO! The ride has stopped and we're stuck up here! We're doomed!

Just kiddin', Jake!

I know the ride operator only does that to heighten the tension.

Oh man, it's back! We just can't get away from that creep.

What?

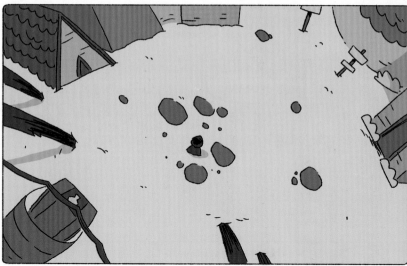

Man, that dude is seriously dampening my mood.

GO AWAY, MOOD-DAMPENER!

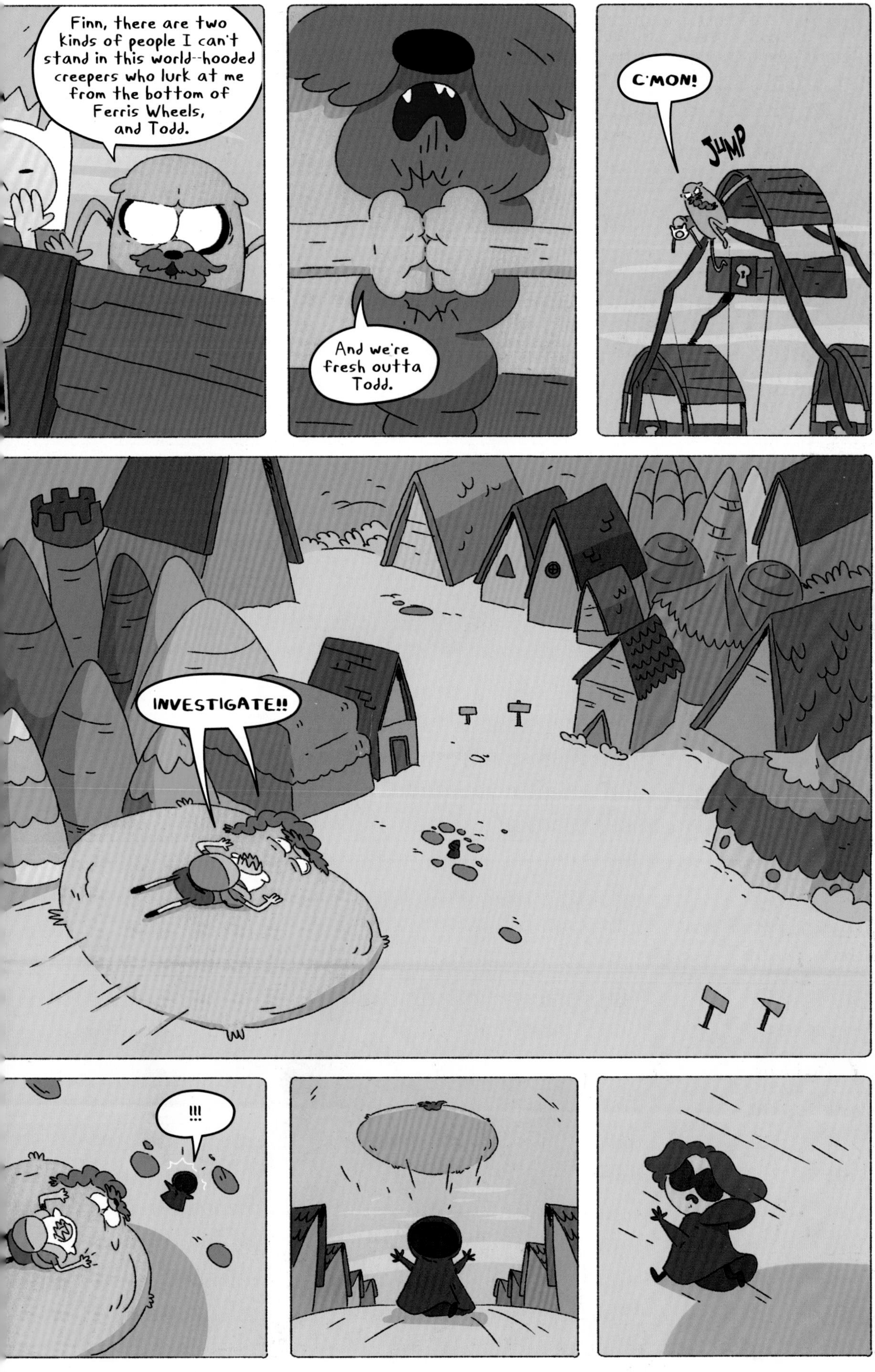
Finn, there are two kinds of people I can't stand in this world--hooded creepers who lurk at me from the bottom of Ferris Wheels, and Todd.
And we're fresh outta Todd.
C'MON!
JUMP
INVESTIGATE!!
!!!

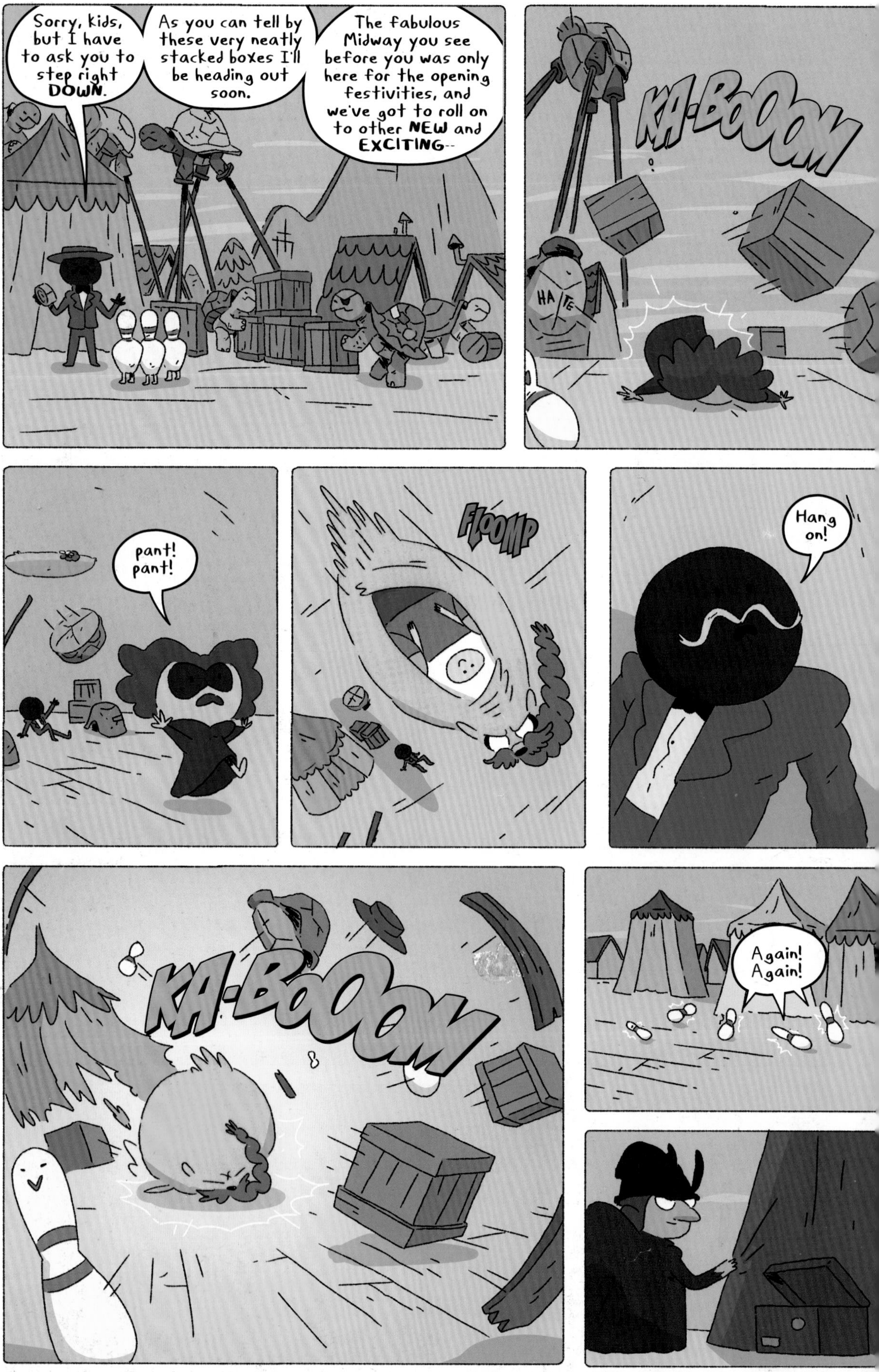
Sorry, kids, but I have to ask you to step right DOWN.
As you can tell by these very neatly stacked boxes I'll be heading out soon.
The fabulous Midway you see before you was only here for the opening festivities, and we've got to roll on to other NEW and EXCITING--
KA-BOOOOM
HATE
pant! pant!
FLOOMP
Hang on!
KA-BOOOOM
Again! Again!

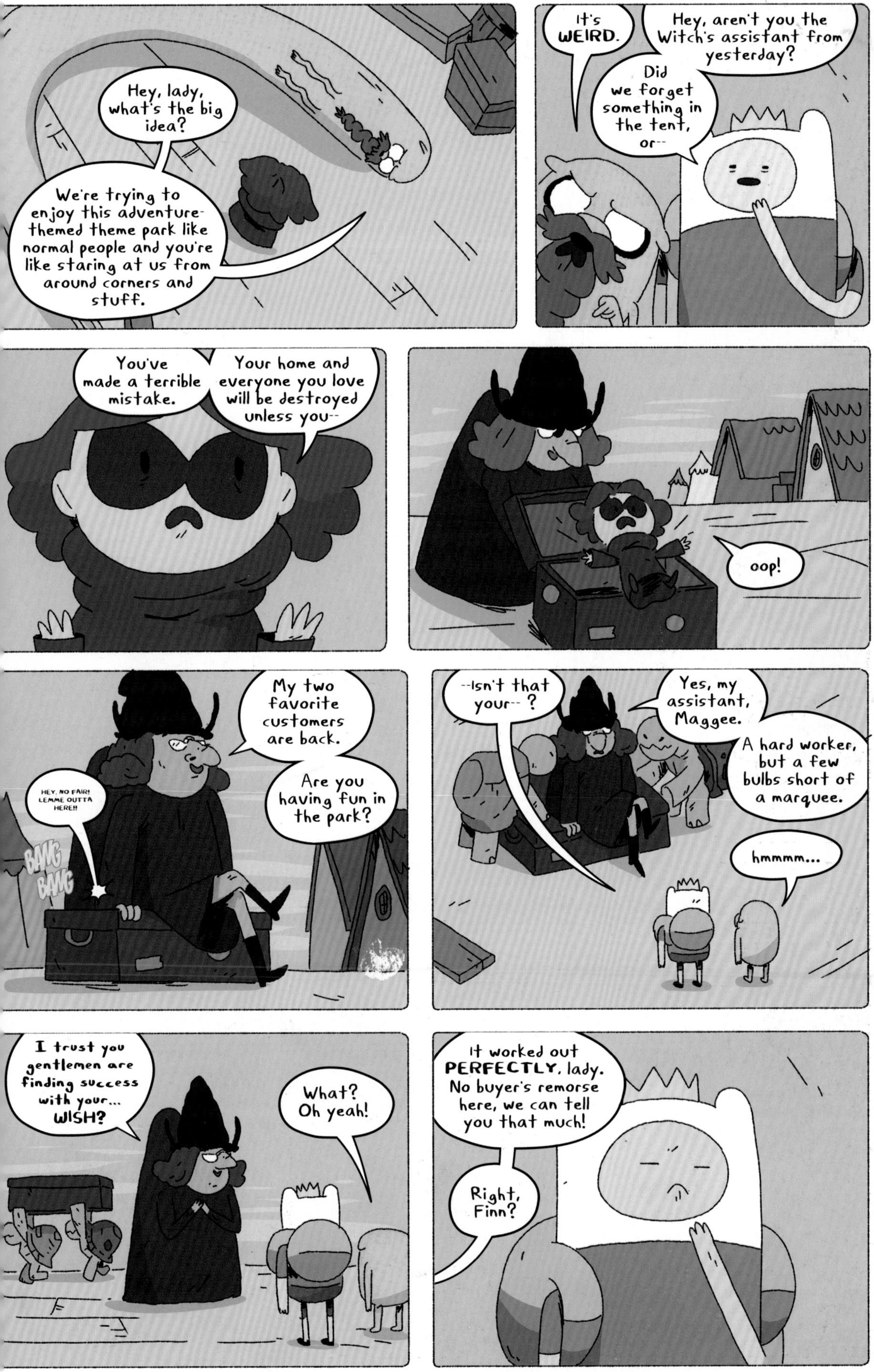
Hey, lady, what's the big idea?
We're trying to enjoy this adventure-themed theme park like normal people and you're like staring at us from around corners and stuff.
It's WEIRD.
Hey, aren't you the Witch's assistant from yesterday?
Did we forget something in the tent, or--
You've made a terrible mistake.
Your home and everyone you love will be destroyed unless you--
oop!
My two favorite customers are back.
Are you having fun in the park?
HEY, NO FAIR! LEMME OUTTA HERE!!
--Isn't that your-- ?
Yes, my assistant, Maggee.
A hard worker, but a few bulbs short of a marquee.
hmmmm...
I trust you gentlemen are finding success with your... WISH?
What? Oh yeah!
It worked out PERFECTLY, lady. No buyer's remorse here, we can tell you that much!
Right, Finn?

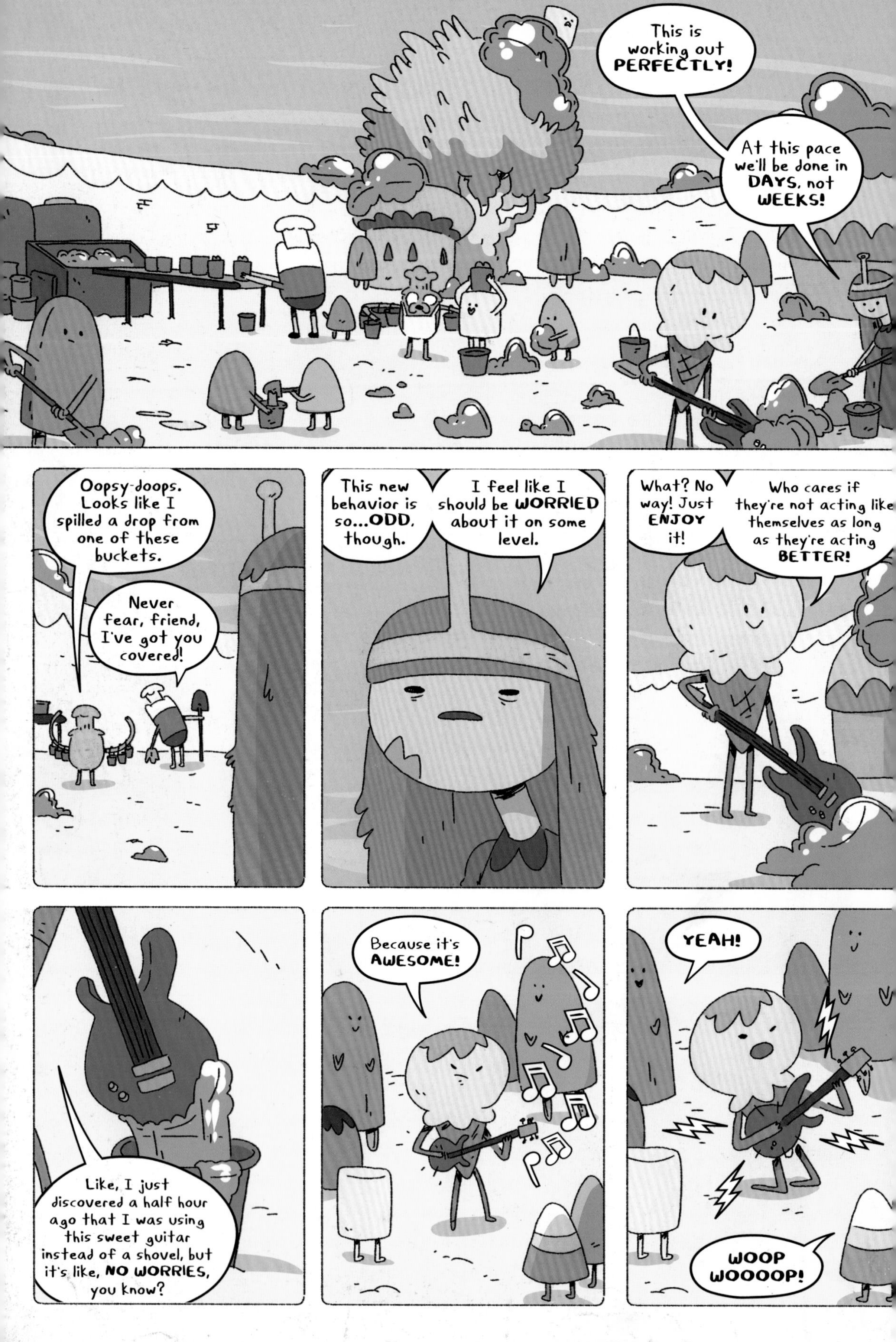
This is working out PERFECTLY!
At this pace we'll be done in DAYS, not WEEKS!
Oopsy-doops. Looks like I spilled a drop from one of these buckets.
Never fear, friend, I've got you covered!
This new behavior is so...ODD, though.
I feel like I should be WORRIED about it on some level.
What? No way! Just ENJOY it!
Who cares if they're not acting like themselves as long as they're acting BETTER!
Like, I just discovered a half hour ago that I was using this sweet guitar instead of a shovel, but it's like, NO WORRIES, you know?
Because it's AWESOME!
YEAH!
WOOP WOOOOP!

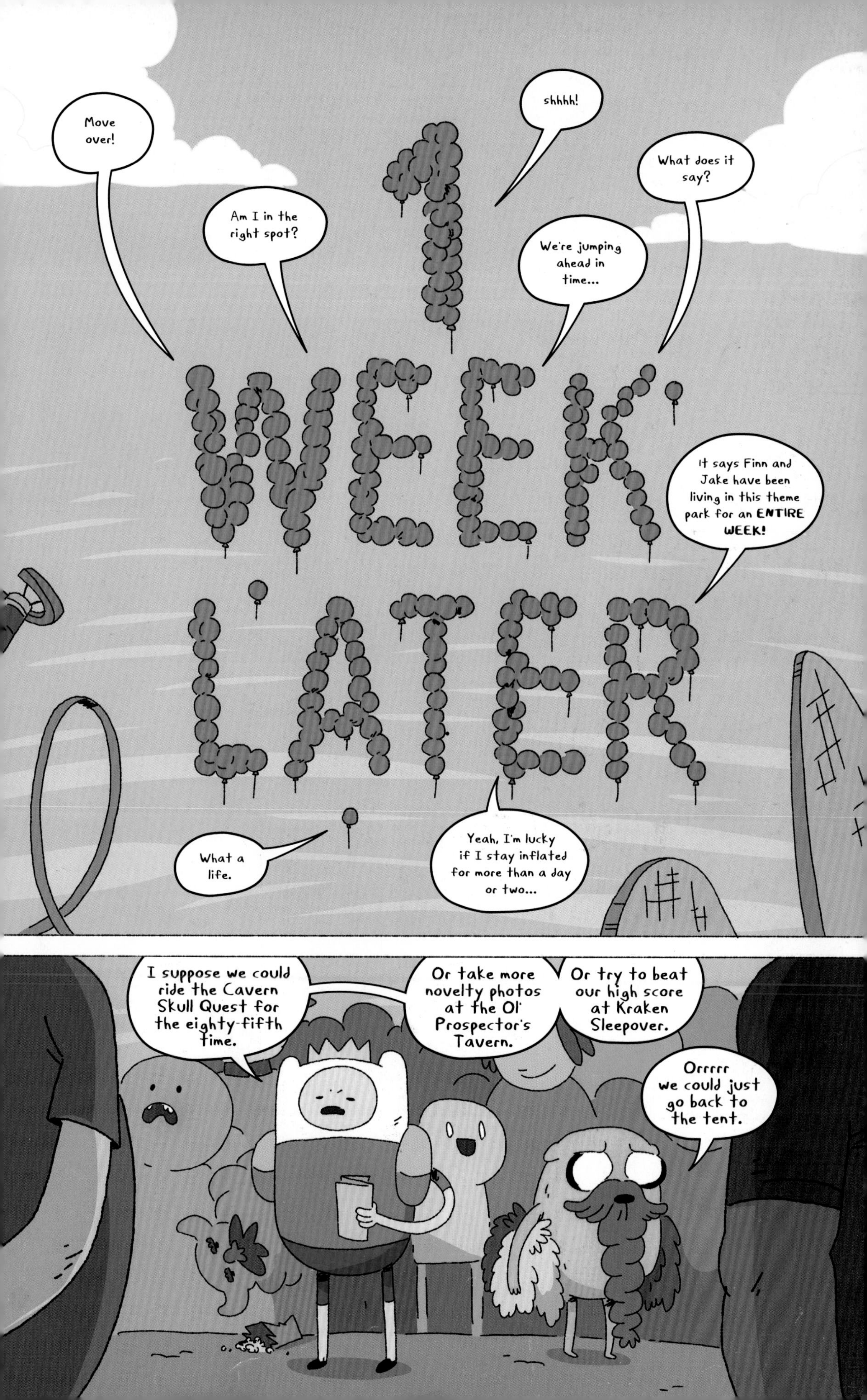
Move over!
Am I in the right spot?
1
shhhh!
What does it say?
We're jumping ahead in time...
WEEK
It says Finn and Jake have been living in this theme park for an ENTIRE WEEK!
LATER
What a life.
Yeah, I'm lucky if I stay inflated for more than a day or two...
I suppose we could ride the Cavern Skull Quest for the eighty-fifth time.
Or take more novelty photos at the Ol' Prospector's Tavern.
Or try to beat our high score at Kraken Sleepover.
Orrrrr we could just go back to the tent.

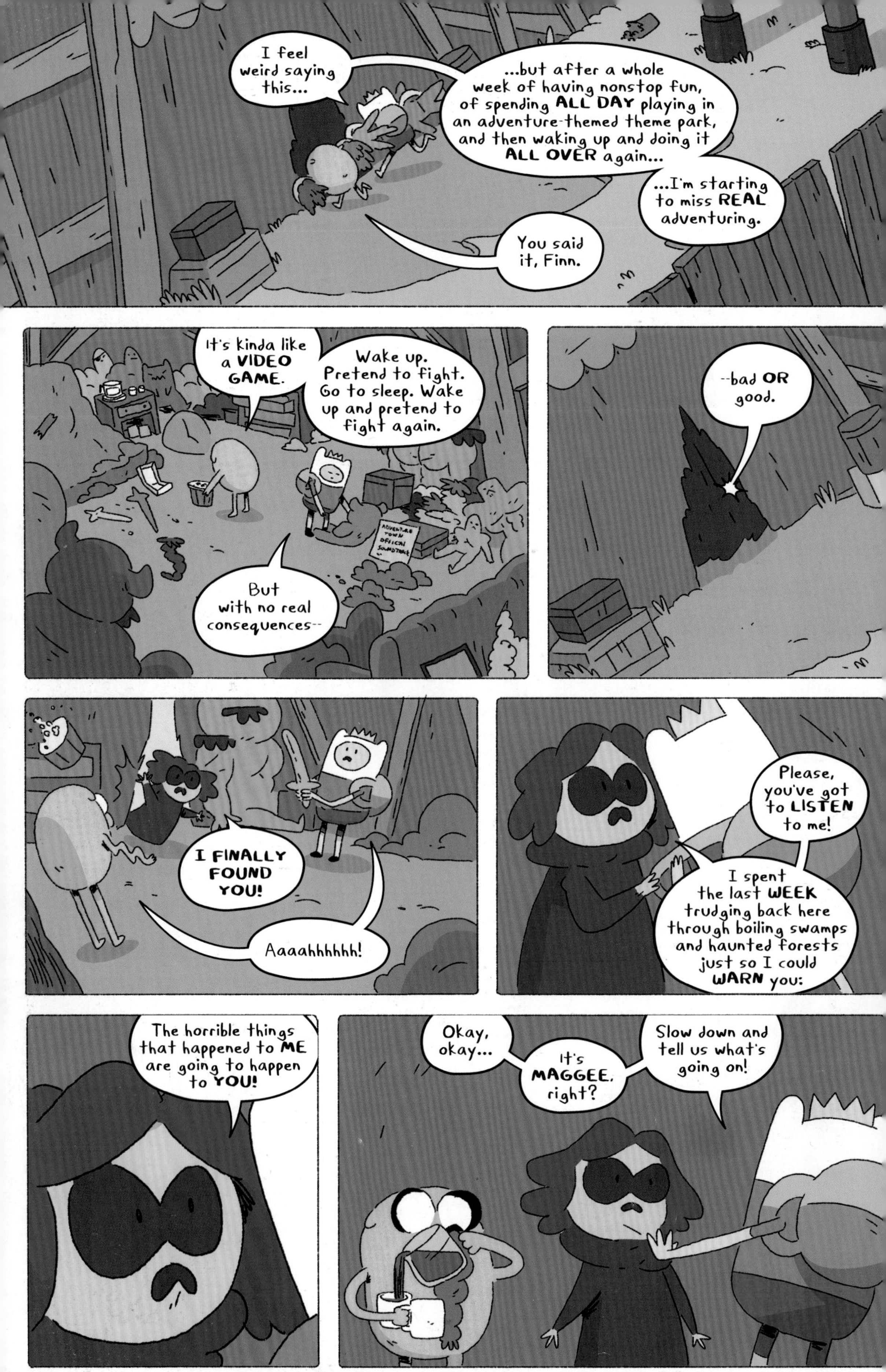
I feel weird saying this...
...but after a whole week of having nonstop fun, of spending ALL DAY playing in an adventure-themed theme park, and then waking up and doing it ALL OVER again...
...I'm starting to miss REAL adventuring.
You said it, Finn.
It's kinda like a VIDEO GAME.
Wake up. Pretend to fight. Go to sleep. Wake up and pretend to fight again.
But with no real consequences--
--bad OR good.
I FINALLY FOUND YOU!
Aaaahhhhhh!
Please, you've got to LISTEN to me!
I spent the last WEEK trudging back here through boiling swamps and haunted forests just so I could WARN you:
The horrible things that happened to ME are going to happen to YOU!
Okay, okay...
It's MAGGEE, right?
Slow down and tell us what's going on!

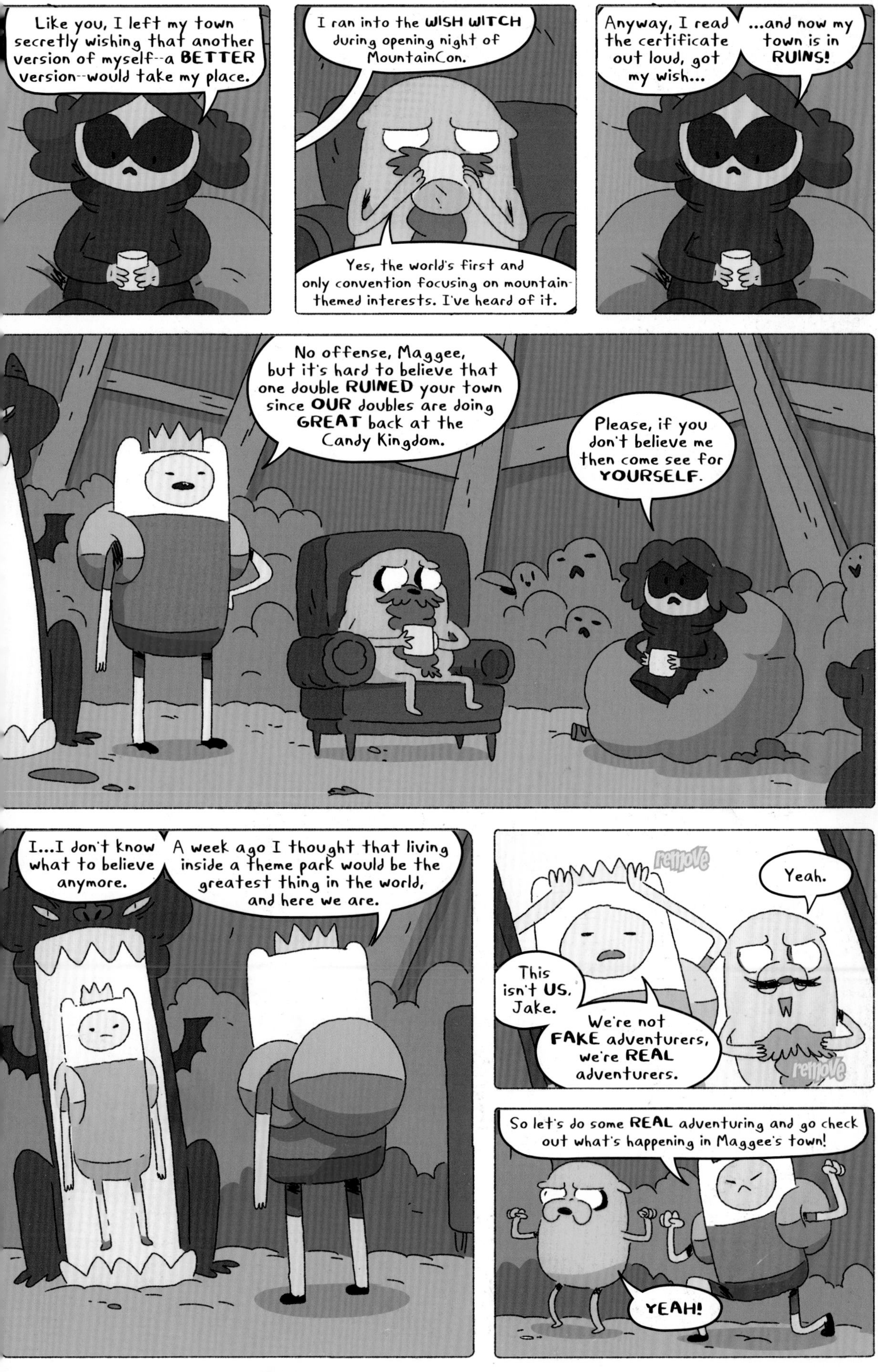

Like you, I left my town secretly wishing that another version of myself--a BETTER version--would take my place.
I ran into the WISH WITCH during opening night of MountainCon.
Yes, the world's first and only convention focusing on mountain-themed interests. I've heard of it.
Anyway, I read the certificate out loud, got my wish...
...and now my town is in RUINS!
No offense, Maggee, but it's hard to believe that one double RUINED your town since OUR doubles are doing GREAT back at the Candy Kingdom.
Please, if you don't believe me then come see for YOURSELF.
I...I don't know what to believe anymore.
A week ago I thought that living inside a theme park would be the greatest thing in the world, and here we are.
Yeah.
This isn't US, Jake.
We're not FAKE adventurers, we're REAL adventurers.
So let's do some REAL adventuring and go check out what's happening in Maggee's town!
YEAH!

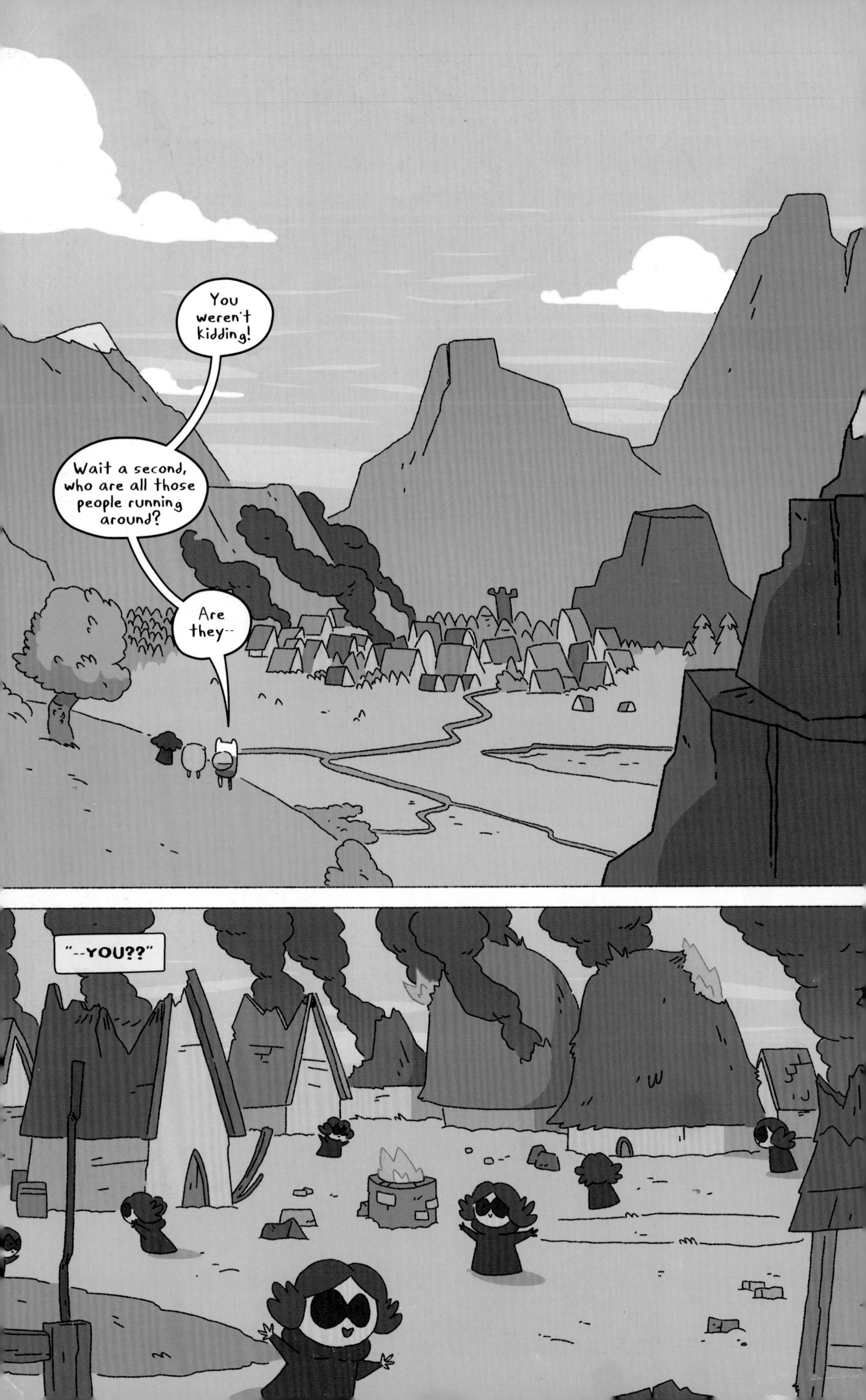
You weren't kidding!
Wait a second, who are all those people running around?
Are they--
"--YOU??"

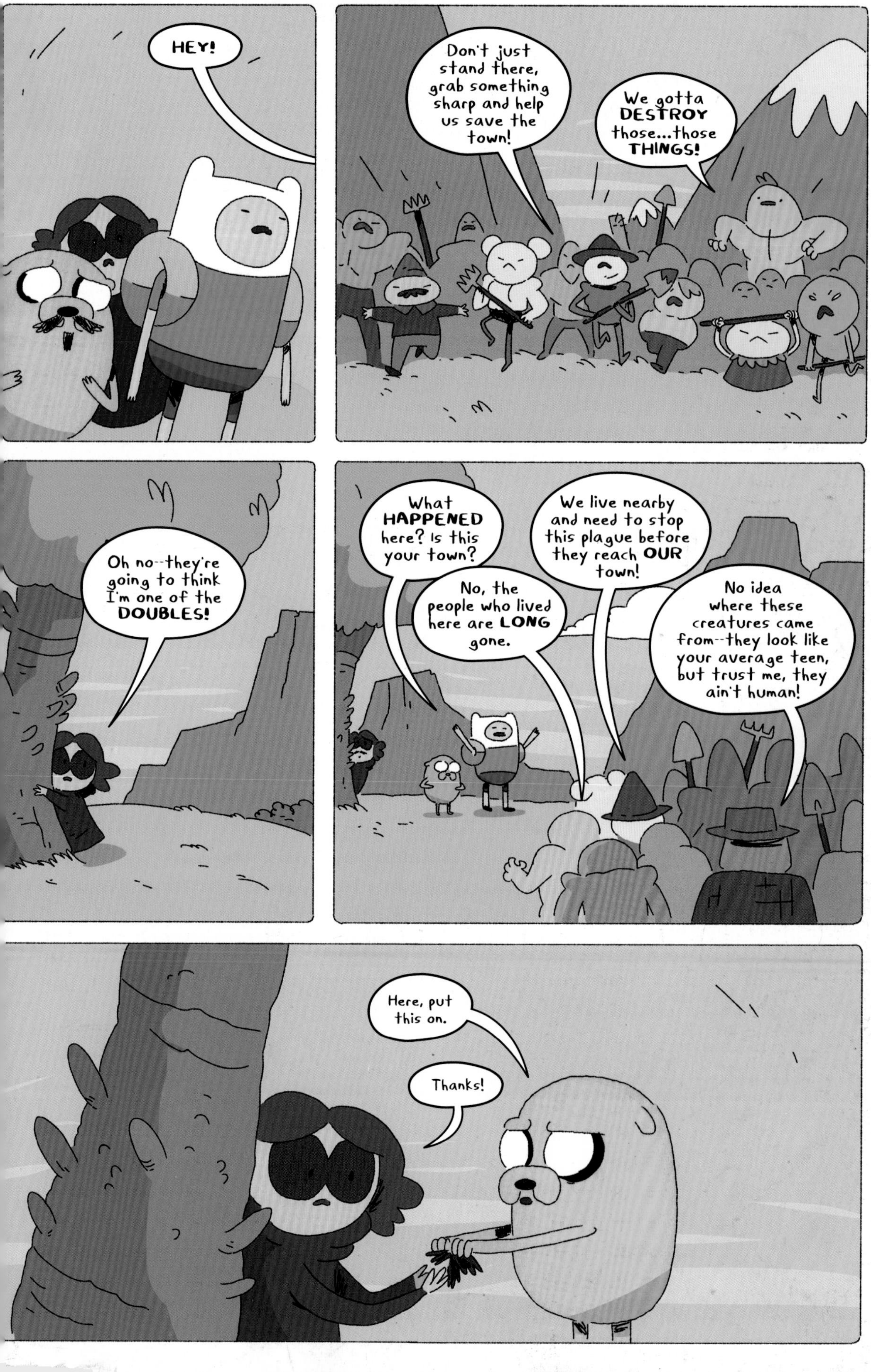
HEY!
Don't just stand there, grab something sharp and help us save the town!
We gotta DESTROY those...those THINGS!
Oh no--they're going to think I'm one of the DOUBLES!
What HAPPENED here? Is this your town?
No, the people who lived here are LONG gone.
We live nearby and need to stop this plague before they reach OUR town!
No idea where these creatures came from--they look like your average teen, but trust me, they ain't human!
Here, put this on.
Thanks!

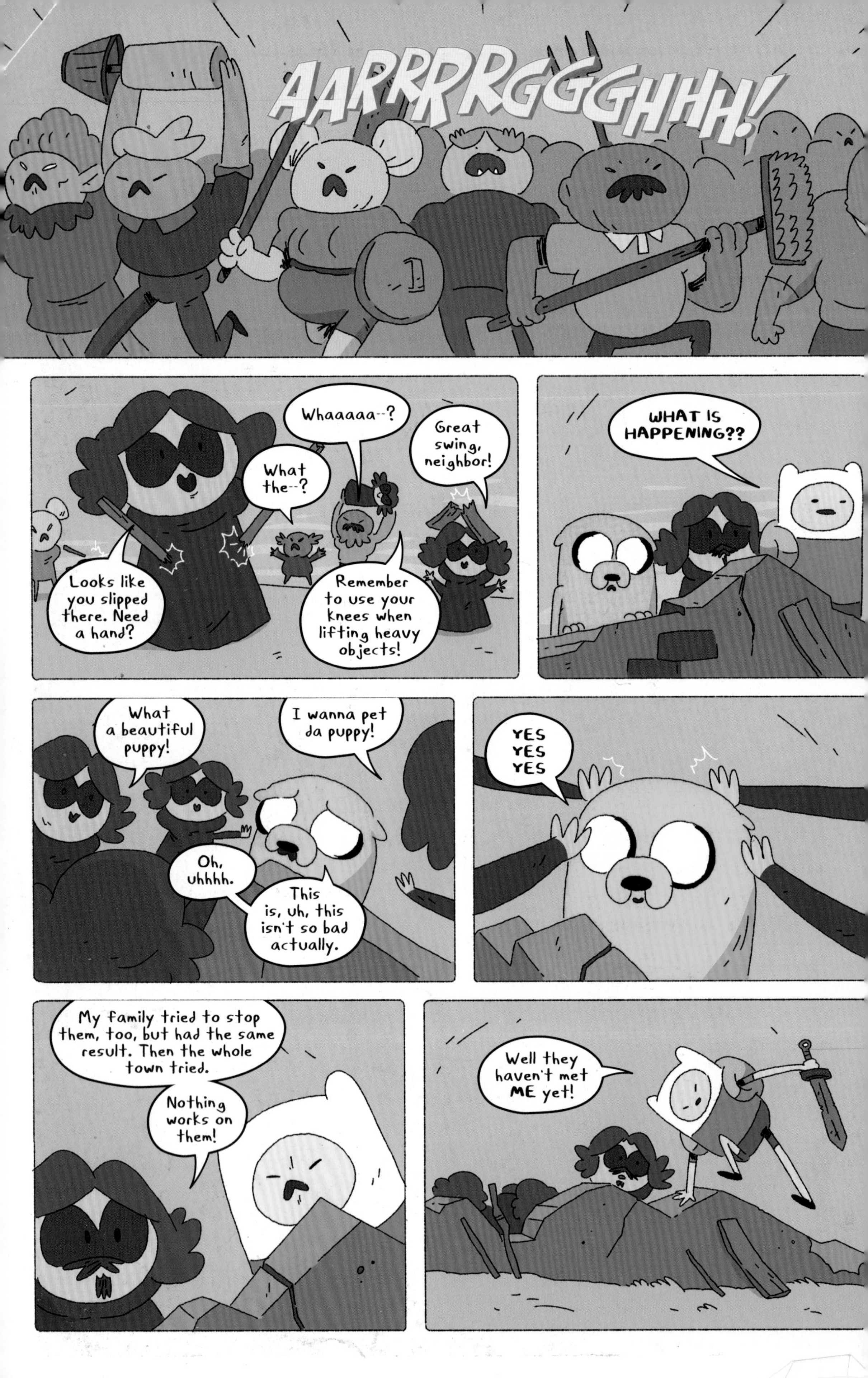
AARRRRGGGHHH!
Whaaaaa--?
Great swing, neighbor!
What the--?
Looks like you slipped there. Need a hand?
Remember to use your knees when lifting heavy objects!
WHAT IS HAPPENING??
What a beautiful puppy!
I wanna pet da puppy!
Oh, uhhhh.
This is, uh, this isn't so bad actually.
YES YES YES
My family tried to stop them, too, but had the same result. Then the whole town tried.
Nothing works on them!
Well they haven't met ME yet!

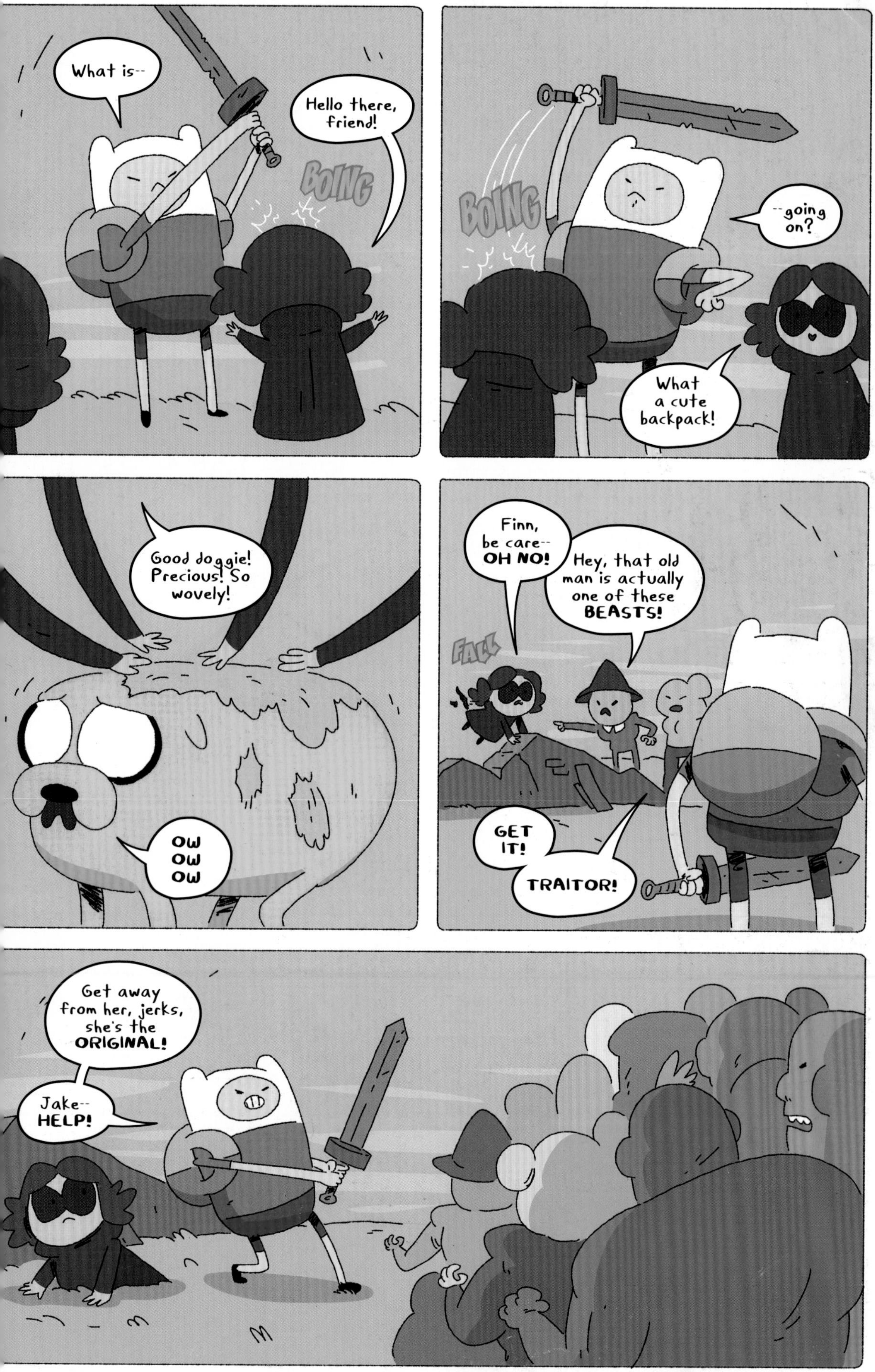
What is--
Hello there, friend!
BOING
BOING
--going on?
What a cute backpack!
Good doggie! Precious! So wovely!
OW OW OW
Finn, be care-- OH NO!
Hey, that old man is actually one of these BEASTS!
GET IT!
TRAITOR!
Get away from her, jerks, she's the ORIGINAL!
Jake-- HELP!

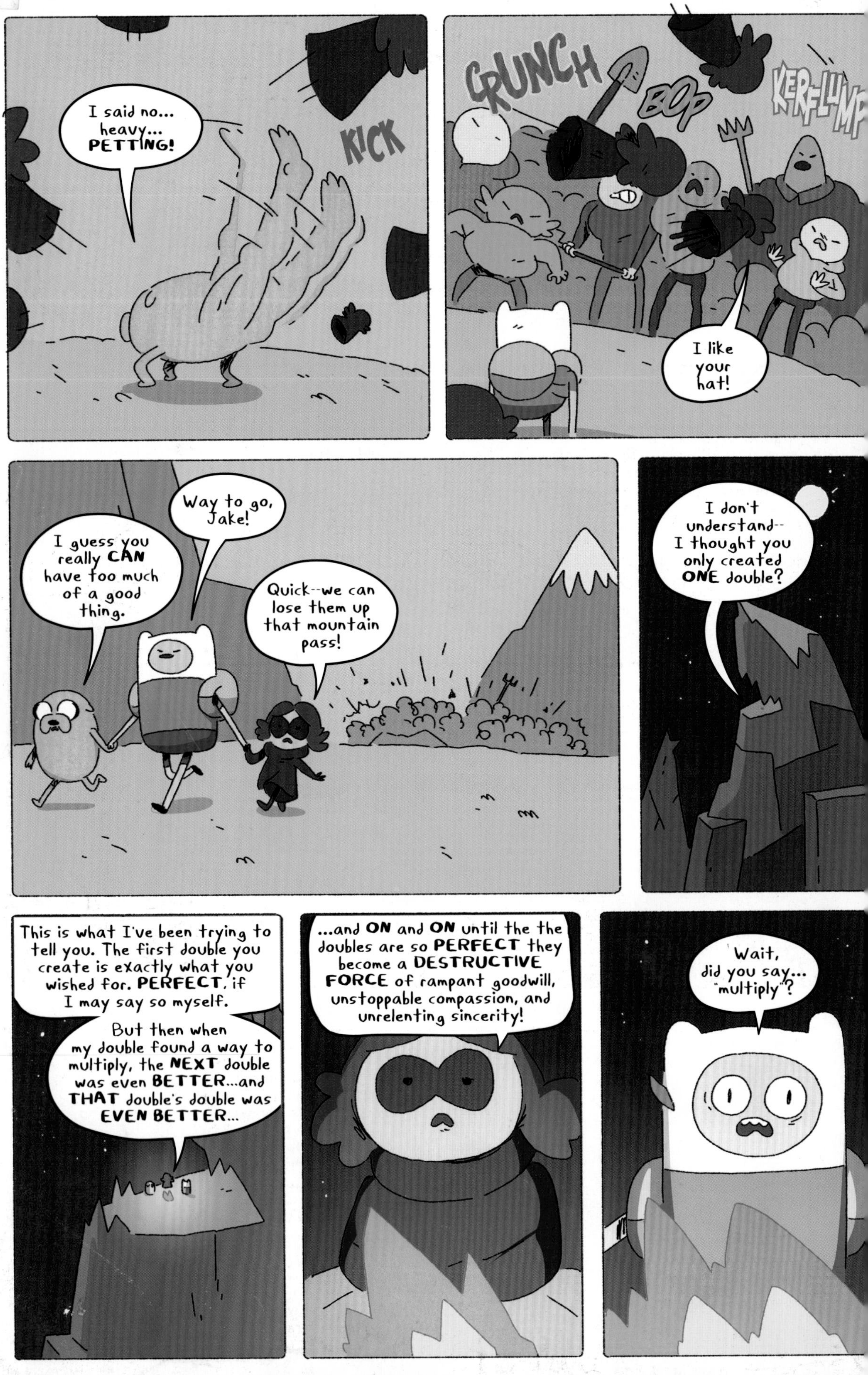
I said no... heavy... PETTING!
KICK
CRUNCH
BOP
KERFLUMP
I like your hat!
I guess you really CAN have too much of a good thing.
Way to go, Jake!
Quick--we can lose them up that mountain pass!
I don't understand-- I thought you only created ONE double?
This is what I've been trying to tell you. The first double you create is exactly what you wished for. PERFECT, if I may say so myself.
But then when my double found a way to multiply, the NEXT double was even BETTER...and THAT double's double was EVEN BETTER...
...and ON and ON until the the doubles are so PERFECT they become a DESTRUCTIVE FORCE of rampant goodwill, unstoppable compassion, and unrelenting sincerity!
Wait, did you say... "multiply"?

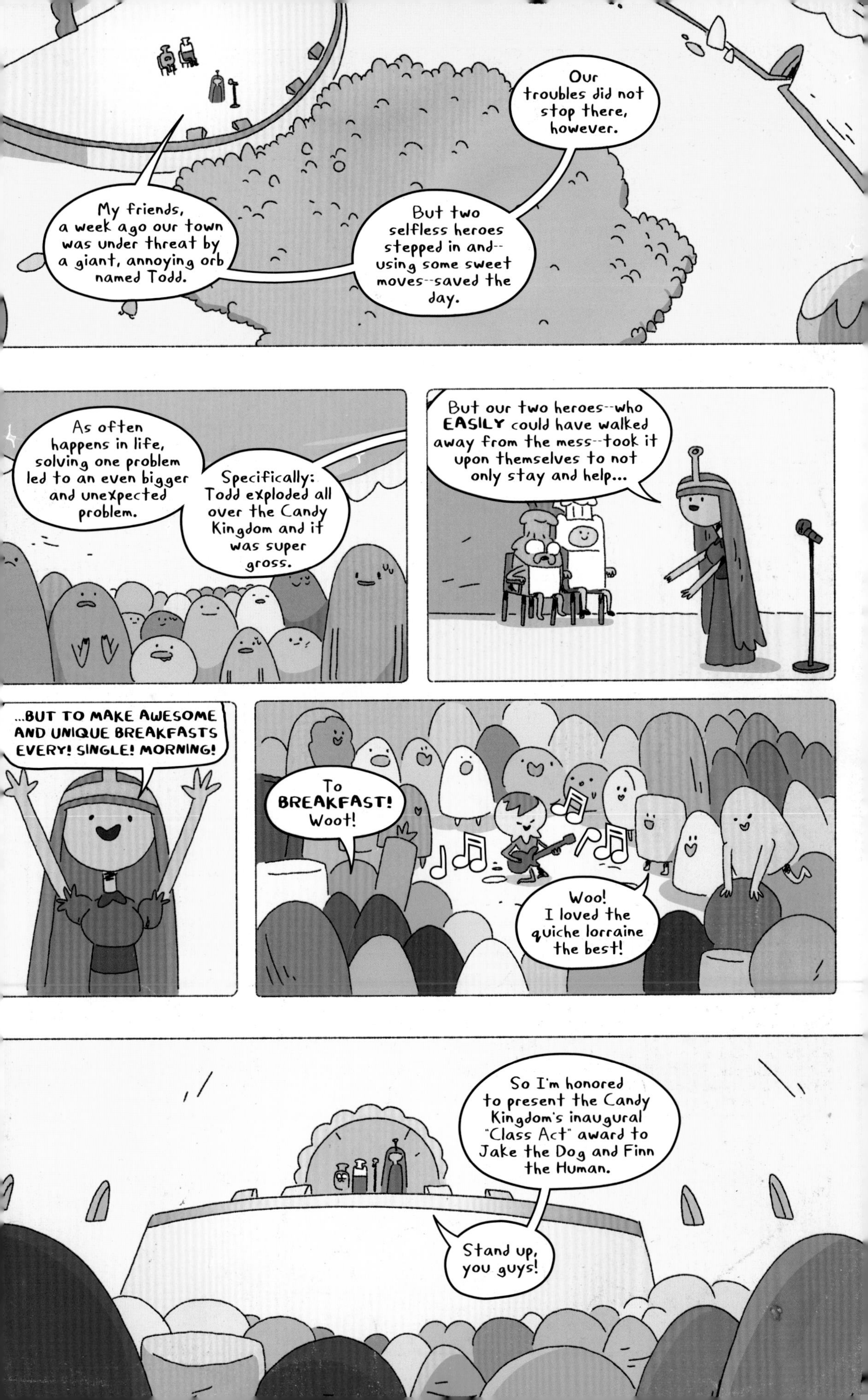
My friends, a week ago our town was under threat by a giant, annoying orb named Todd.
But two selfless heroes stepped in and--using some sweet moves--saved the day.
Our troubles did not stop there, however.
As often happens in life, solving one problem led to an even bigger and unexpected problem.
Specifically: Todd exploded all over the Candy Kingdom and it was super gross.
But our two heroes--who EASILY could have walked away from the mess--took it upon themselves to not only stay and help...
...BUT TO MAKE AWESOME AND UNIQUE BREAKFASTS EVERY! SINGLE! MORNING!
To BREAKFAST! Woot!
Woo! I loved the quiche lorraine the best!
So I'm honored to present the Candy Kingdom's inaugural "Class Act" award to Jake the Dog and Finn the Human.
Stand up, you guys!

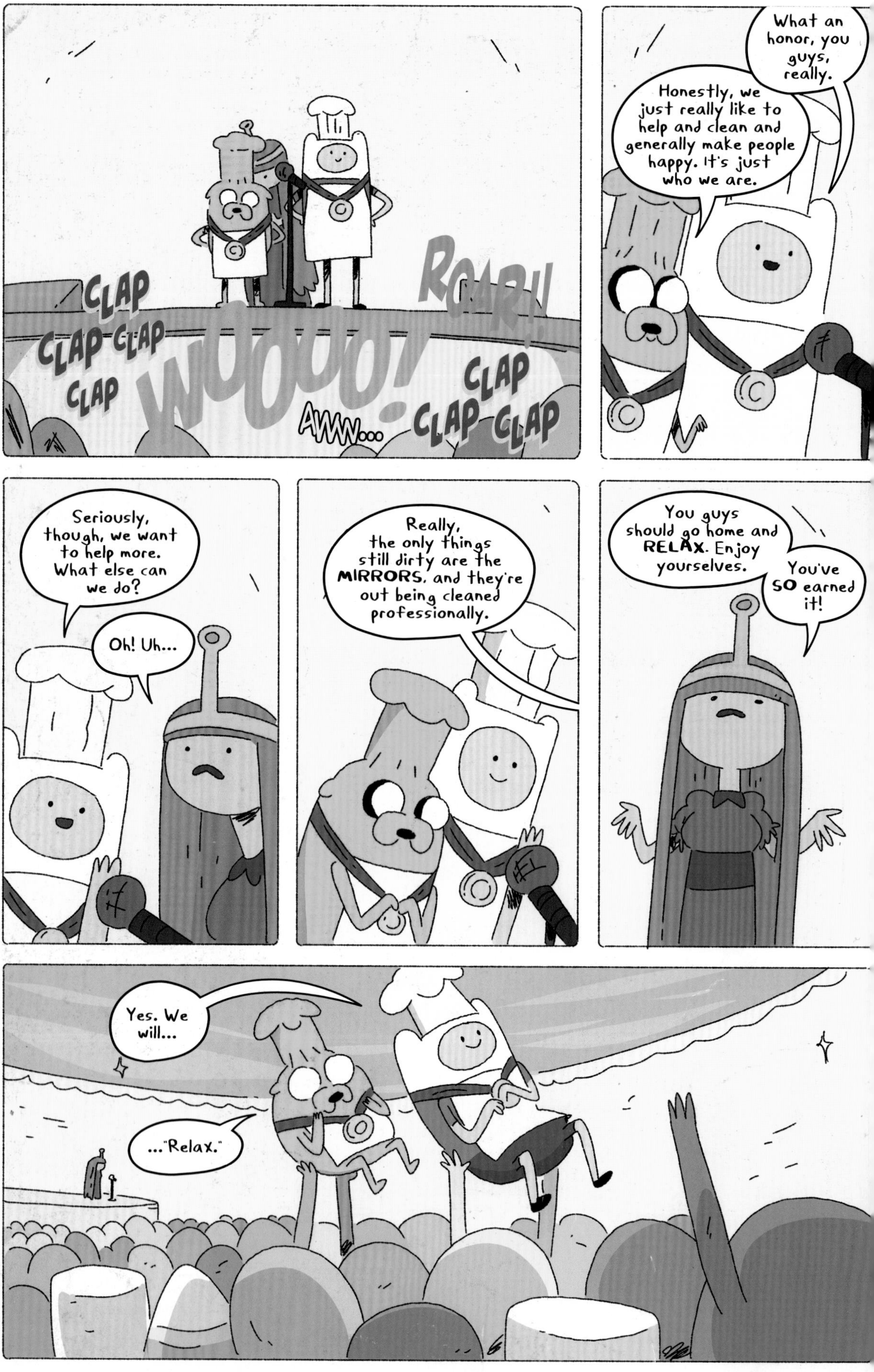
CLAP
CLAP CLAP
CLAP
WOOOO!
AWW...
ROAR!!
CLAP
CLAP CLAP
Honestly, we just really like to help and clean and generally make people happy. It's just who we are.
What an honor, you guys, really.
Seriously, though, we want to help more. What else can we do?
Oh! Uh...
Really, the only things still dirty are the MIRRORS, and they're out being cleaned professionally.
You guys should go home and RELAX. Enjoy yourselves.
You've SO earned it!
Yes. We will...
..."Relax."

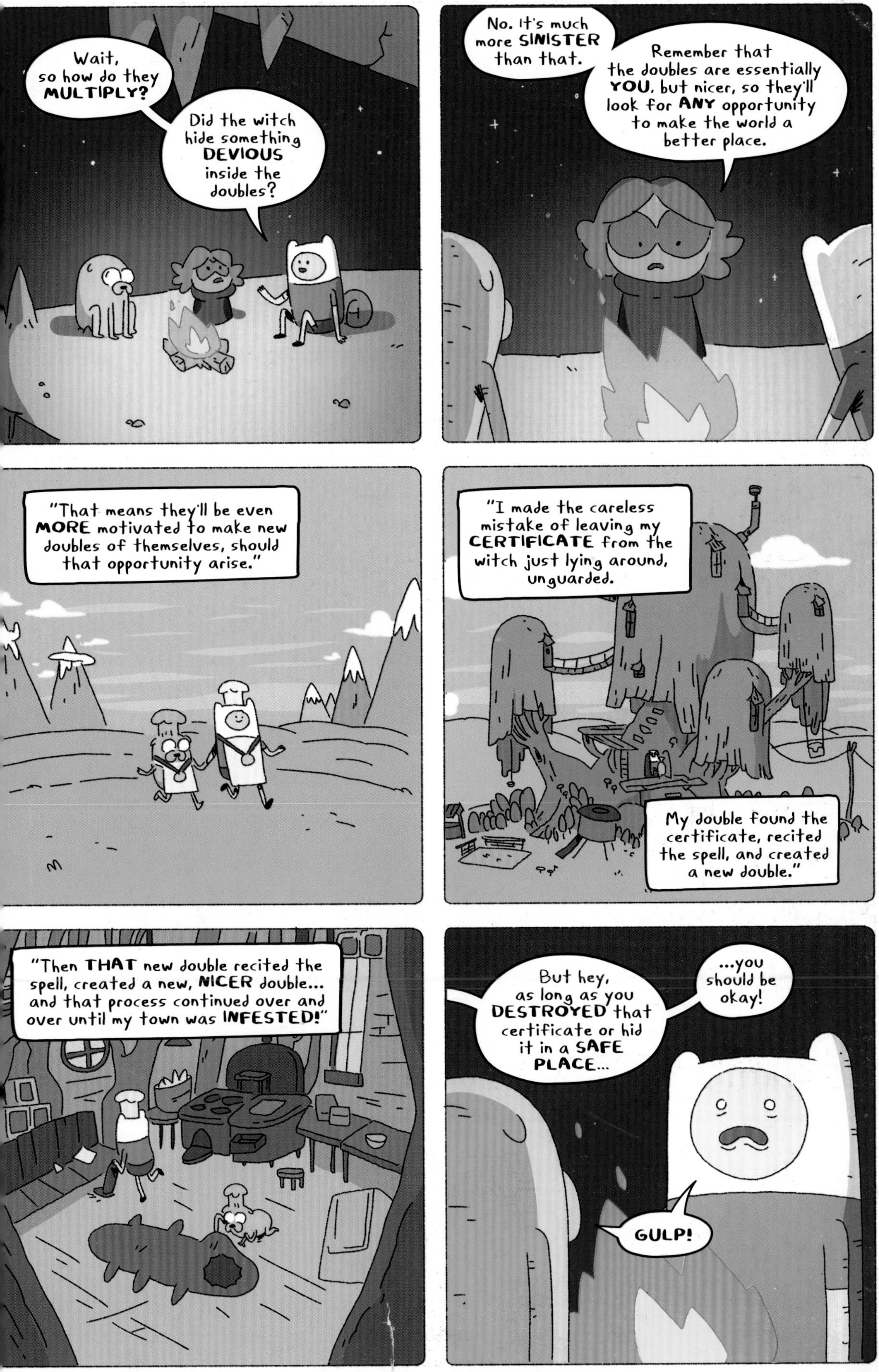
Wait, so how do they MULTIPLY?
Did the witch hide something DEVIOUS inside the doubles?
No. It's much more SINISTER than that.
Remember that the doubles are essentially YOU, but nicer, so they'll look for ANY opportunity to make the world a better place.
"That means they'll be even MORE motivated to make new doubles of themselves, should that opportunity arise."
"I made the careless mistake of leaving my CERTIFICATE from the witch just lying around, unguarded.
My double found the certificate, recited the spell, and created a new double."
"Then THAT new double recited the spell, created a new, NICER double... and that process continued over and over until my town was INFESTED!"
But hey, as long as you DESTROYED that certificate or hid it in a SAFE PLACE...
...you should be okay!
GULP!

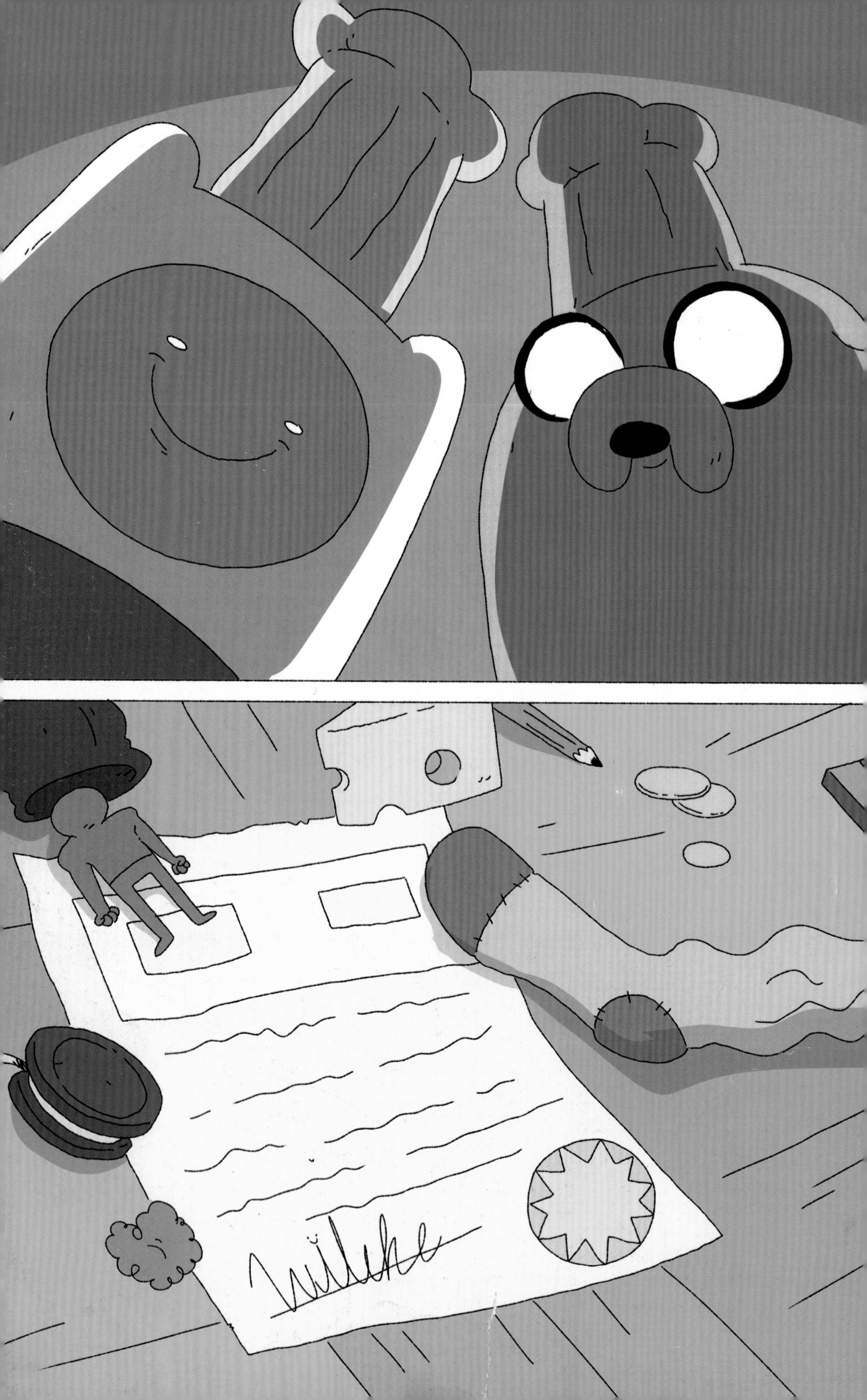

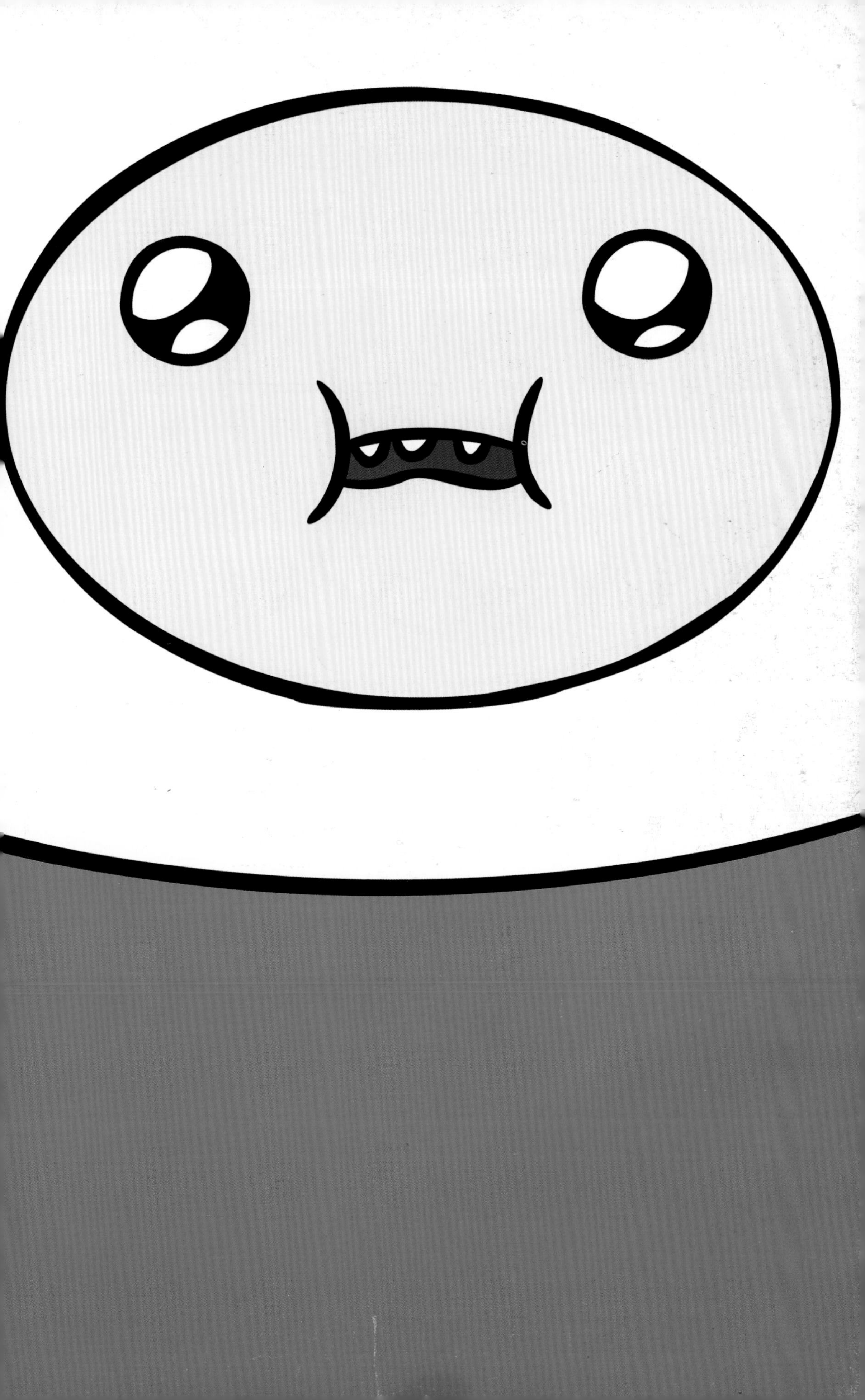

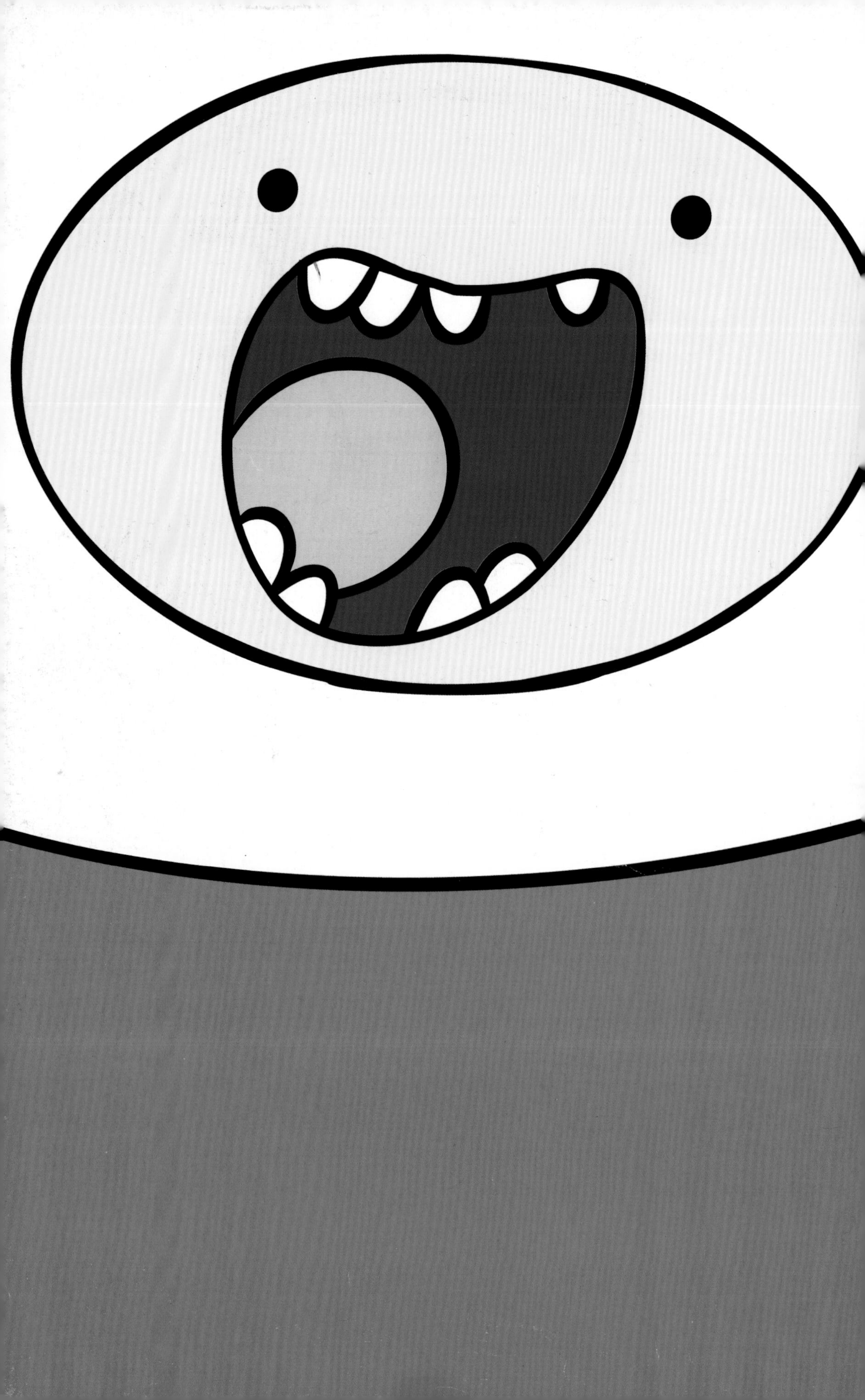

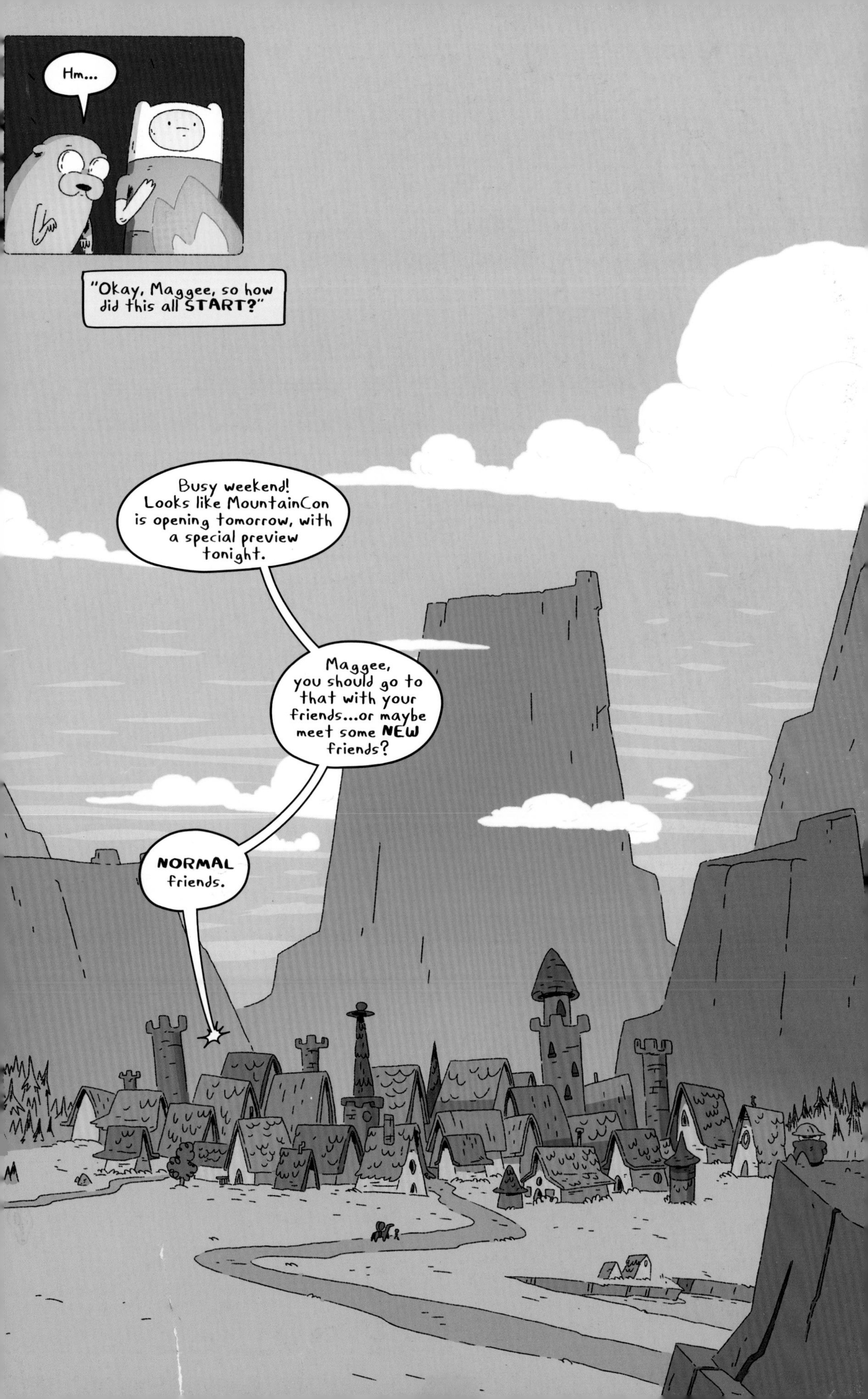
Hm...
"Okay, Maggee, so how did this all START?"
Busy weekend! Looks like MountainCon is opening tomorrow, with a special preview tonight.
Maggee, you should go to that with your friends...or maybe meet some NEW friends?
NORMAL friends.

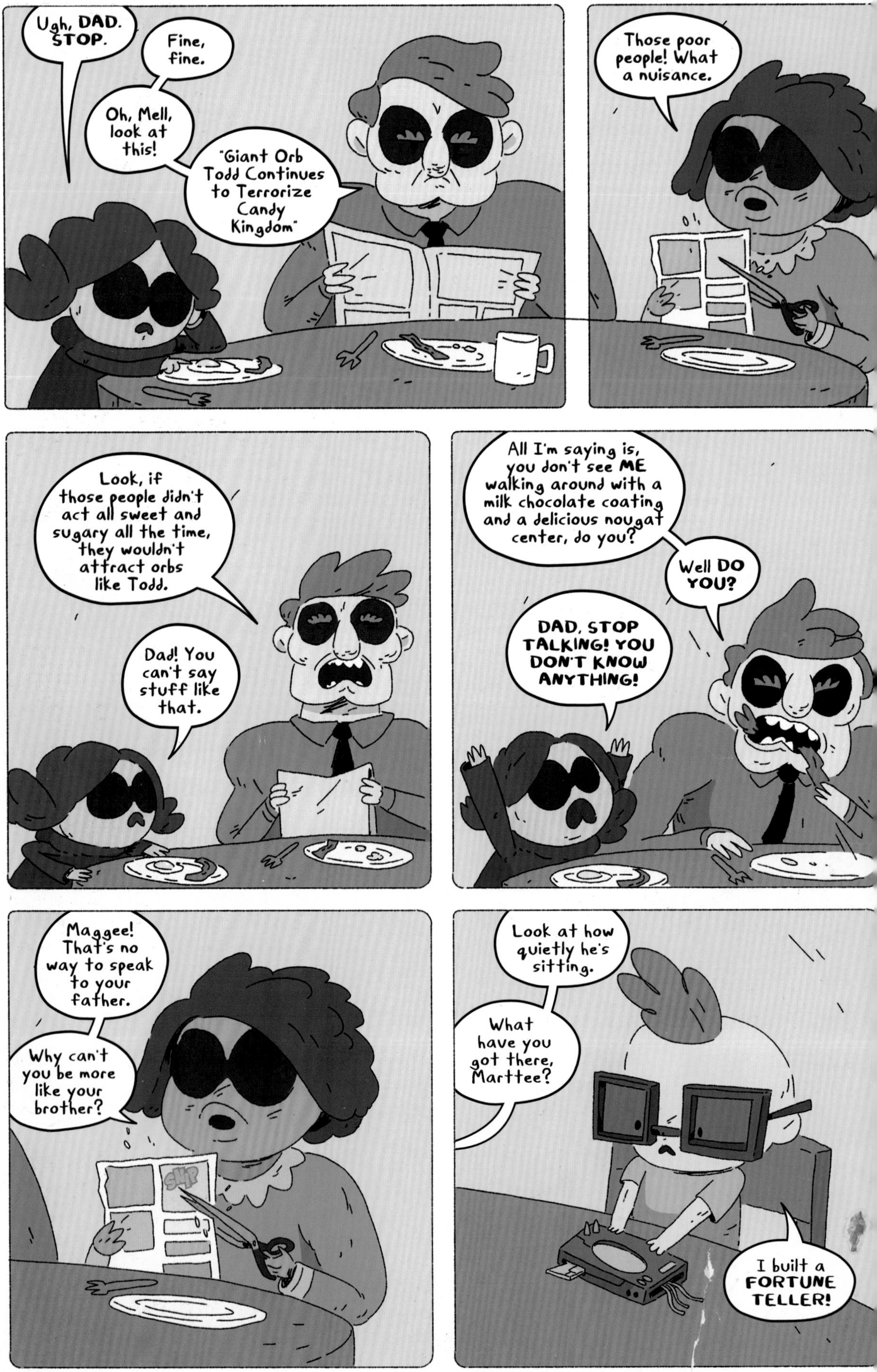

Ugh, DAD. STOP.
Fine, fine.
Oh, Mell, look at this!
"Giant Orb Todd Continues to Terrorize Candy Kingdom"
Those poor people! What a nuisance.
Look, if those people didn't act all sweet and sugary all the time, they wouldn't attract orbs like Todd.
Dad! You can't say stuff like that.
All I'm saying is, you don't see ME walking around with a milk chocolate coating and a delicious nougat center, do you?
Well DO YOU?
DAD, STOP TALKING! YOU DON'T KNOW ANYTHING!
Maggee! That's no way to speak to your father.
Why can't you be more like your brother?
SNIP
Look at how quietly he's sitting.
What have you got there, Marttee?
I built a FORTUNE TELLER!

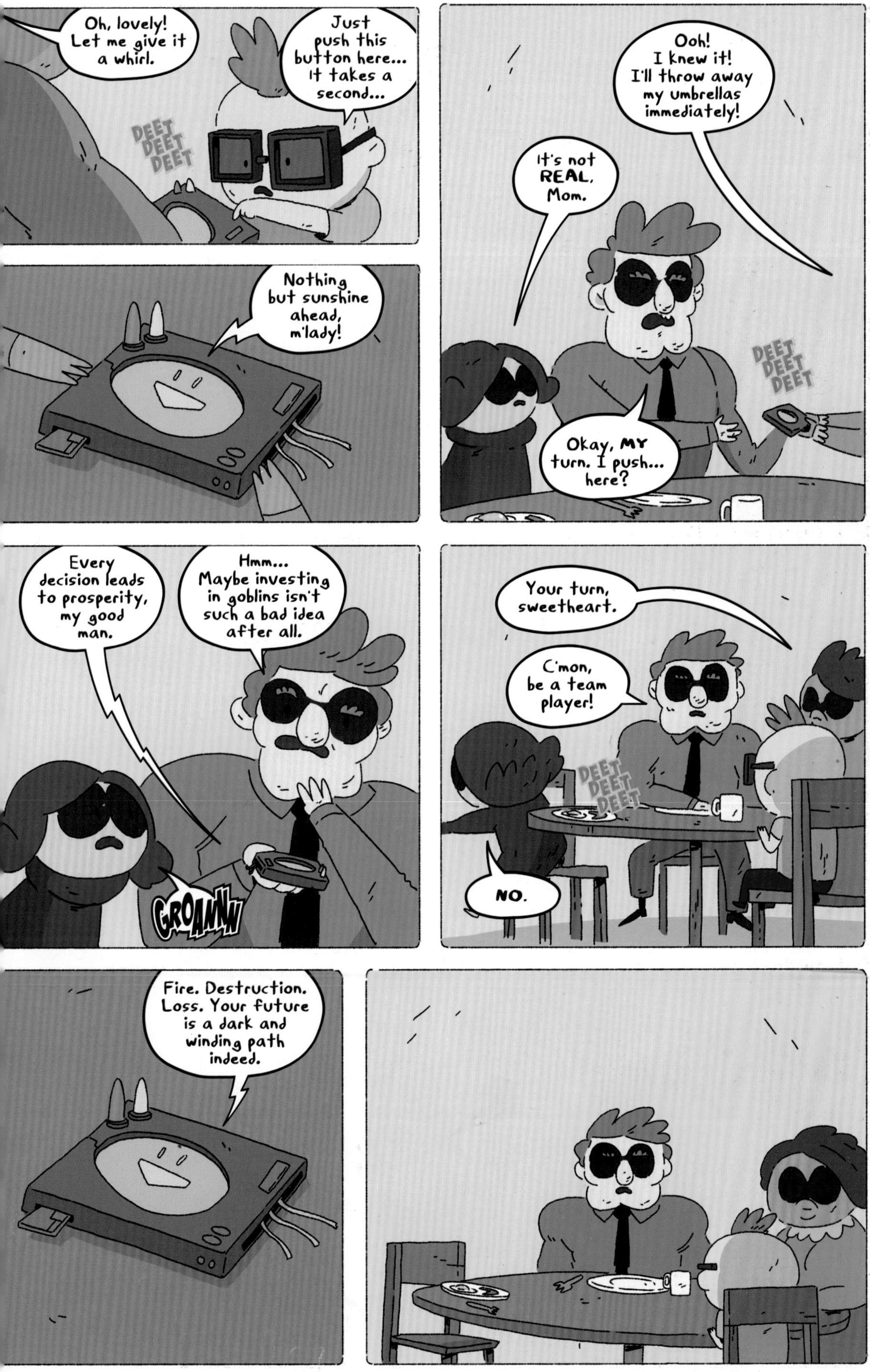
Oh, lovely! Let me give it a whirl.
Just push this button here... It takes a second...
DEET DEET DEET
Ooh! I knew it! I'll throw away my umbrellas immediately!
It's not REAL, Mom.
Nothing but sunshine ahead, m'lady!
DEET DEET DEET
Okay, MY turn. I push... here?
Every decision leads to prosperity, my good man.
Hmm... Maybe investing in goblins isn't such a bad idea after all.
GROANNN
Your turn, sweetheart.
C'mon, be a team player!
DEET DEET DEET
NO.
Fire. Destruction. Loss. Your future is a dark and winding path indeed.

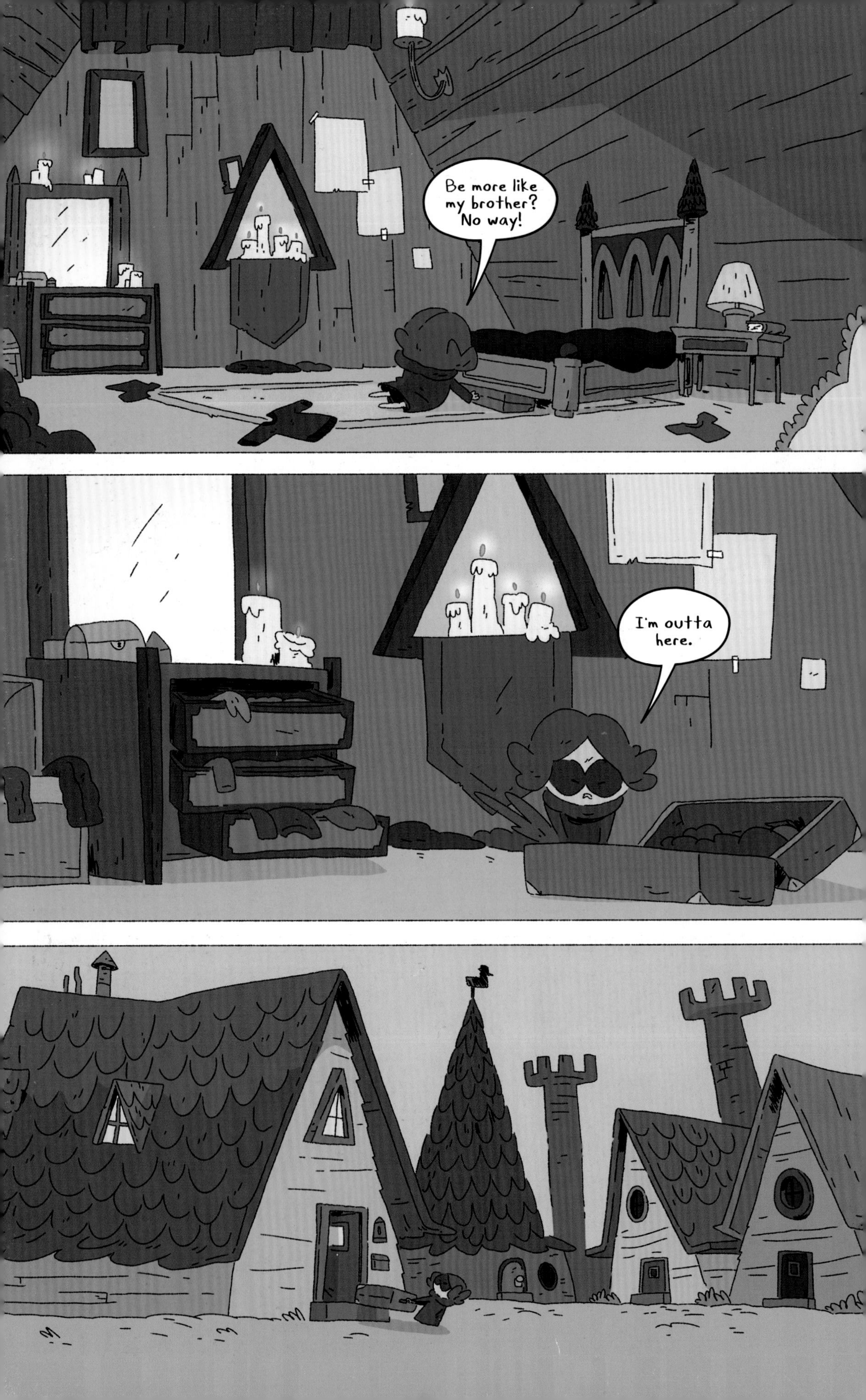
Be more like my brother? No way!
I'm outta here.

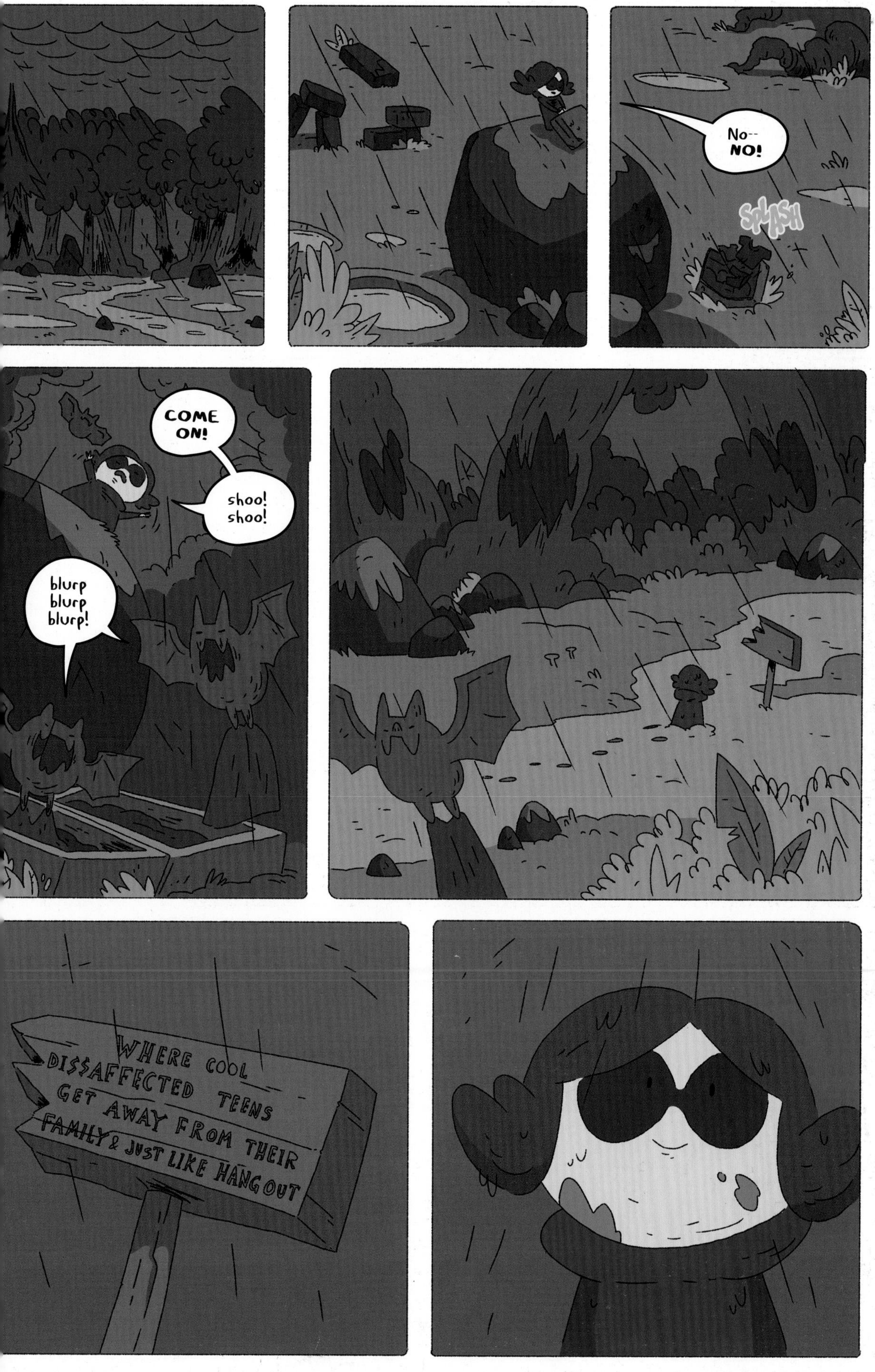
No--
NO!
SPLASH
COME ON!
shoo! shoo!
blurp blurp blurp!
WHERE COOL DI$$AFFECTED TEENS GET AWAY FROM THEIR ~~FAMILY~~ & JUST LIKE HANG OUT

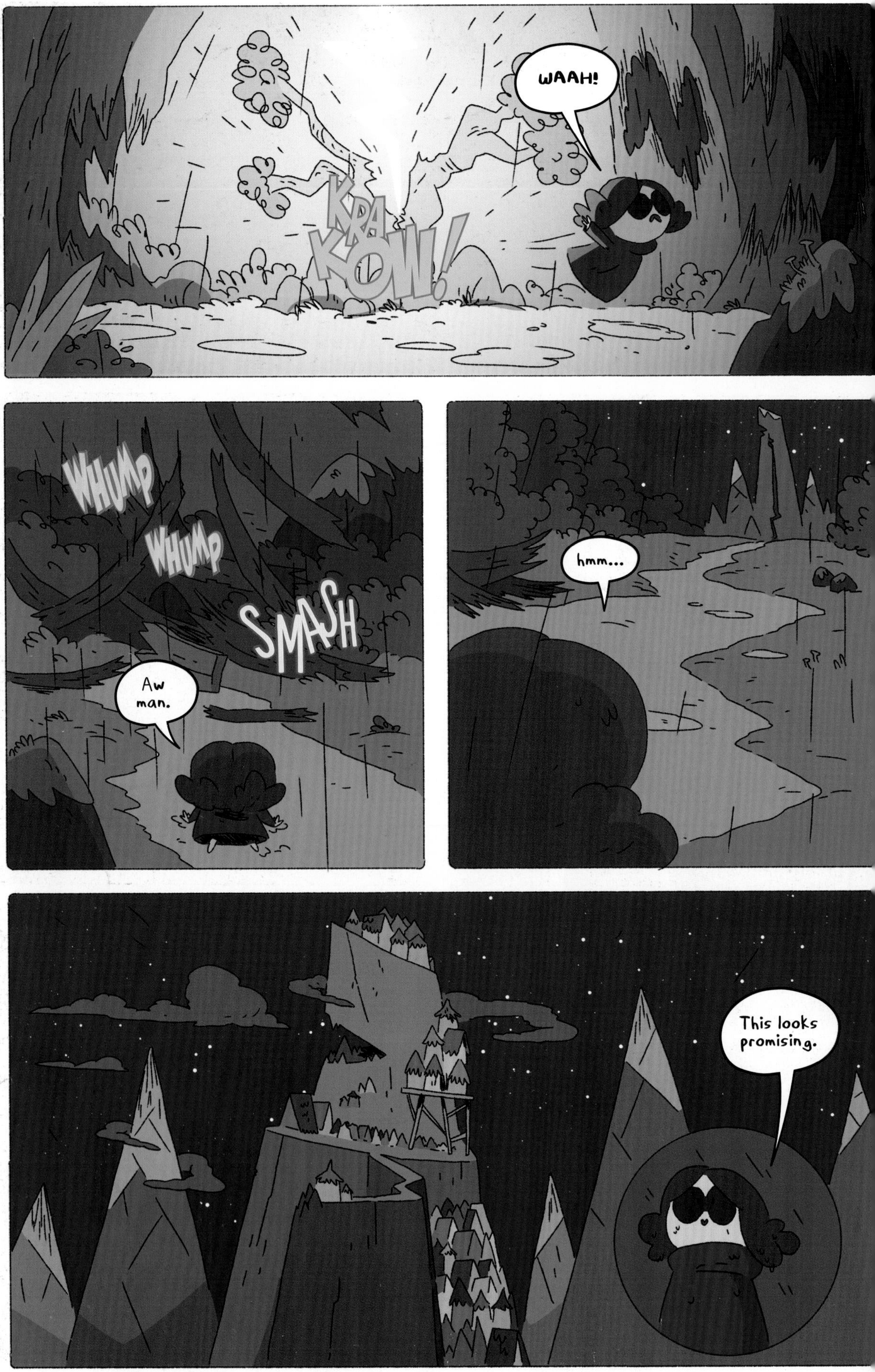
WAAH!
KRA KOW!
WHUMP
WHUMP
SMASH
Aw man.
hmm...
This looks promising.

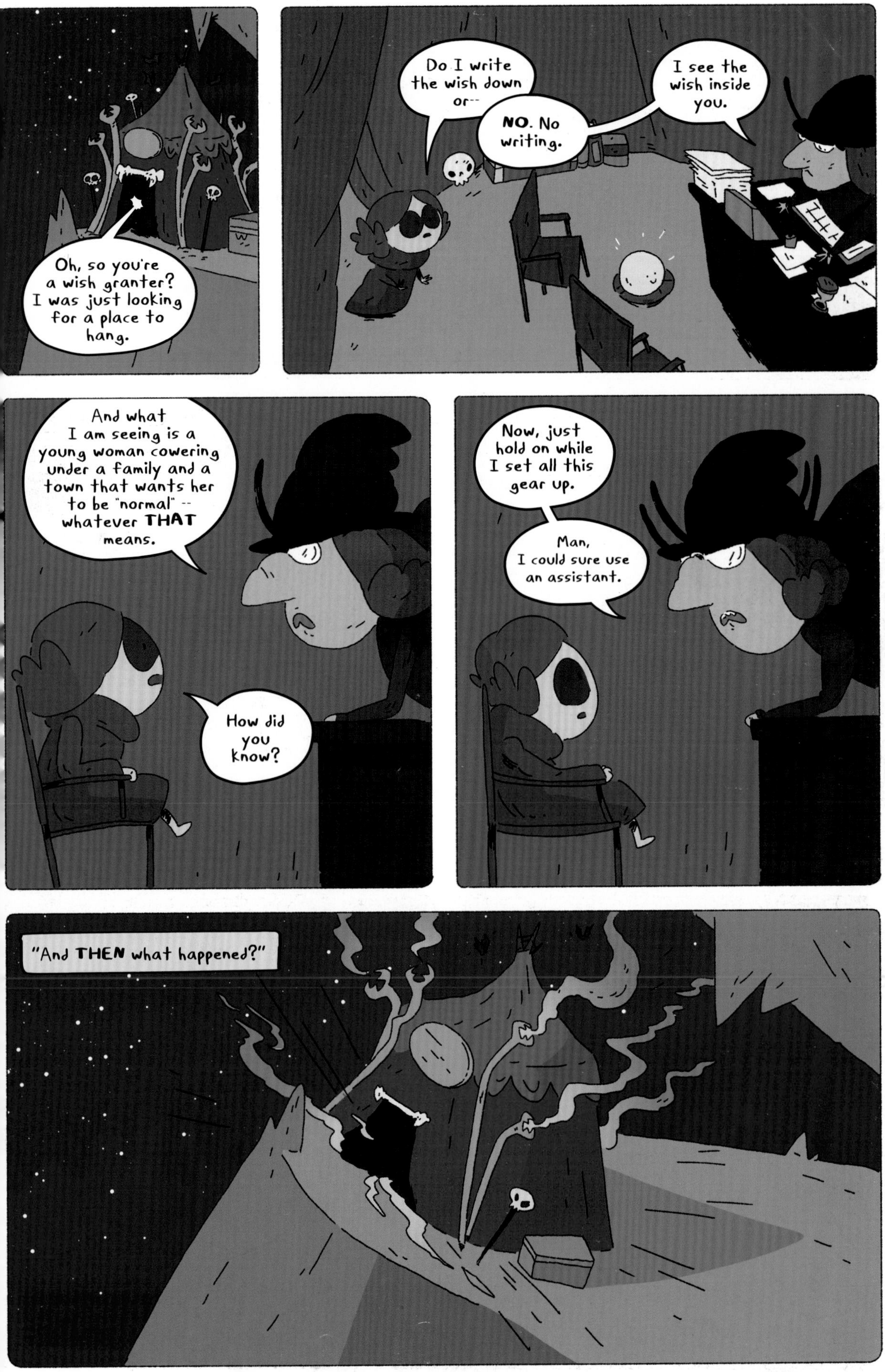
Oh, so you're a wish granter? I was just looking for a place to hang.
Do I write the wish down or--
NO. No writing.
I see the wish inside you.
And what I am seeing is a young woman cowering under a family and a town that wants her to be "normal" -- whatever THAT means.
How did you know?
Now, just hold on while I set all this gear up.
Man, I could sure use an assistant.
"And THEN what happened?"

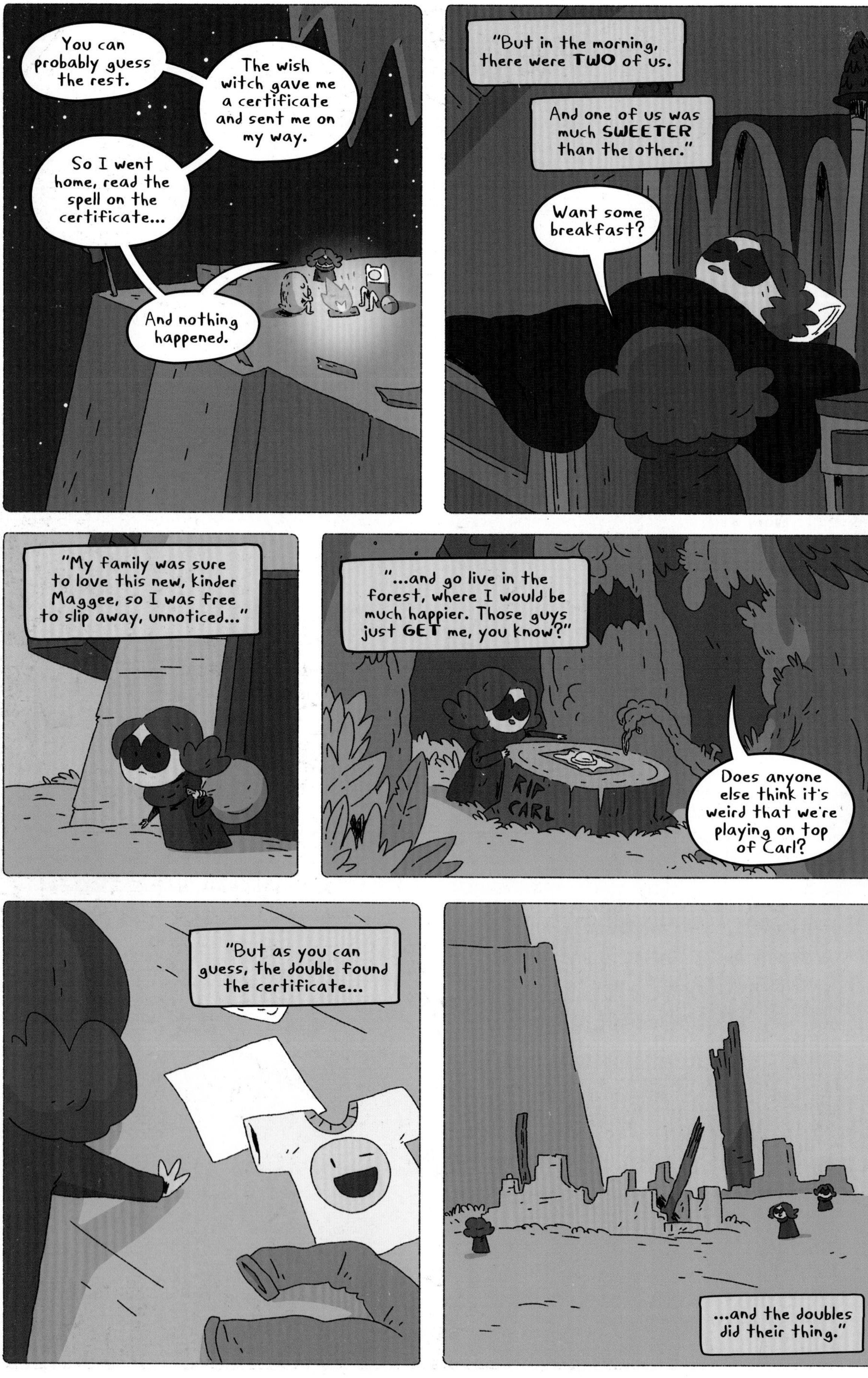
You can probably guess the rest.
The wish witch gave me a certificate and sent me on my way.
So I went home, read the spell on the certificate...
And nothing happened.
"But in the morning, there were TWO of us.
And one of us was much SWEETER than the other."
Want some breakfast?
"My family was sure to love this new, kinder Maggee, so I was free to slip away, unnoticed..."
"...and go live in the forest, where I would be much happier. Those guys just GET me, you know?"
RIP CARL
Does anyone else think it's weird that we're playing on top of Carl?
"But as you can guess, the double found the certificate...
...and the doubles did their thing."

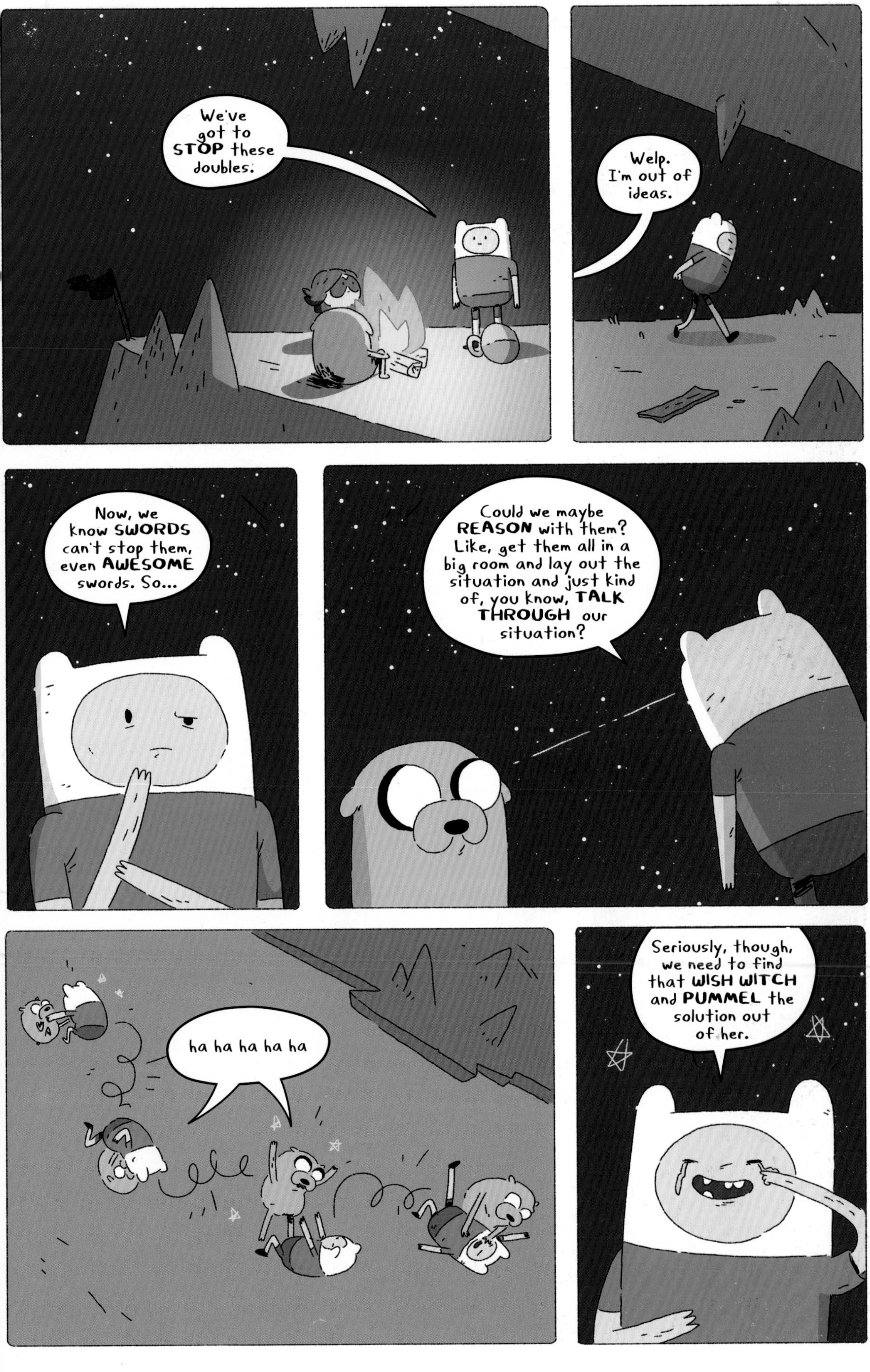
We've got to STOP these doubles.
Welp. I'm out of ideas.
Now, we know SWORDS can't stop them, even AWESOME swords. So...
Could we maybe REASON with them? Like, get them all in a big room and lay out the situation and just kind of, you know, TALK THROUGH our situation?
ha ha ha ha ha
Seriously, though, we need to find that WISH WITCH and PUMMEL the solution out of her.

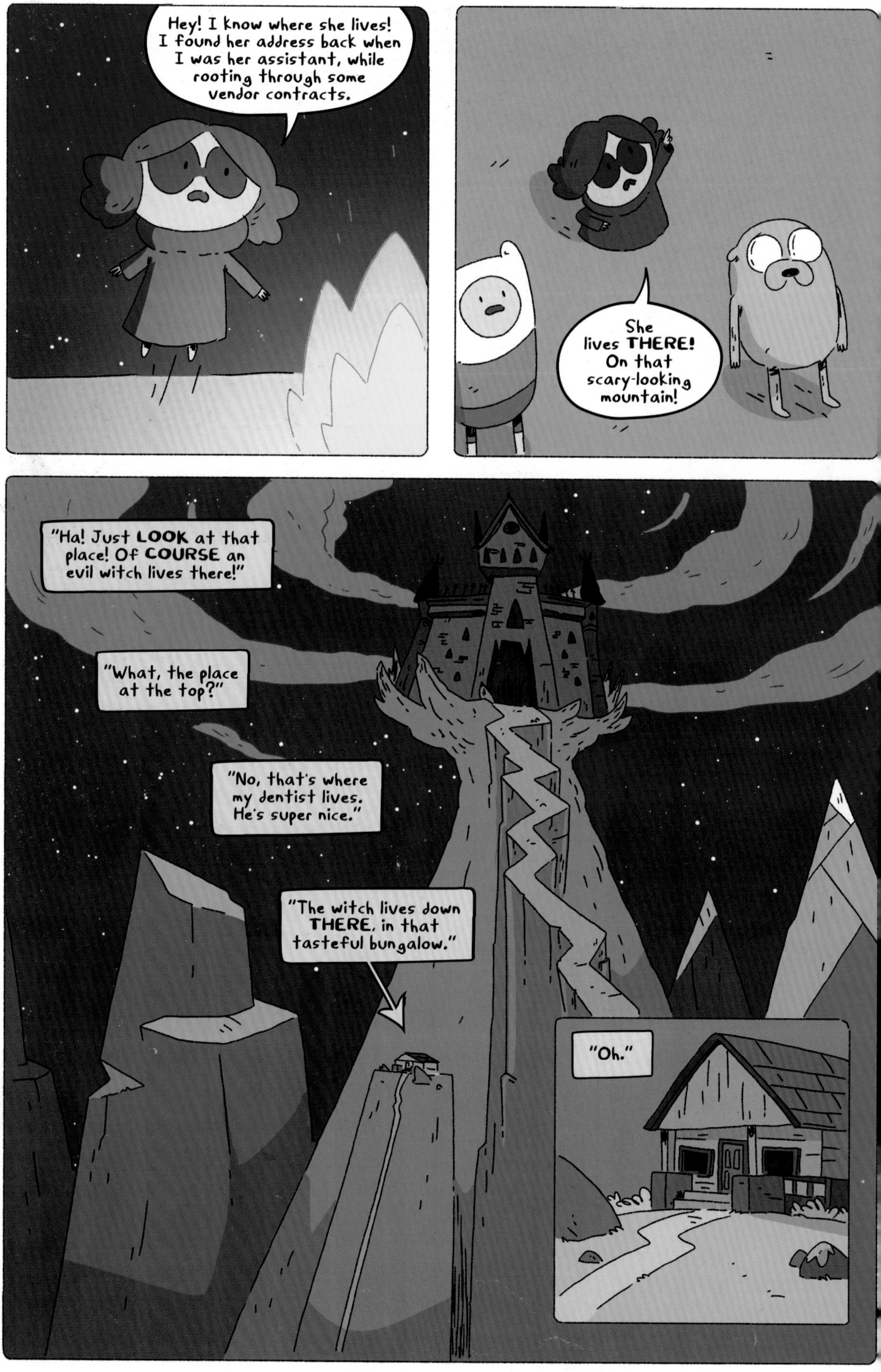
Hey! I know where she lives! I found her address back when I was her assistant, while rooting through some vendor contracts.
She lives THERE! On that scary-looking mountain!
"Ha! Just LOOK at that place! Of COURSE an evil witch lives there!"
"What, the place at the top?"
"No, that's where my dentist lives. He's super nice."
"The witch lives down THERE, in that tasteful bungalow."
"Oh."

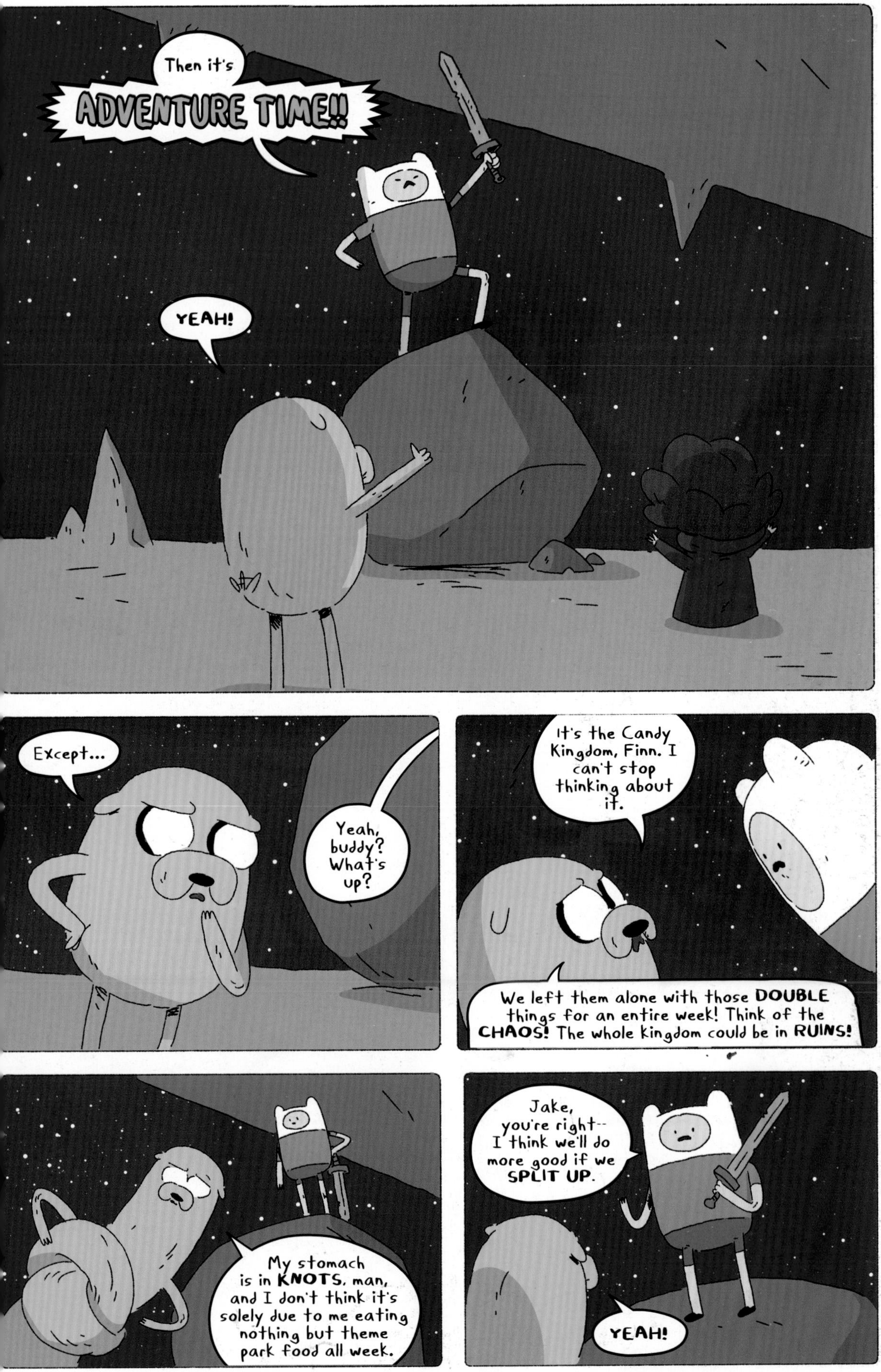
Then it's
ADVENTURE TIME!!
YEAH!
Except...
Yeah, buddy? What's up?
It's the Candy Kingdom, Finn. I can't stop thinking about it.
We left them alone with those DOUBLE things for an entire week! Think of the CHAOS! The whole kingdom could be in RUINS!
My stomach is in KNOTS, man, and I don't think it's solely due to me eating nothing but theme park food all week.
Jake, you're right-- I think we'll do more good if we SPLIT UP.
YEAH!

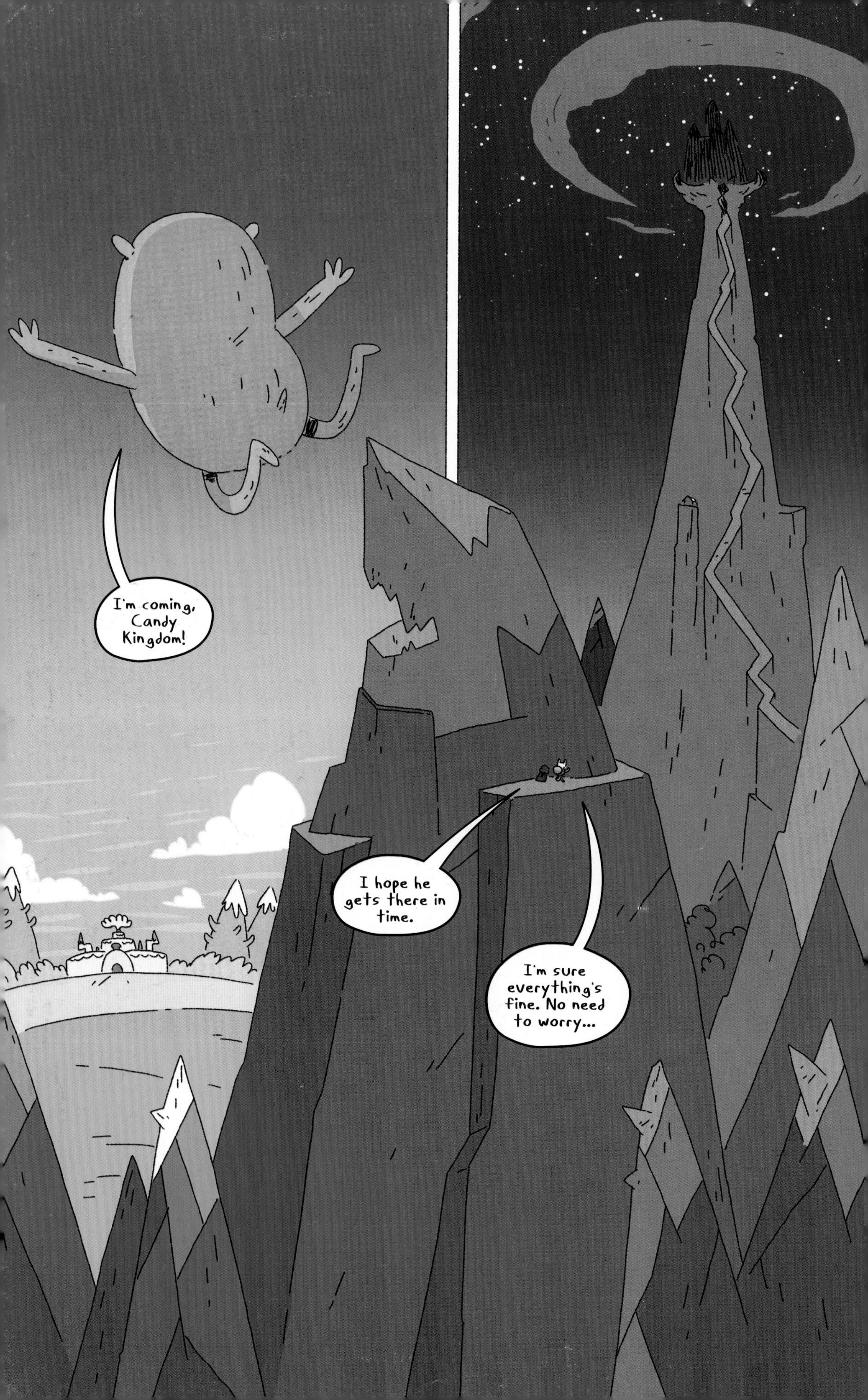
I'm coming, Candy Kingdom!
I hope he gets there in time.
I'm sure everything's fine. No need to worry...

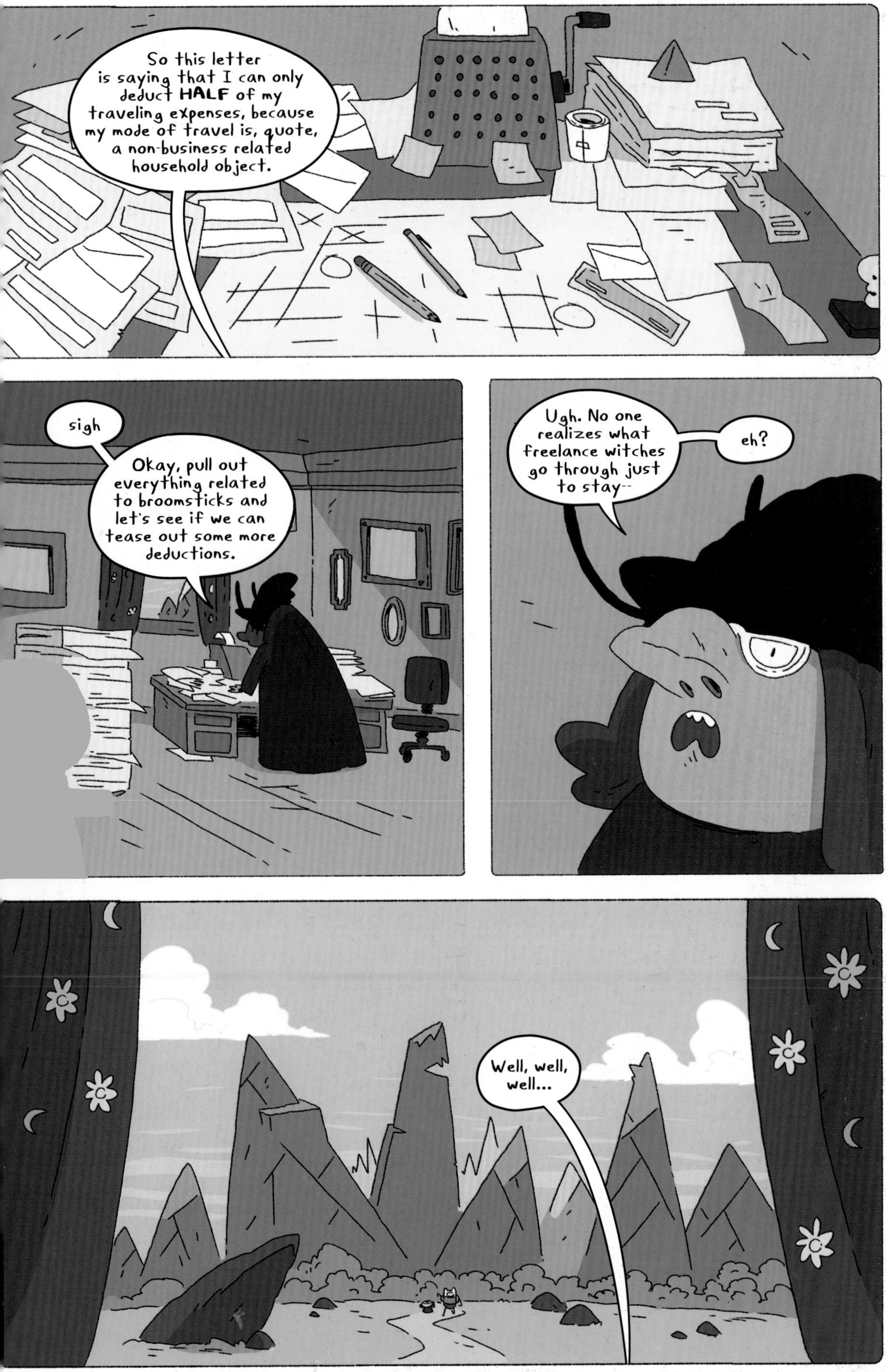
So this letter is saying that I can only deduct HALF of my traveling expenses, because my mode of travel is, quote, a non-business related household object.
sigh
Okay, pull out everything related to broomsticks and let's see if we can tease out some more deductions.
Ugh. No one realizes what freelance witches go through just to stay--
eh?
Well, well, well...

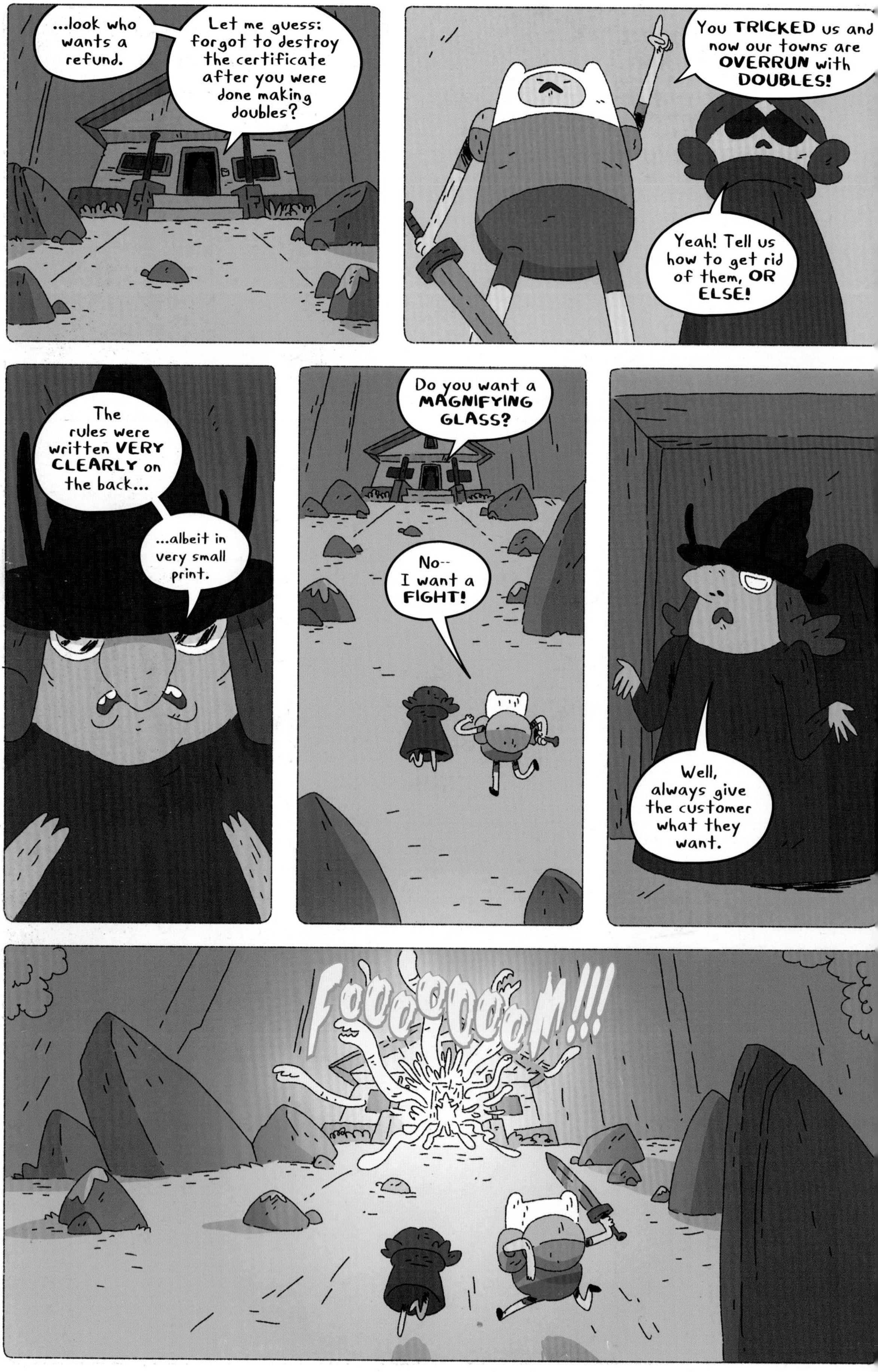
...look who wants a refund.
Let me guess: forgot to destroy the certificate after you were done making doubles?
You TRICKED us and now our towns are OVERRUN with DOUBLES!
Yeah! Tell us how to get rid of them, OR ELSE!
The rules were written VERY CLEARLY on the back...
...albeit in very small print.
Do you want a MAGNIFYING GLASS?
No-- I want a FIGHT!
Well, always give the customer what they want.
FOOOOOOOOM!!!

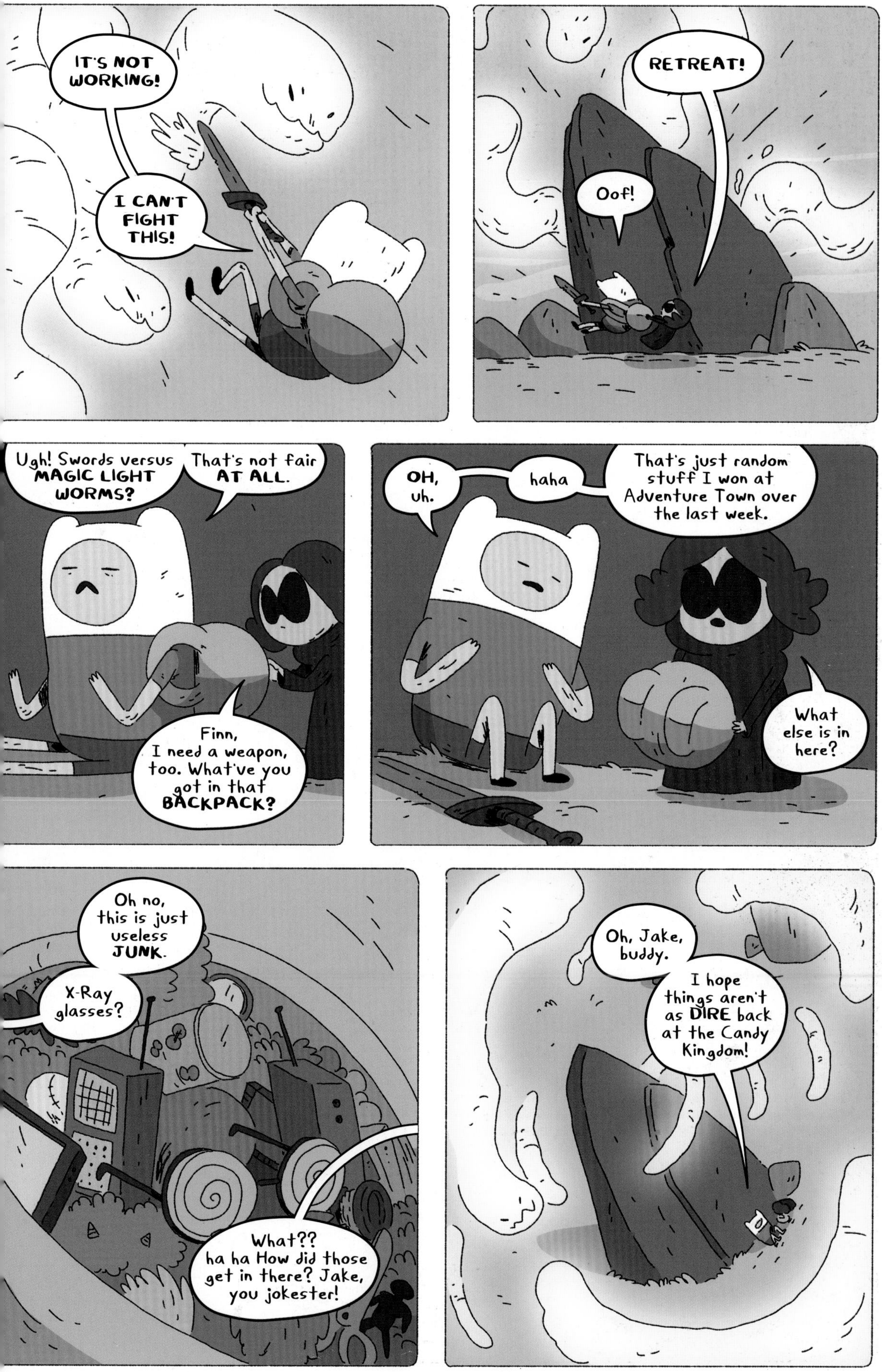

IT'S NOT WORKING!
I CAN'T FIGHT THIS!
RETREAT!
Oof!
Ugh! Swords versus MAGIC LIGHT WORMS?
That's not fair AT ALL.
Finn, I need a weapon, too. What've you got in that BACKPACK?
OH, uh.
haha
That's just random stuff I won at Adventure Town over the last week.
What else is in here?
Oh no, this is just useless JUNK.
X-Ray glasses?
What?? ha ha How did those get in there? Jake, you jokester!
Oh, Jake, buddy.
I hope things aren't as DIRE back at the Candy Kingdom!

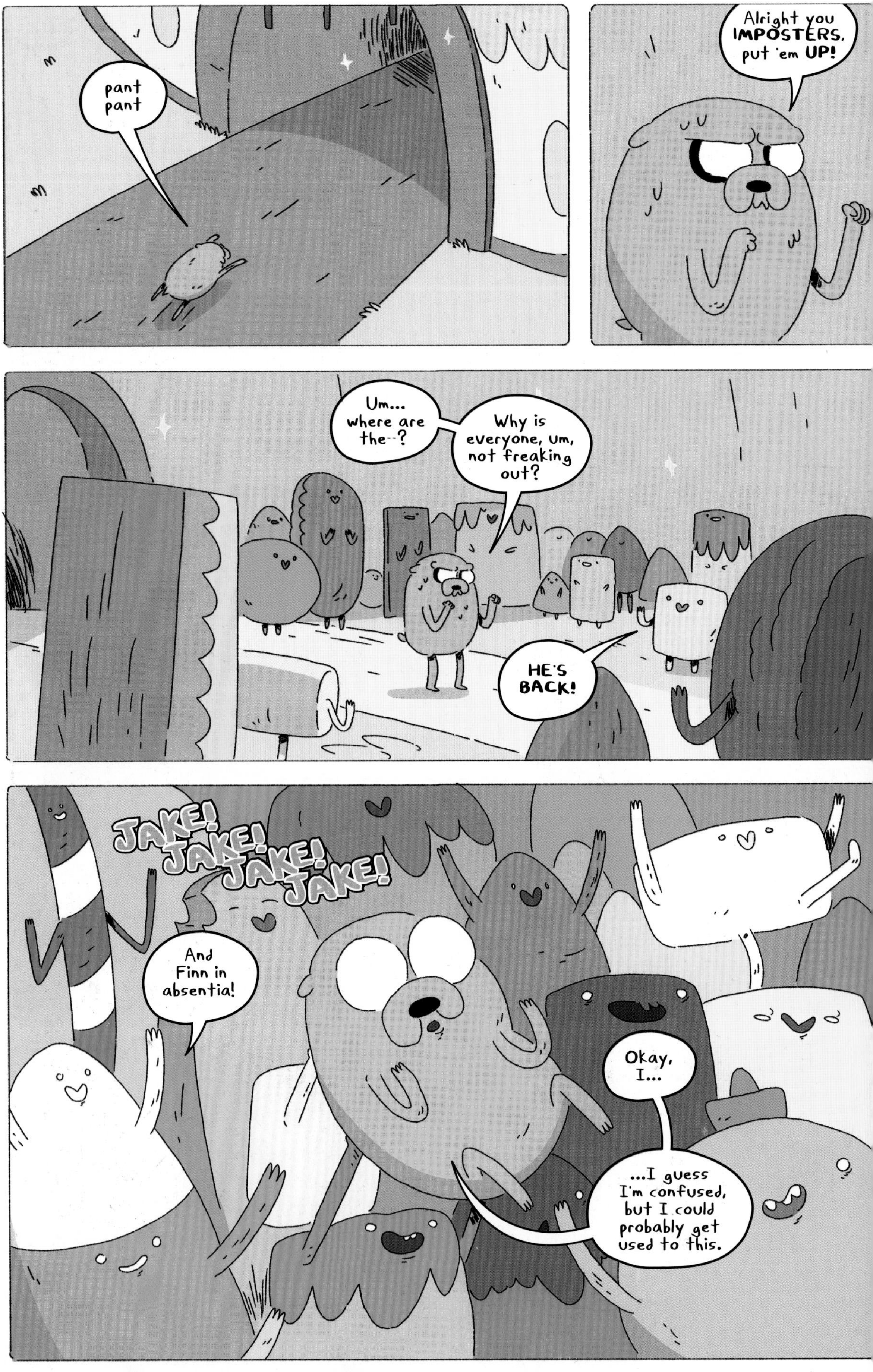
pant pant
Alright you IMPOSTERS, put 'em UP!
Um... where are the--?
Why is everyone, um, not freaking out?
HE'S BACK!
JAKE! JAKE! JAKE! JAKE!
And Finn in absentia!
Okay, I...
...I guess I'm confused, but I could probably get used to this.

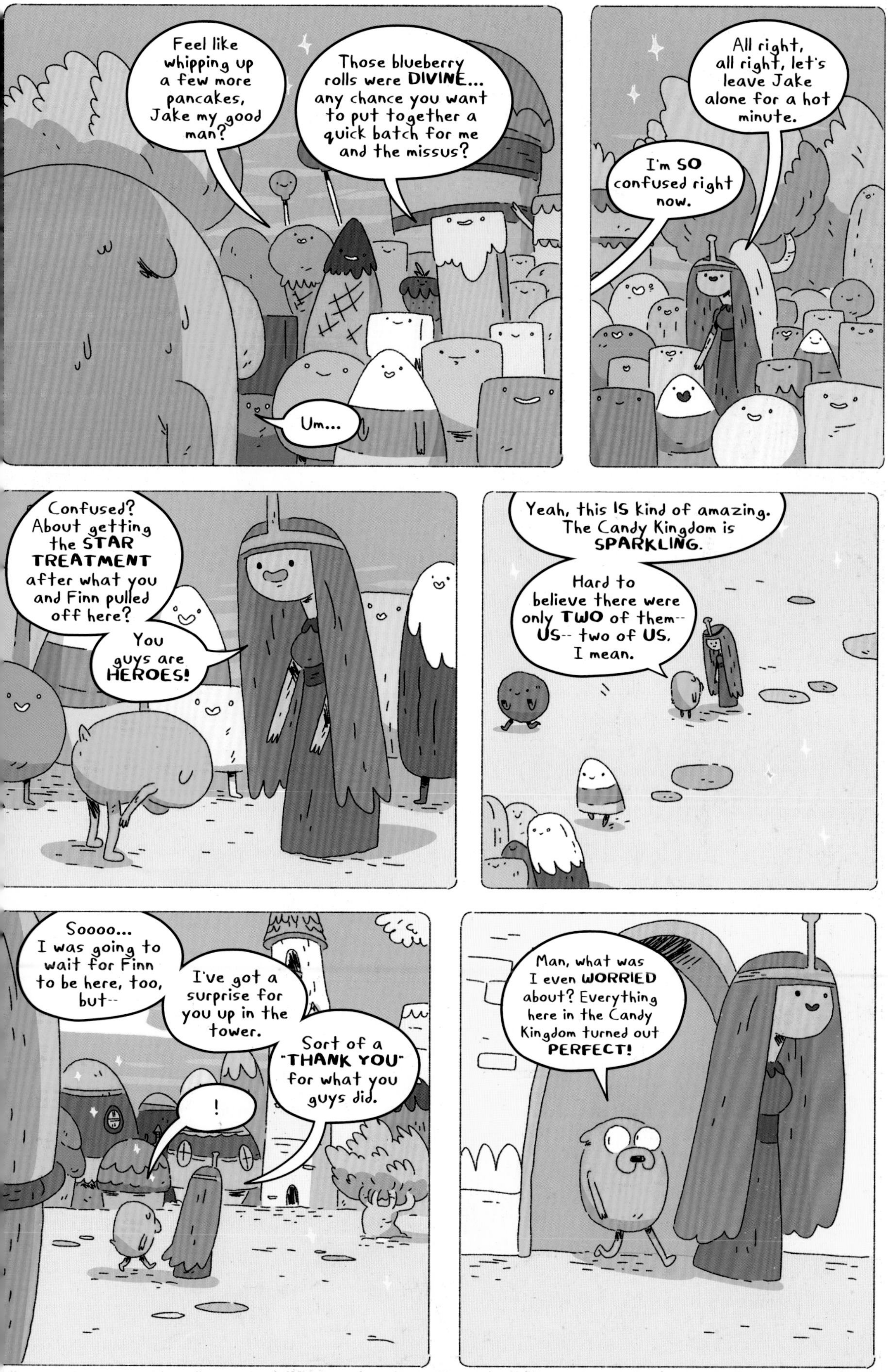
Feel like whipping up a few more pancakes, Jake my good man?
Those blueberry rolls were DIVINE... any chance you want to put together a quick batch for me and the missus?
Um...
All right, all right, let's leave Jake alone for a hot minute.
I'm SO confused right now.
Confused? About getting the STAR TREATMENT after what you and Finn pulled off here?
You guys are HEROES!
Yeah, this IS kind of amazing. The Candy Kingdom is SPARKLING.
Hard to believe there were only TWO of them-- US-- two of US, I mean.
Soooo... I was going to wait for Finn to be here, too, but--
I've got a surprise for you up in the tower.
Sort of a "THANK YOU" for what you guys did.
!
Man, what was I even WORRIED about? Everything here in the Candy Kingdom turned out PERFECT!

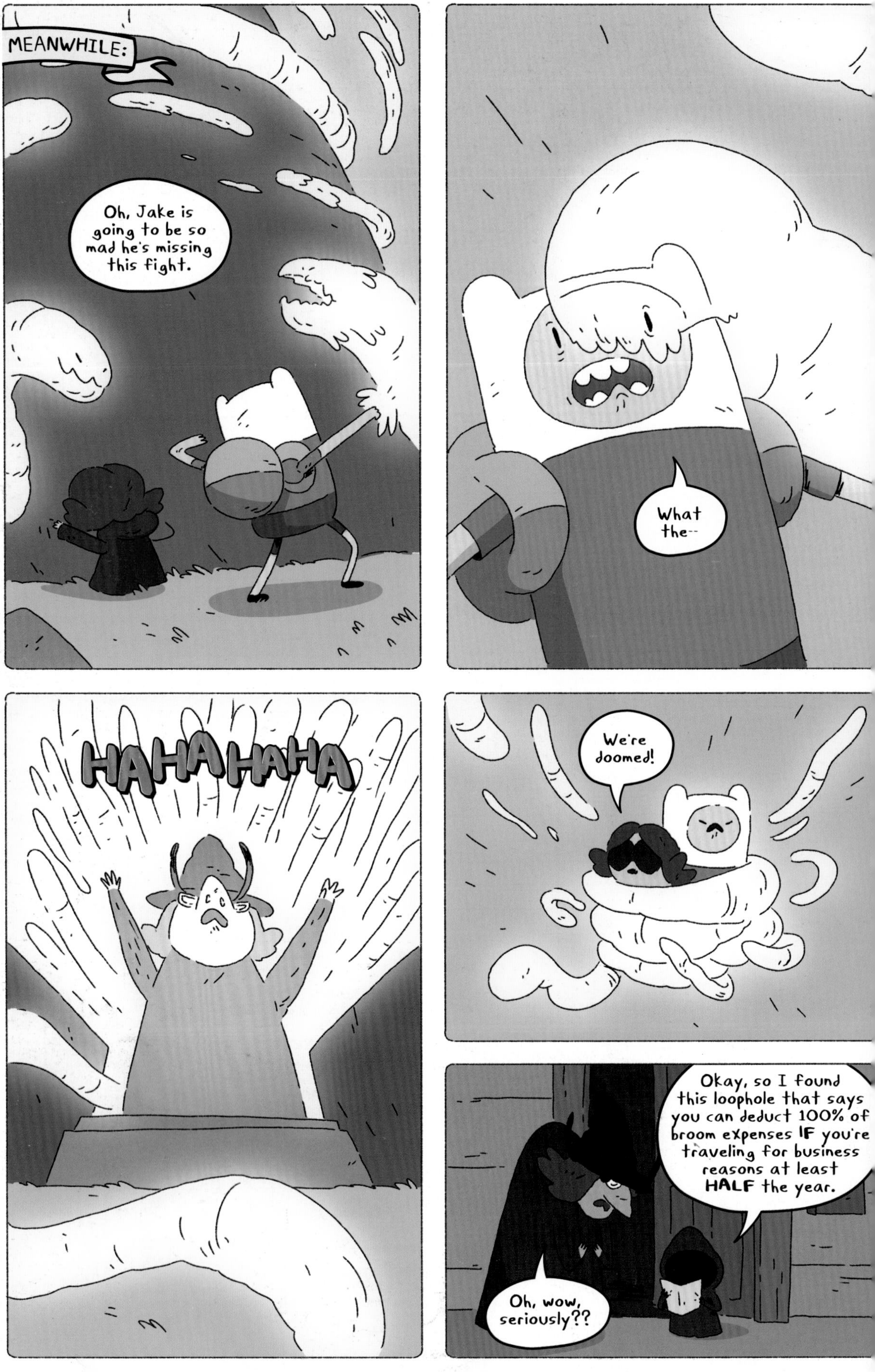
MEANWHILE:
Oh, Jake is going to be so mad he's missing this fight.
What the--
HAHAHAHA
We're doomed!
Okay, so I found this loophole that says you can deduct 100% of broom expenses **IF** you're traveling for business reasons at least **HALF** the year.
Oh, wow, seriously??

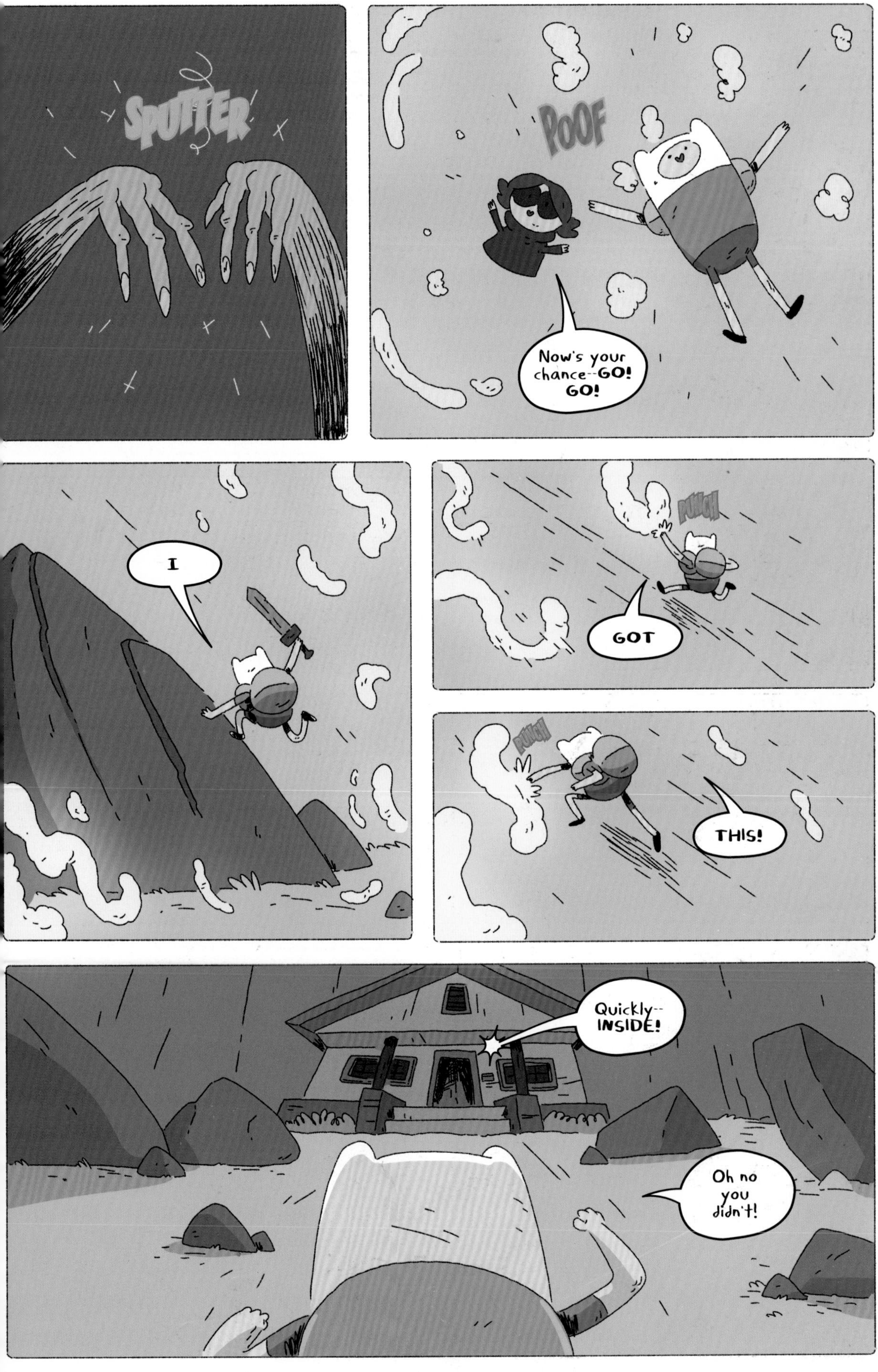
SPUTTER
POOF
Now's your chance--GO! GO!
I
PUNCH
GOT
PUNCH
THIS!
Quickly--INSIDE!
Oh no you didn't!

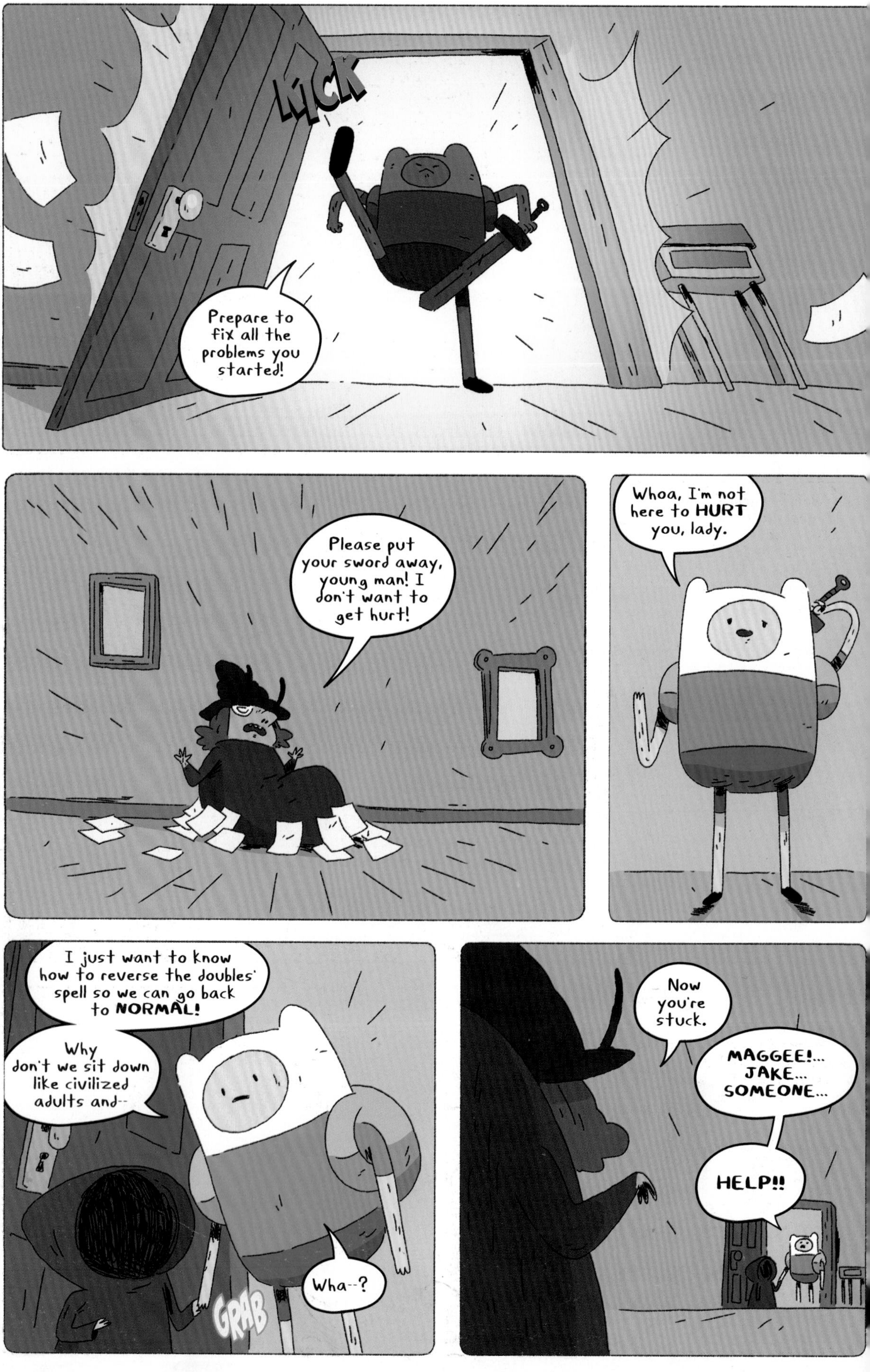
KICK
Prepare to fix all the problems you started!
Please put your sword away, young man! I don't want to get hurt!
Whoa, I'm not here to HURT you, lady.
I just want to know how to reverse the doubles' spell so we can go back to NORMAL!
Why don't we sit down like civilized adults and--
GRAB
Wha--?
Now you're stuck.
MAGGEE!... JAKE... SOMEONE...
HELP!!

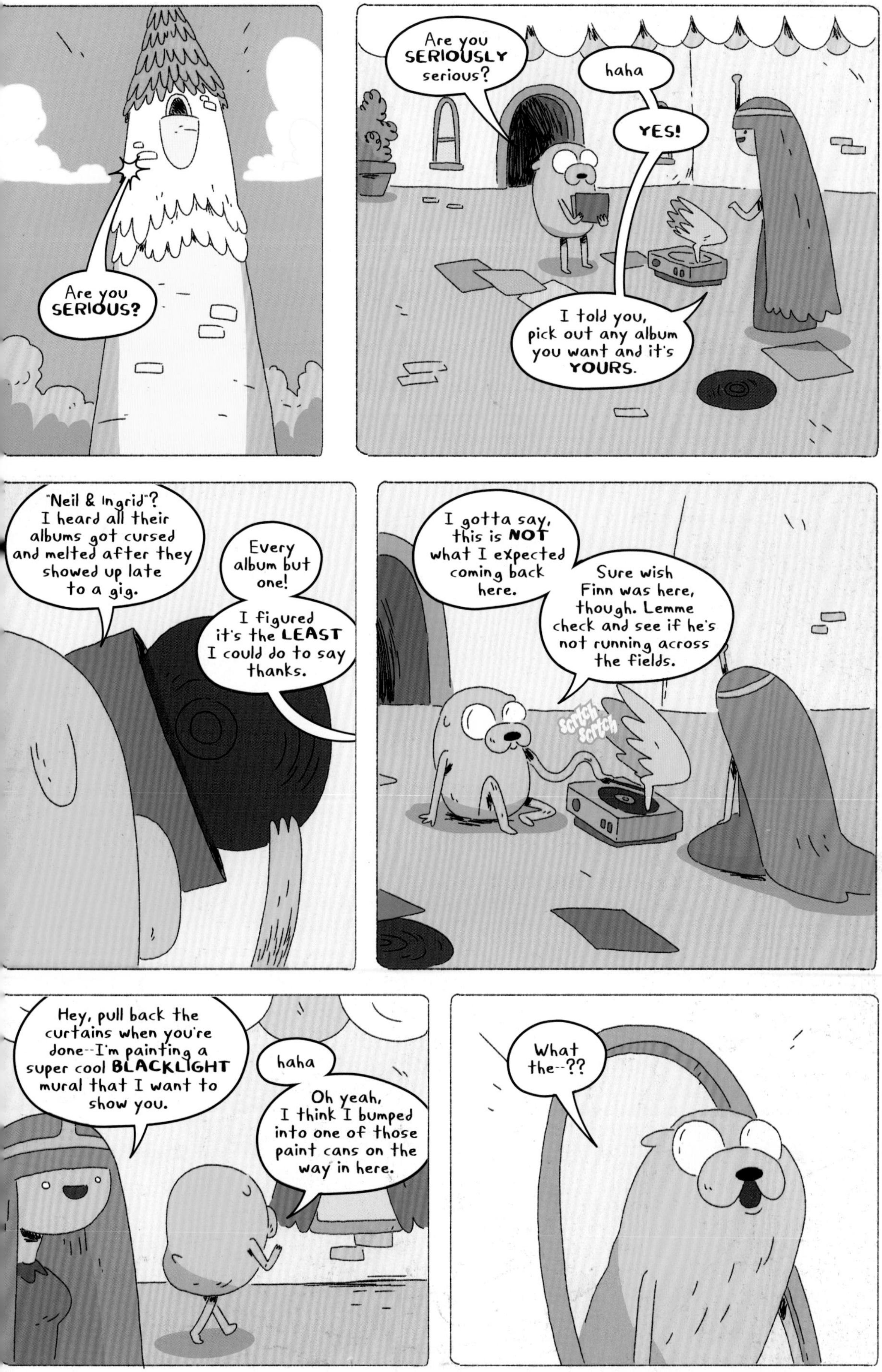

Are you SERIOUS?
Are you SERIOUSLY serious?
haha
YES!
I told you, pick out any album you want and it's YOURS.
"Neil & Ingrid"? I heard all their albums got cursed and melted after they showed up late to a gig.
Every album but one!
I figured it's the LEAST I could do to say thanks.
I gotta say, this is NOT what I expected coming back here.
Sure wish Finn was here, though. Lemme check and see if he's not running across the fields.
scritch scritch
Hey, pull back the curtains when you're done--I'm painting a super cool BLACKLIGHT mural that I want to show you.
haha
Oh yeah, I think I bumped into one of those paint cans on the way in here.
What the--??

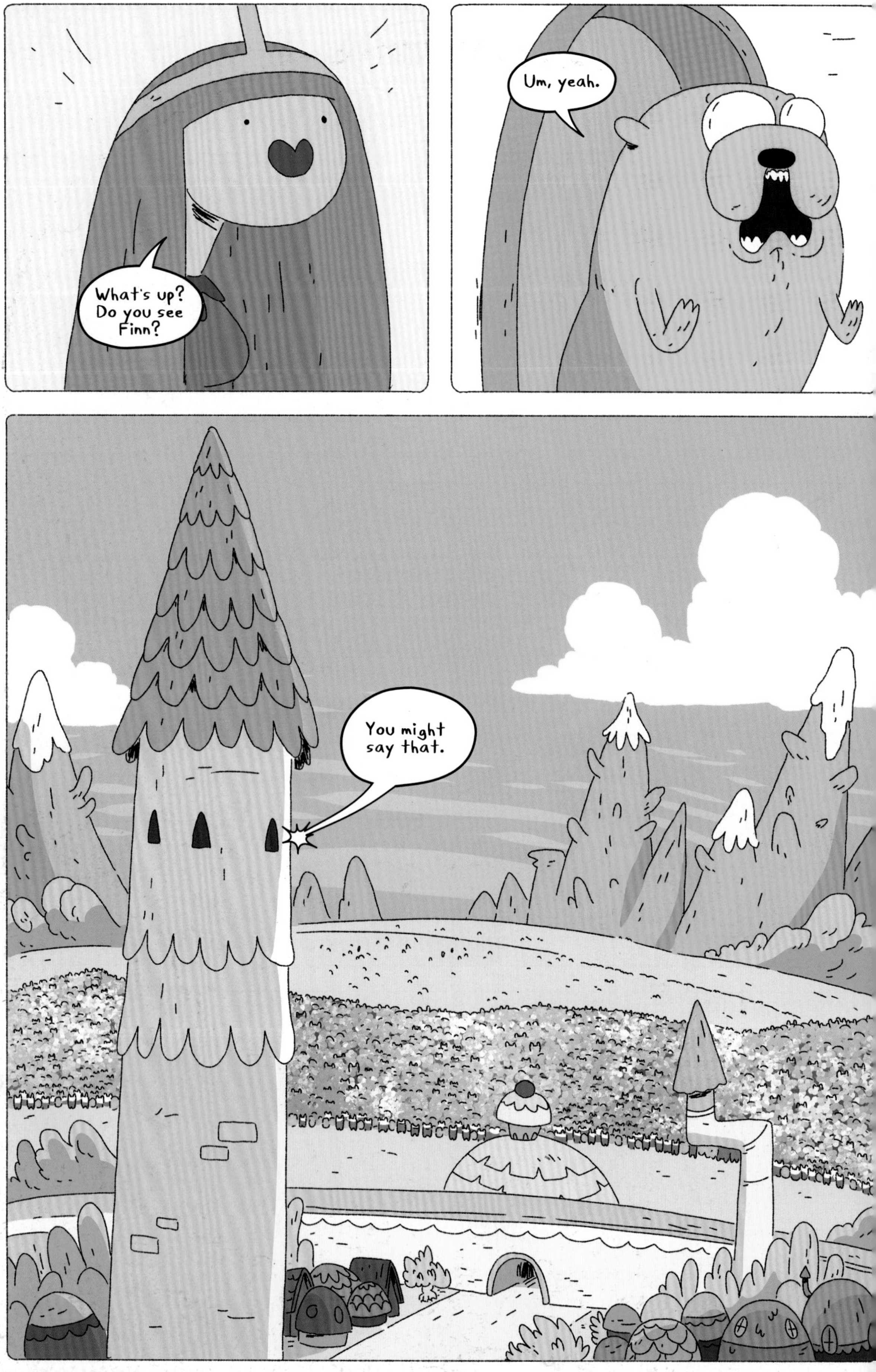
What's up? Do you see Finn?
Um, yeah.
You might say that.

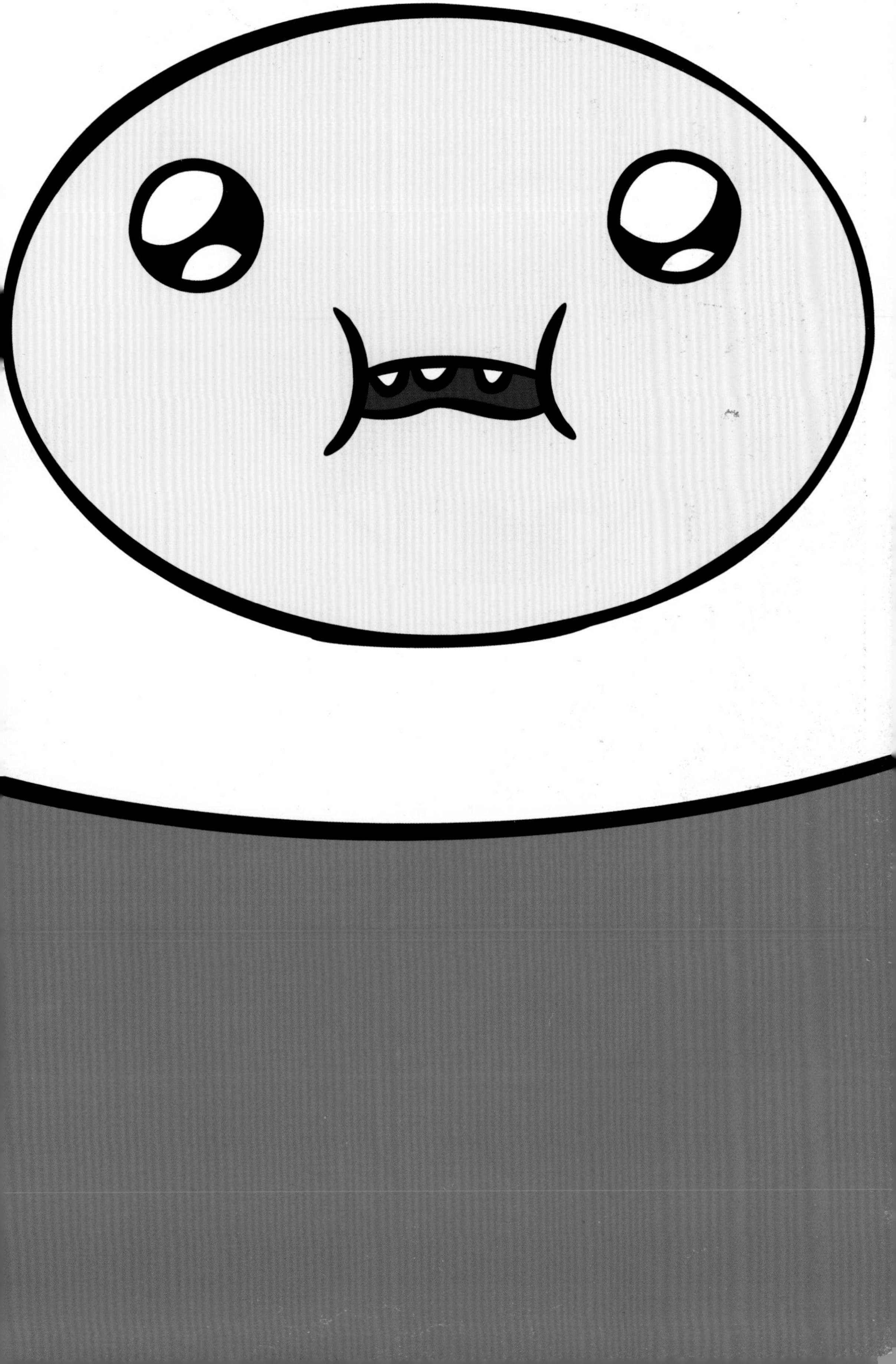

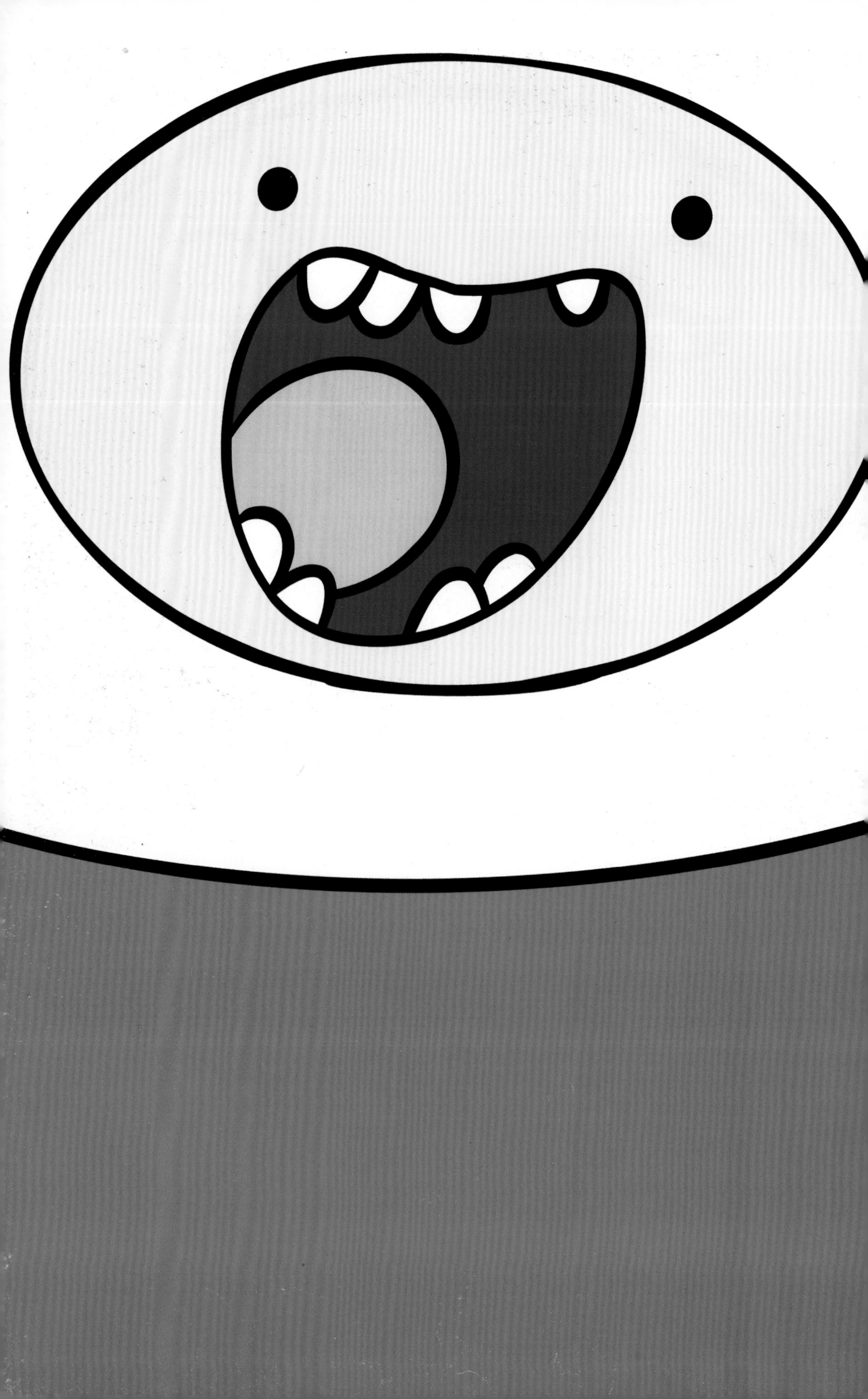

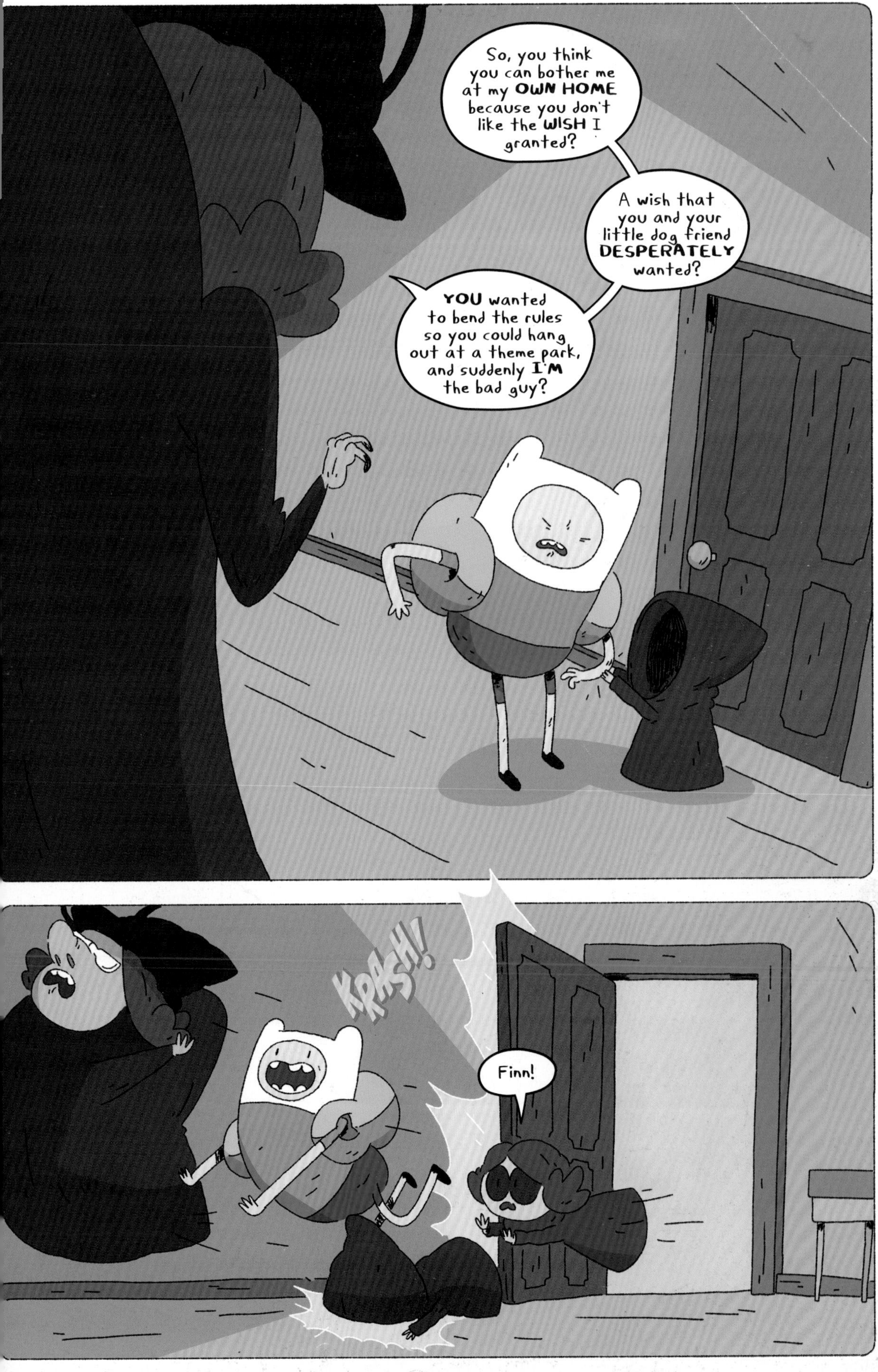
So, you think you can bother me at my OWN HOME because you don't like the WISH I granted?
A wish that you and your little dog friend DESPERATELY wanted?
YOU wanted to bend the rules so you could hang out at a theme park, and suddenly I'M the bad guy?
KRASH!
Finn!

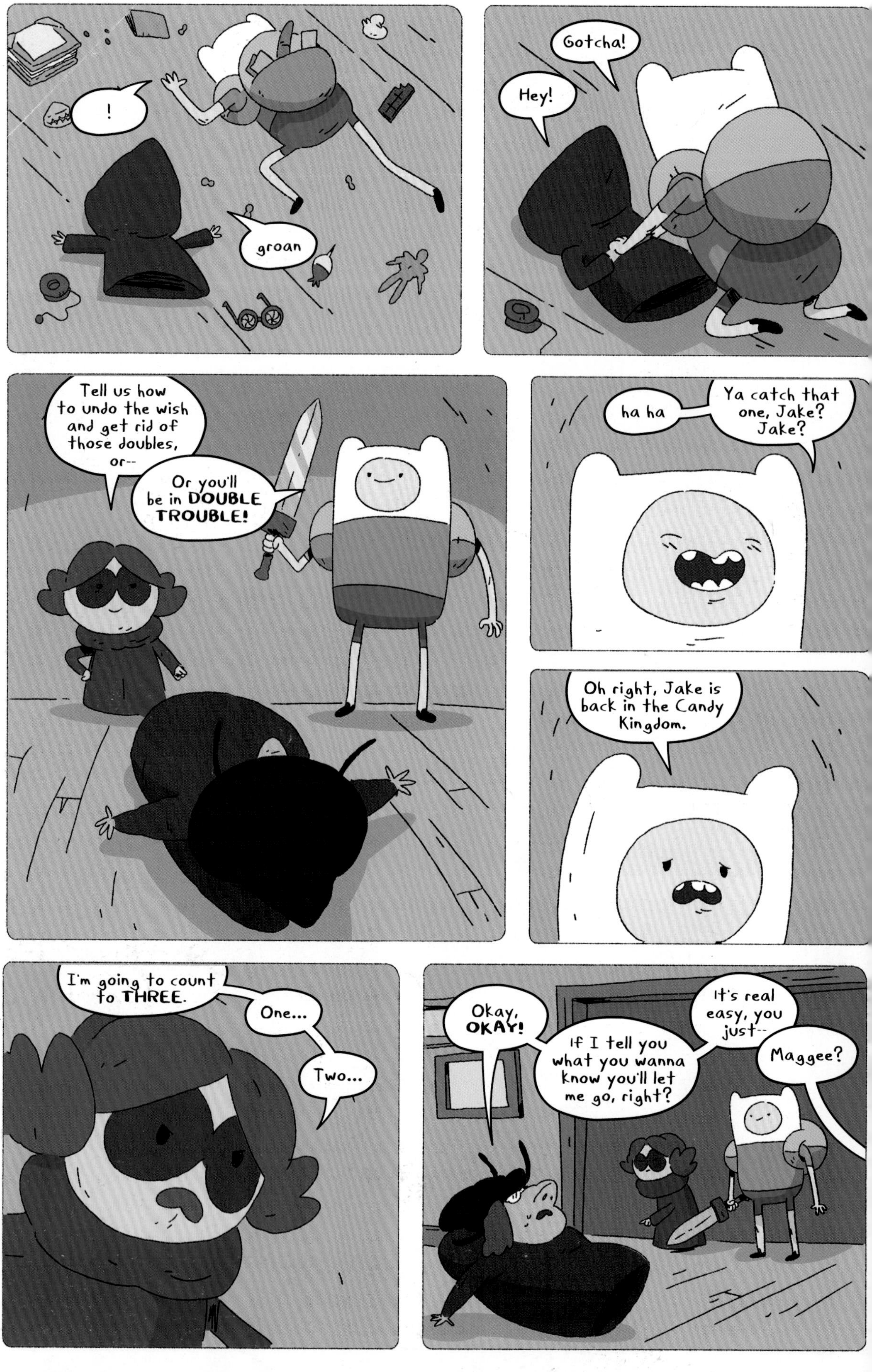
!
groan
Gotcha!
Hey!
Tell us how to undo the wish and get rid of those doubles, or--
Or you'll be in DOUBLE TROUBLE!
ha ha
Ya catch that one, Jake? Jake?
Oh right, Jake is back in the Candy Kingdom.
I'm going to count to THREE.
One...
Two...
Okay, OKAY!
If I tell you what you wanna know you'll let me go, right?
It's real easy, you just--
Maggee?

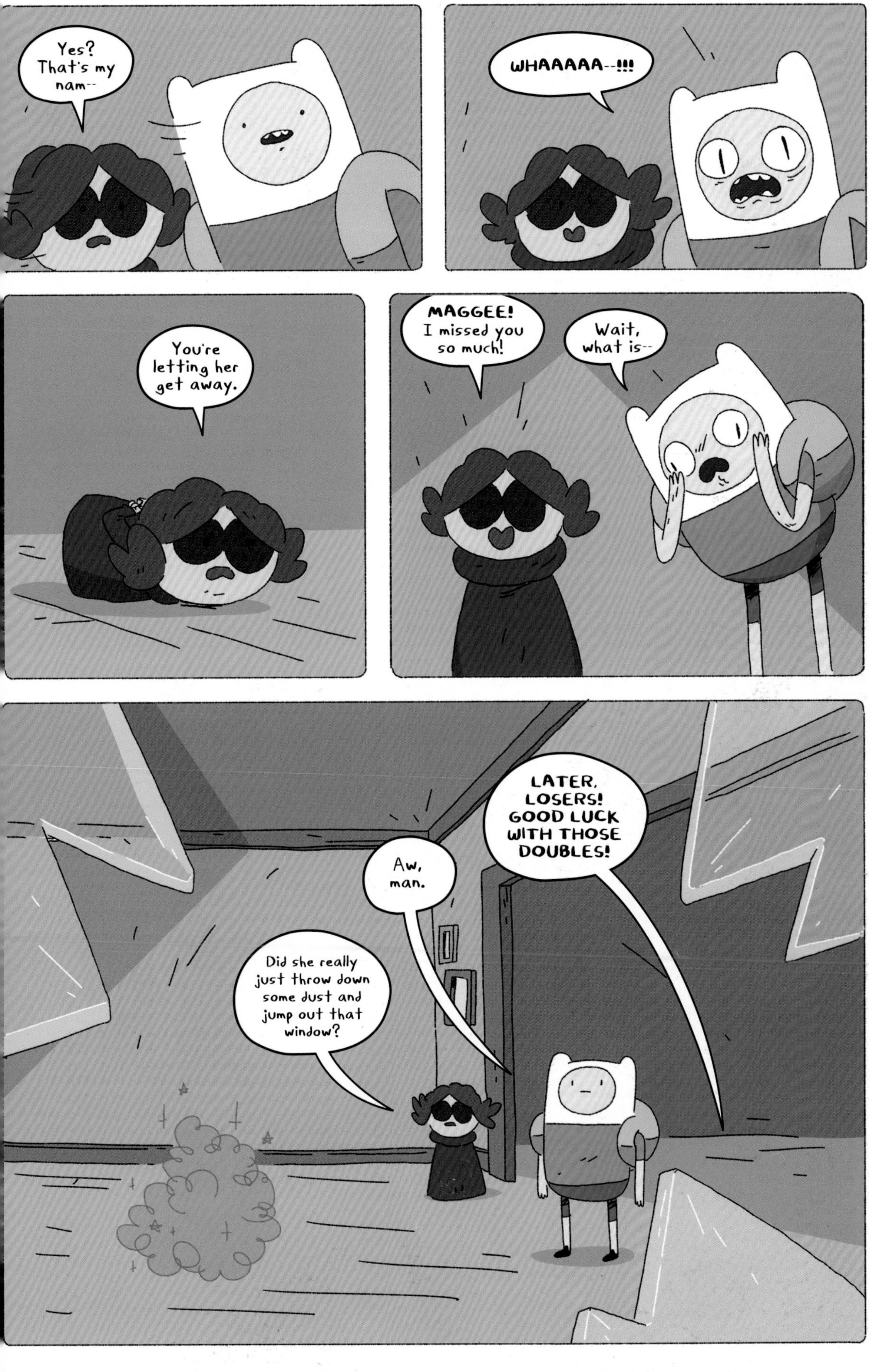
Yes? That's my nam--
WHAAAAA--!!!
You're letting her get away.
MAGGEE! I missed you so much!
Wait, what is--
LATER, LOSERS! GOOD LUCK WITH THOSE DOUBLES!
Aw, man.
Did she really just throw down some dust and jump out that window?

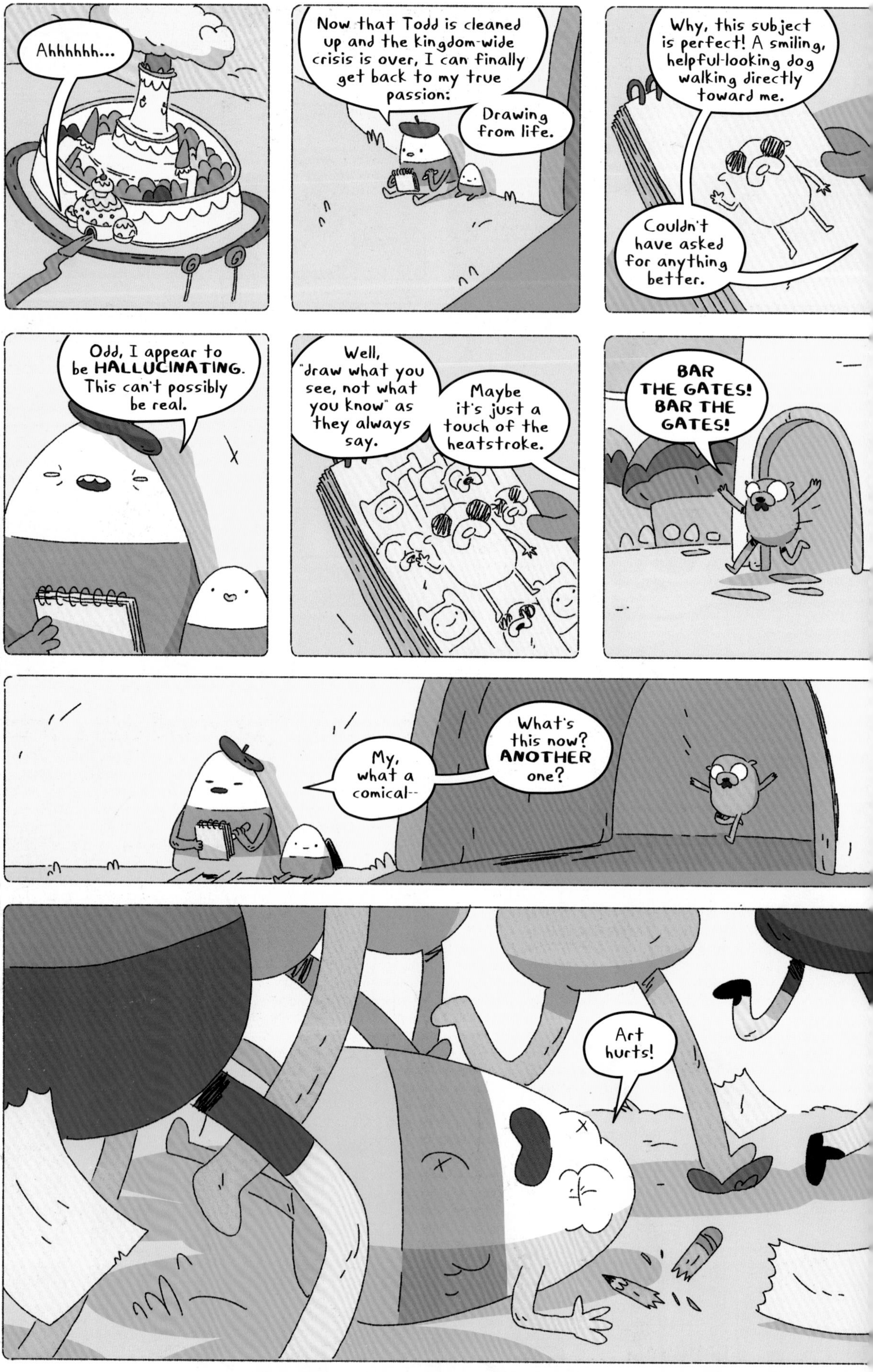
Ahhhhhh...
Now that Todd is cleaned up and the kingdom-wide crisis is over, I can finally get back to my true passion:
Drawing from life.
Why, this subject is perfect! A smiling, helpful-looking dog walking directly toward me.
Couldn't have asked for anything better.
Odd, I appear to be **HALLUCINATING**. This can't possibly be real.
Well, "draw what you see, not what you know" as they always say.
Maybe it's just a touch of the heatstroke.
**BAR THE GATES! BAR THE GATES!**
My, what a comical--
What's this now? **ANOTHER** one?
Art hurts!

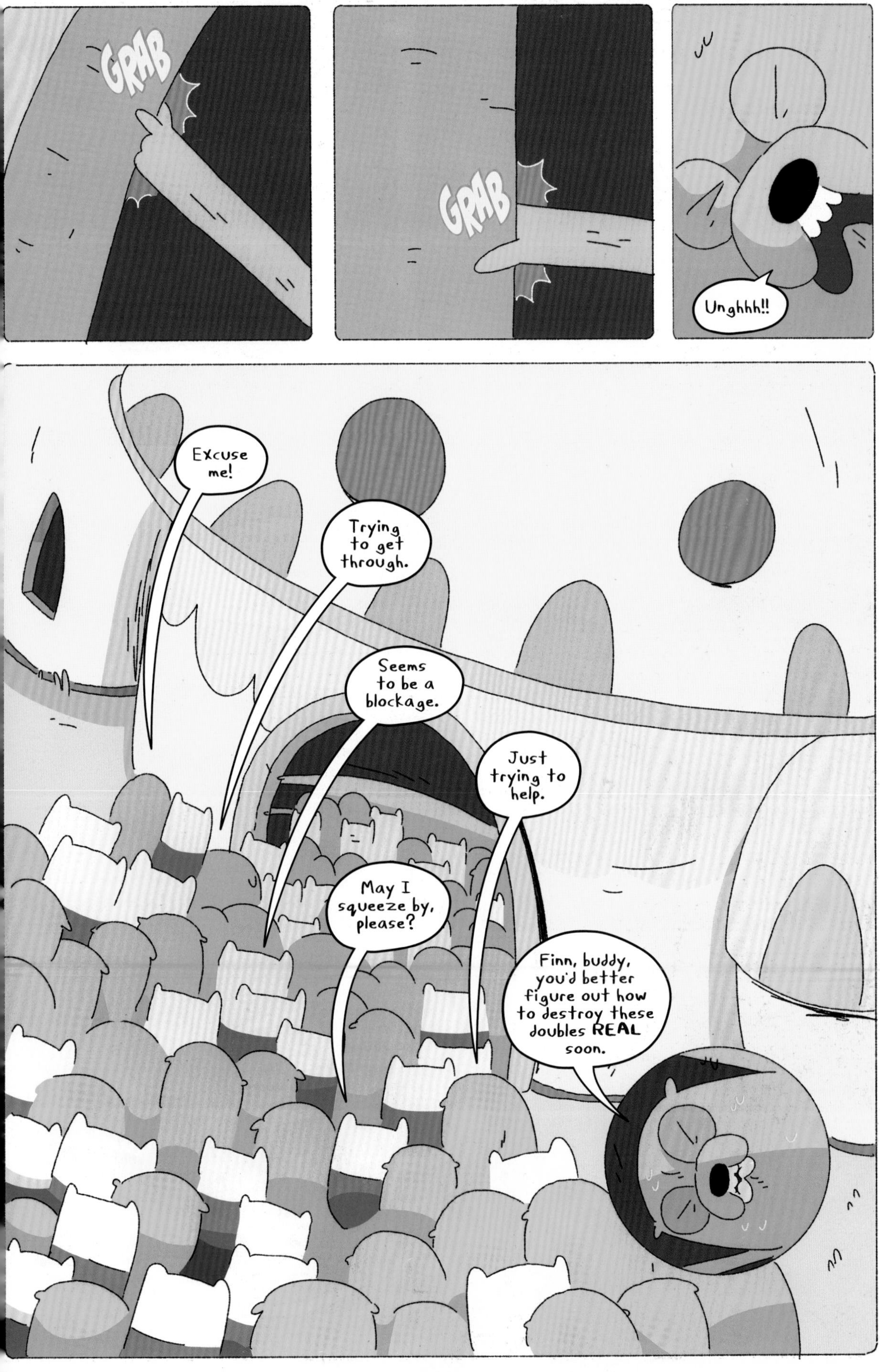
GRAB
GRAB
Unghhh!!
Excuse me!
Trying to get through.
Seems to be a blockage.
Just trying to help.
May I squeeze by, please?
Finn, buddy, you'd better figure out how to destroy these doubles REAL soon.

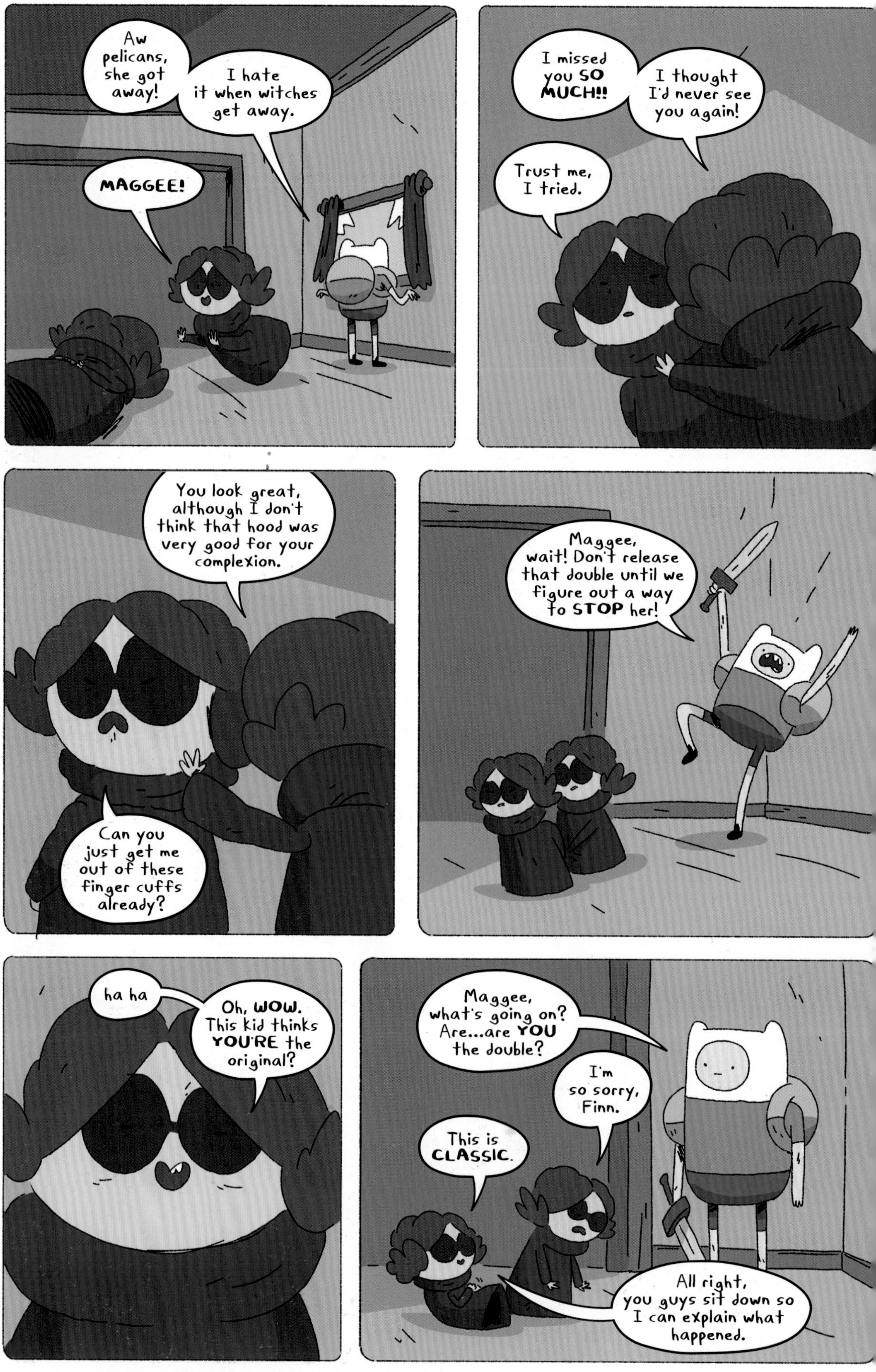
Aw pelicans, she got away!
I hate it when witches get away.
MAGGEE!
I missed you SO MUCH!!
I thought I'd never see you again!
Trust me, I tried.
You look great, although I don't think that hood was very good for your complexion.
Can you just get me out of these finger cuffs already?
Maggee, wait! Don't release that double until we figure out a way to STOP her!
ha ha
Oh, WOW. This kid thinks YOU'RE the original?
Maggee, what's going on? Are...are YOU the double?
I'm so sorry, Finn.
This is CLASSIC.
All right, you guys sit down so I can explain what happened.

So...I've never told anyone this, but back when I lived with my family I felt totally out of place, and--

Right, right. I've heard this part already.

You find the witch and ask her to make a version of you that's slightly nicer so your parents will like her. Like YOU, I mean.

Right.

Right.

So once my double--this girl--was in place, I took off and started working for the witch. She's like the only person who really GETS me.

So that's YOU! You're the FIRST DOUBLE!

Uh-huh.

I wanted to be helpful, but I didn't want to pretend I was someone else.

I left in search of the REAL Maggee.

I wanted to show you that your parents want YOU. The REAL you. Surly, contrarian nature and all.

But when YOU told the story back on the mountain you made it sound like YOU were the original Maggee.

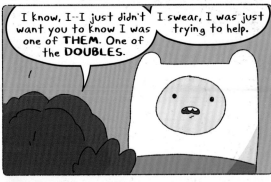

I know, I--I just didn't want you to know I was one of THEM. One of the DOUBLES.

I swear, I was just trying to help.

That's what they all say.

Literally, all of them.

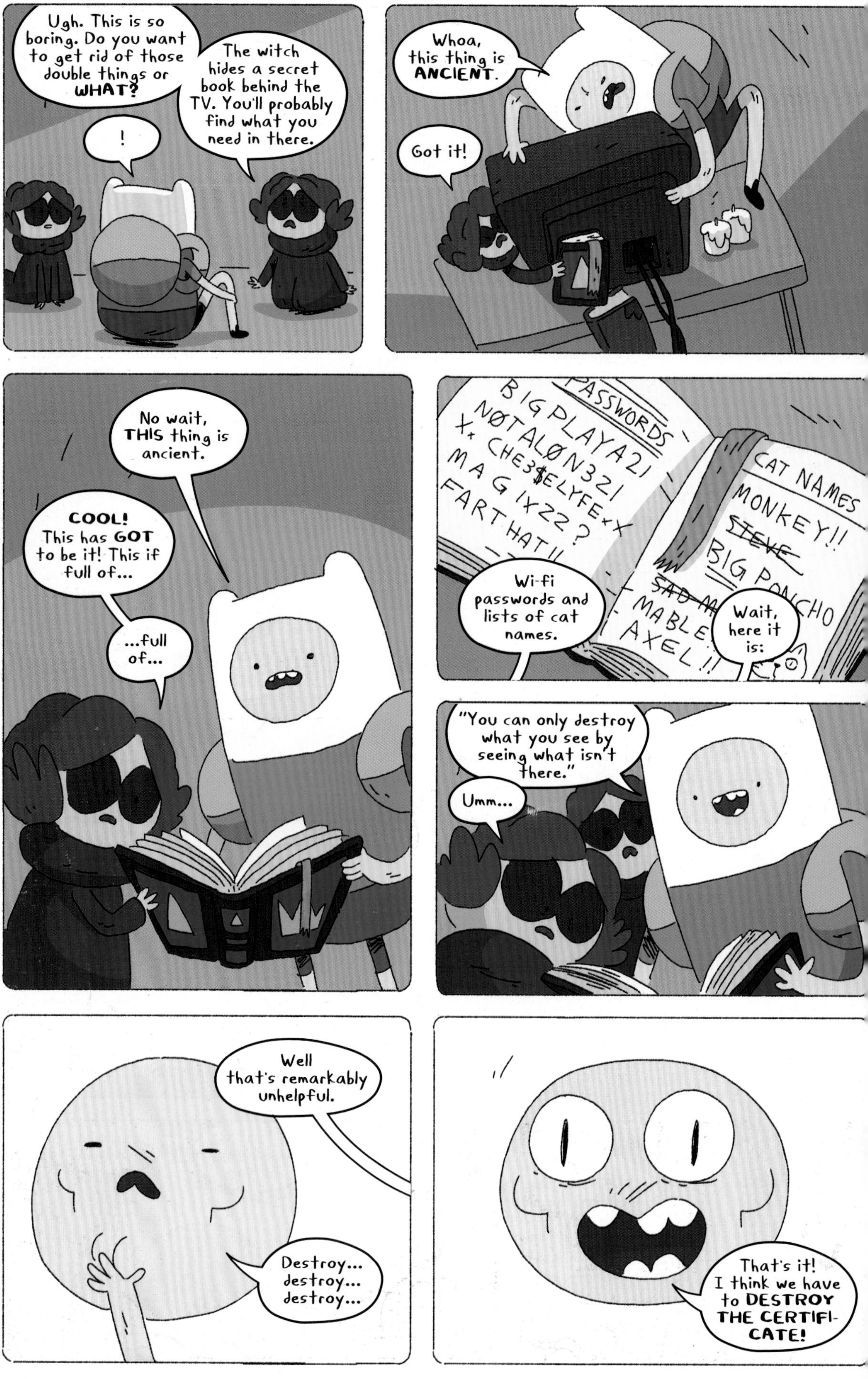
Ugh. This is so boring. Do you want to get rid of those double things or WHAT?
The witch hides a secret book behind the TV. You'll probably find what you need in there.
!
Whoa, this thing is ANCIENT.
Got it!
No wait, THIS thing is ancient.
COOL! This has GOT to be it! This if full of...
...full of...
PASSWORDS
BIGPLAYA21
NØTALØN321
X+CHE3$ELYFE+X
MAGIX22?
FARTHAT!!
CAT NAMES
MONKEY!!
STEVE
BIG PONCHO
MABLE
AXEL!!
Wi-fi passwords and lists of cat names.
Wait, here it is:
"You can only destroy what you see by seeing what isn't there."
Umm...
Well that's remarkably unhelpful.
Destroy... destroy... destroy...
That's it! I think we have to DESTROY THE CERTIFICATE!

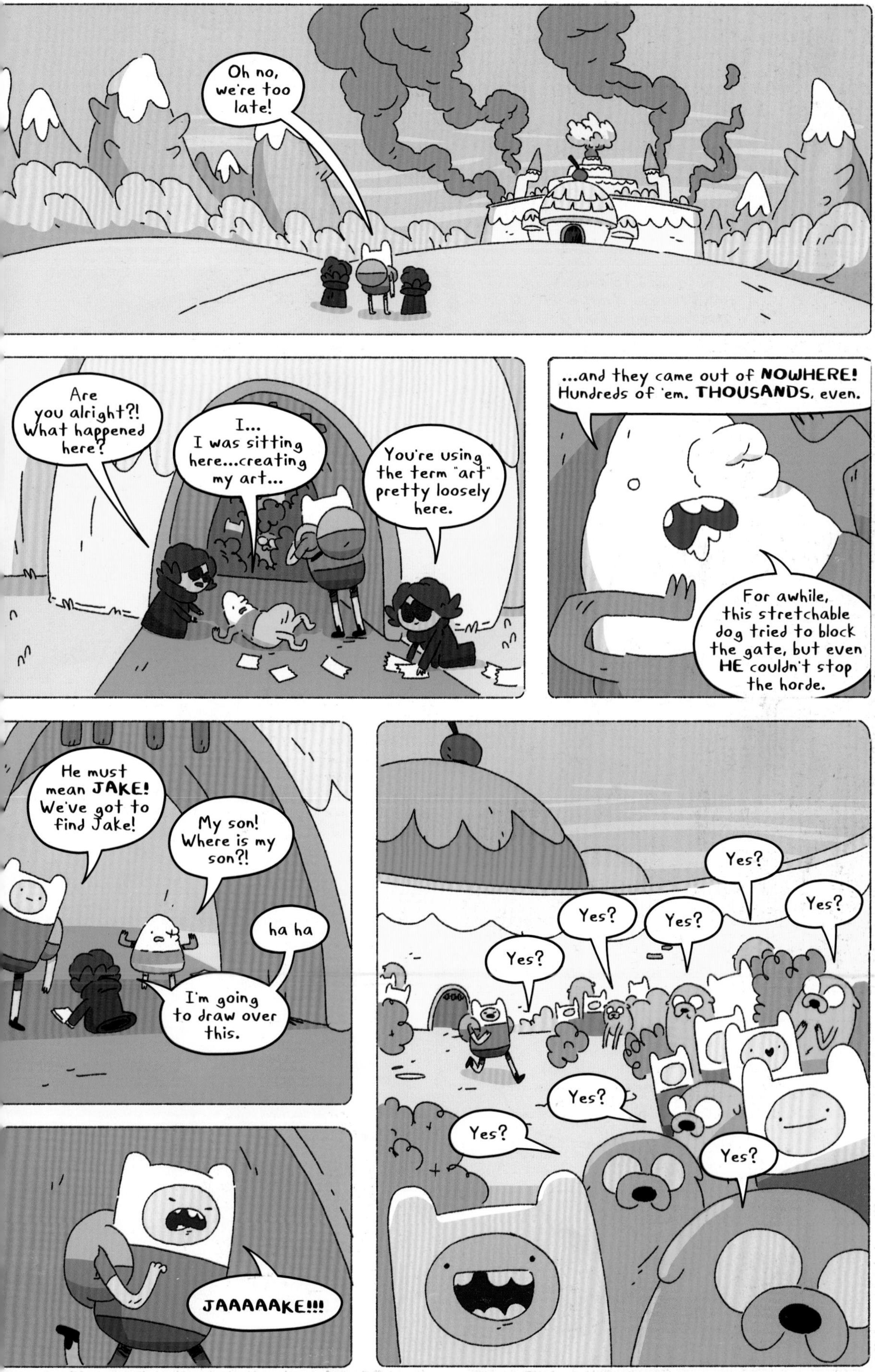
Oh no, we're too late!
Are you alright?! What happened here?
I... I was sitting here...creating my art...
You're using the term "art" pretty loosely here.
...and they came out of NOWHERE! Hundreds of 'em. THOUSANDS, even.
For awhile, this stretchable dog tried to block the gate, but even HE couldn't stop the horde.
He must mean JAKE! We've got to find Jake!
My son! Where is my son?!
ha ha
I'm going to draw over this.
JAAAAAKE!!!
Yes?
Yes?
Yes?
Yes?
Yes?
Yes?
Yes?
Yes?

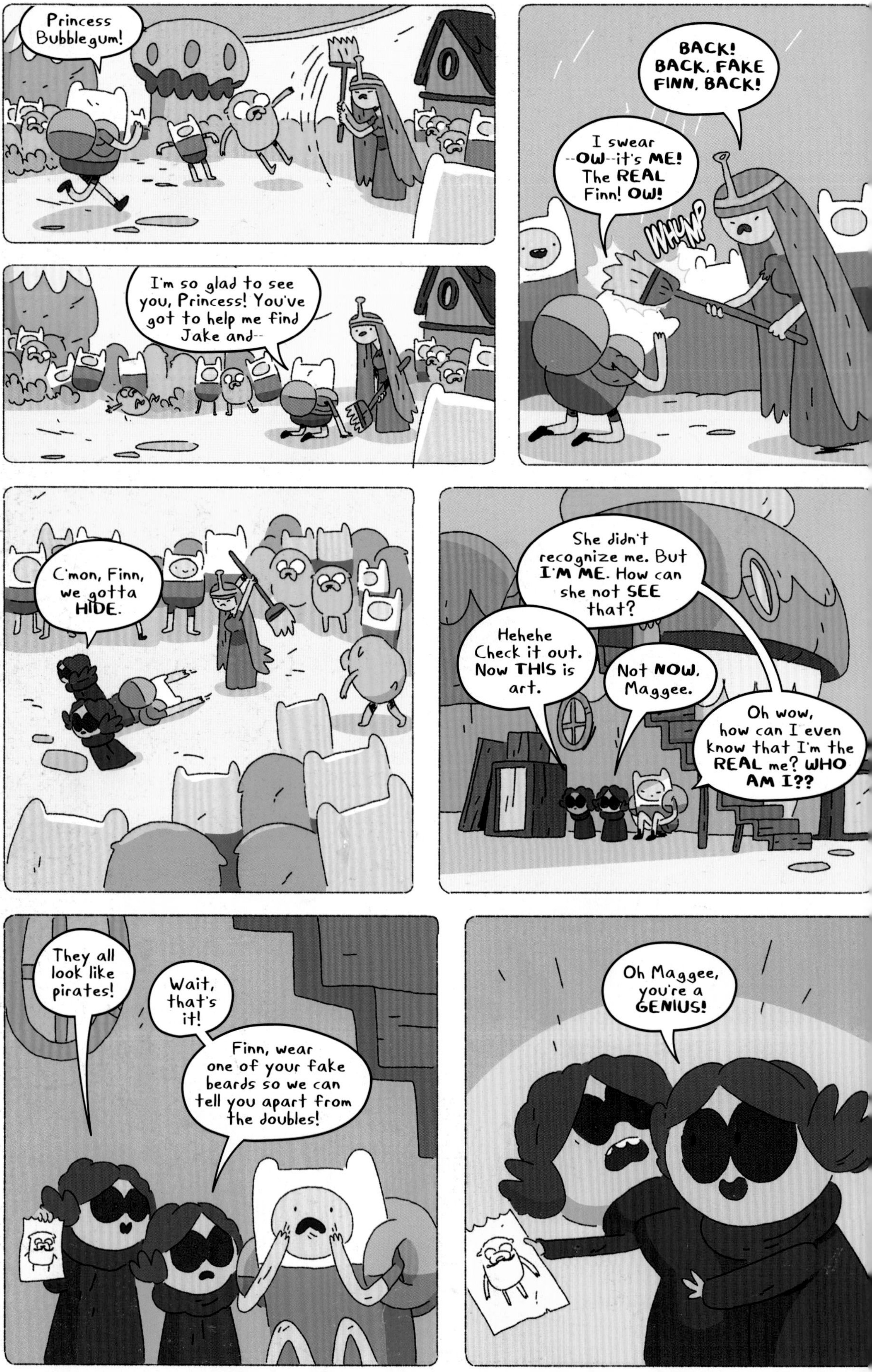
Princess Bubblegum!
I'm so glad to see you, Princess! You've got to help me find Jake and--
BACK! BACK, FAKE FINN, BACK!
I swear --OW--it's ME! The REAL Finn! OW!
WHUMP
C'mon, Finn, we gotta HIDE.
She didn't recognize me. But I'M ME. How can she not SEE that?
Hehehe Check it out. Now THIS is art.
Not NOW, Maggee.
Oh wow, how can I even know that I'm the REAL me? WHO AM I??
They all look like pirates!
Wait, that's it!
Finn, wear one of your fake beards so we can tell you apart from the doubles!
Oh Maggee, you're a GENIUS!

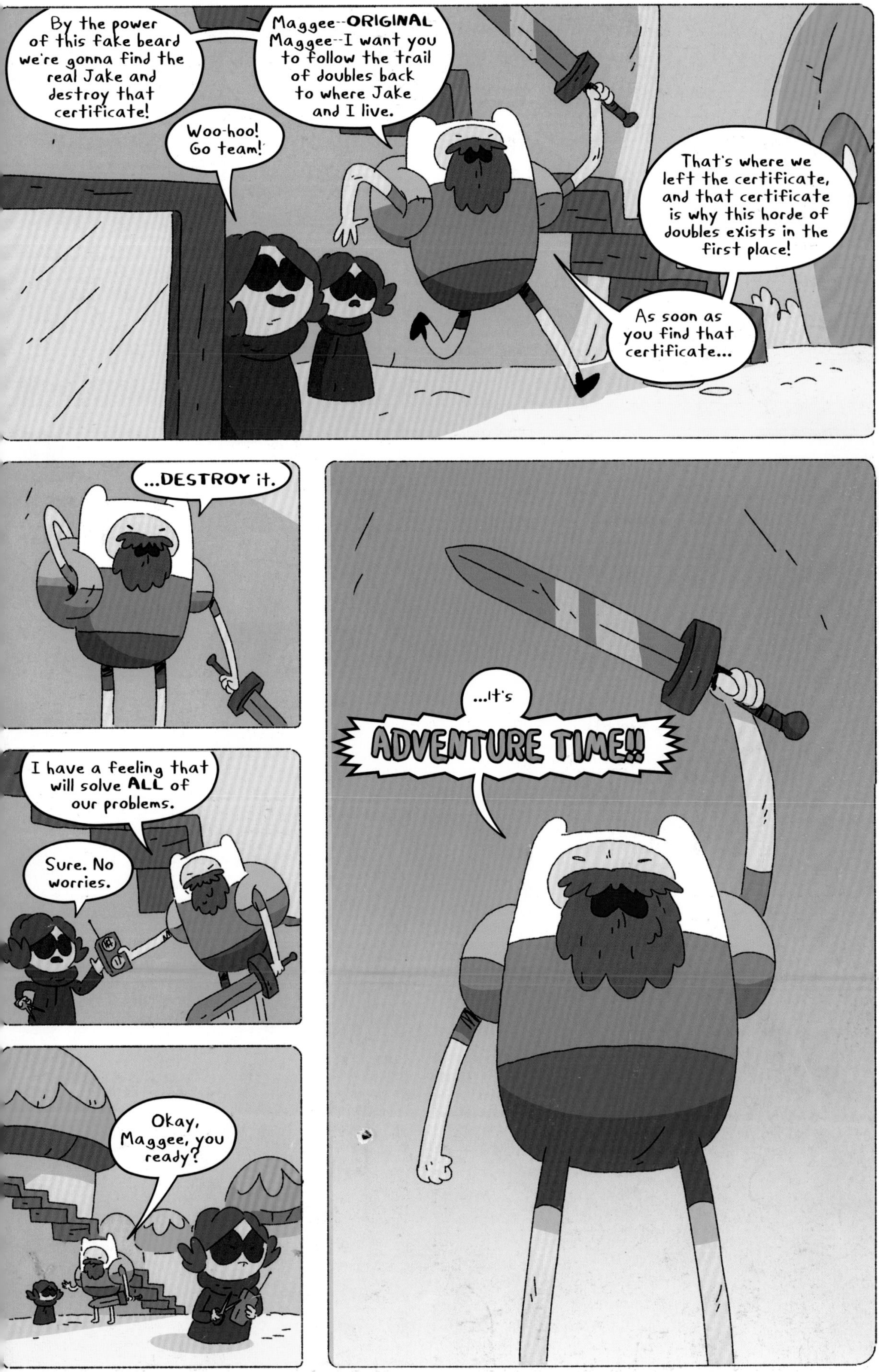
By the power of this fake beard we're gonna find the real Jake and destroy that certificate!
Maggee--ORIGINAL Maggee--I want you to follow the trail of doubles back to where Jake and I live.
Woo-hoo! Go team!
That's where we left the certificate, and that certificate is why this horde of doubles exists in the first place!
As soon as you find that certificate...
...DESTROY it.
I have a feeling that will solve ALL of our problems.
Sure. No worries.
Okay, Maggee, you ready?
...It's
ADVENTURE TIME!!

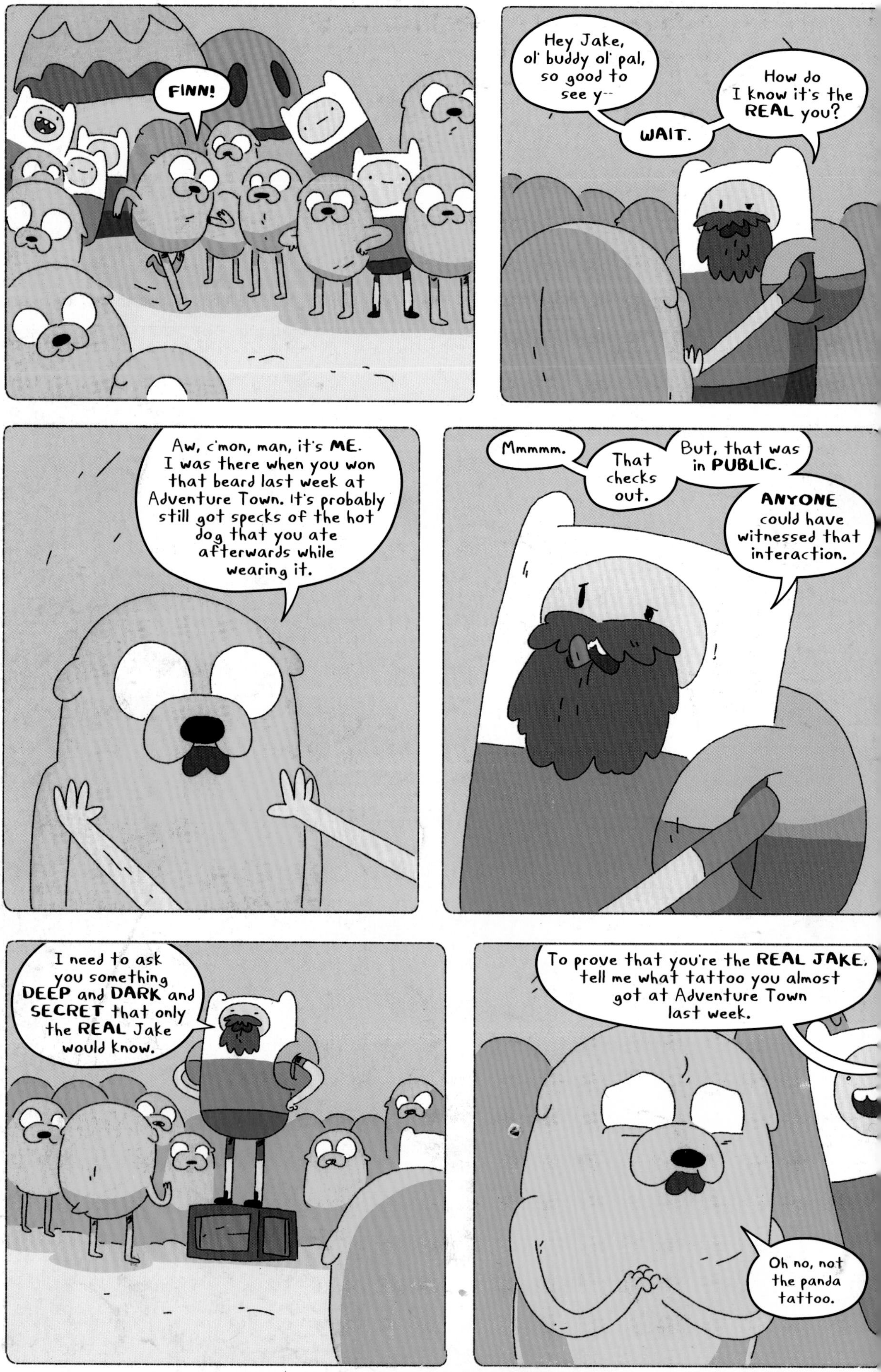
FINN!
Hey Jake, ol' buddy ol' pal, so good to see y--
WAIT.
How do I know it's the REAL you?
Aw, c'mon, man, it's ME. I was there when you won that beard last week at Adventure Town. It's probably still got specks of the hot dog that you ate afterwards while wearing it.
Mmmmm.
That checks out.
But, that was in PUBLIC.
ANYONE could have witnessed that interaction.
I need to ask you something DEEP and DARK and SECRET that only the REAL Jake would know.
To prove that you're the REAL JAKE, tell me what tattoo you almost got at Adventure Town last week.
Oh no, not the panda tattoo.

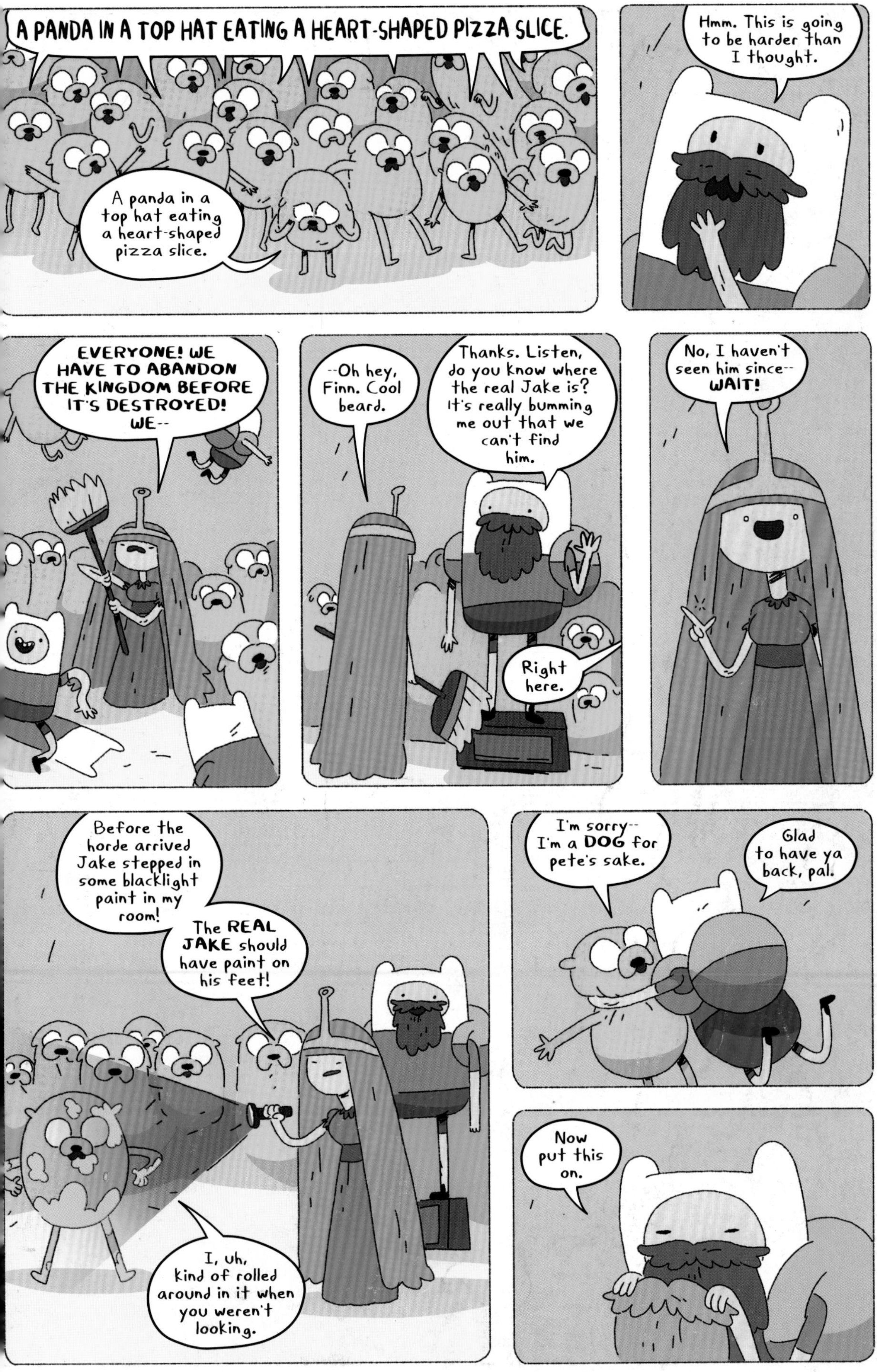
A PANDA IN A TOP HAT EATING A HEART-SHAPED PIZZA SLICE.
A panda in a top hat eating a heart-shaped pizza slice.
Hmm. This is going to be harder than I thought.
EVERYONE! WE HAVE TO ABANDON THE KINGDOM BEFORE IT'S DESTROYED! WE--
--Oh hey, Finn. Cool beard.
Thanks. Listen, do you know where the real Jake is? It's really bumming me out that we can't find him.
Right here.
No, I haven't seen him since-- WAIT!
Before the horde arrived Jake stepped in some blacklight paint in my room!
The REAL JAKE should have paint on his feet!
I, uh, kind of rolled around in it when you weren't looking.
I'm sorry-- I'm a DOG for pete's sake.
Glad to have ya back, pal.
Now put this on.

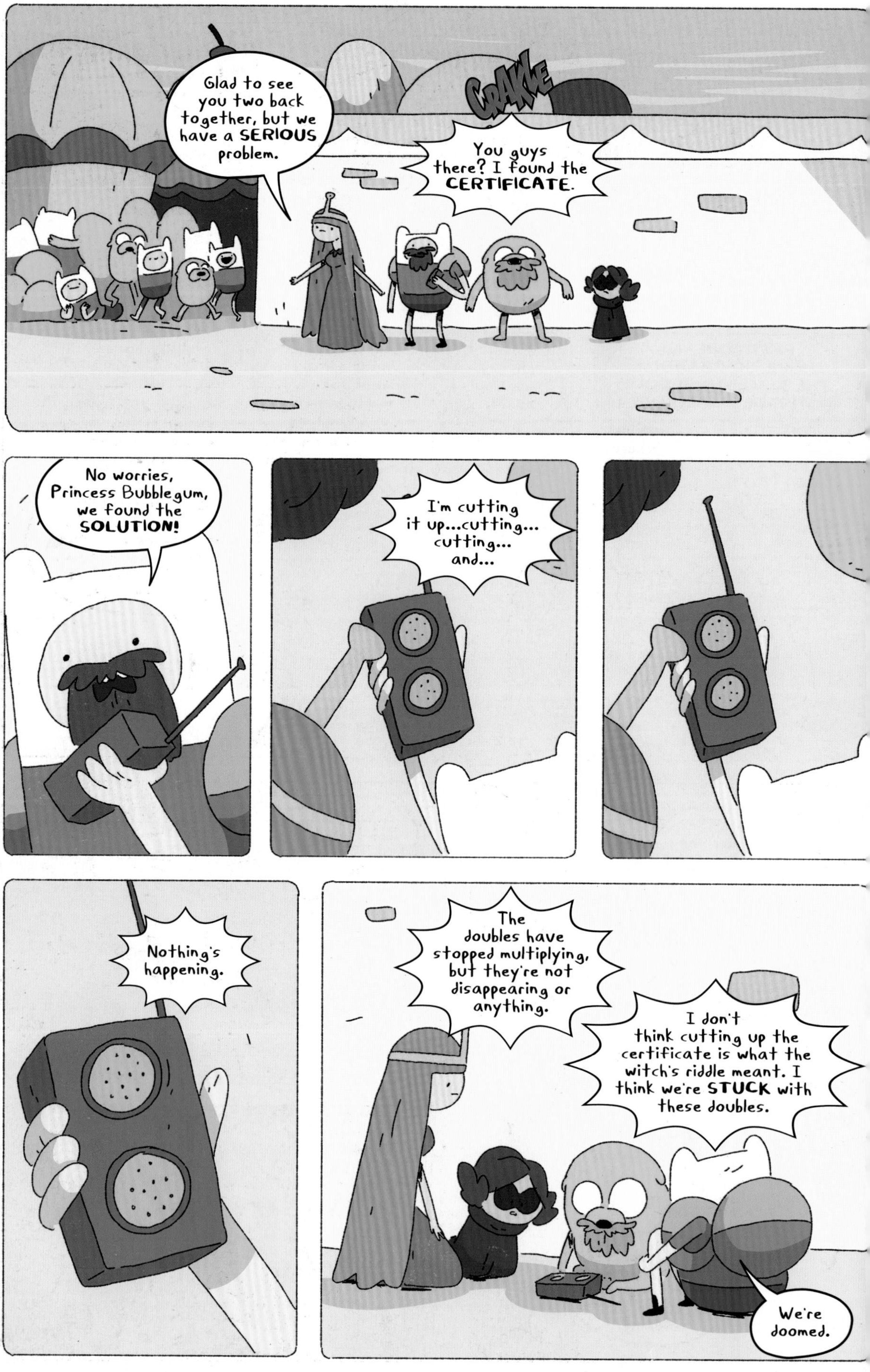
Glad to see you two back together, but we have a SERIOUS problem.
CRAKLE
You guys there? I found the CERTIFICATE.
No worries, Princess Bubblegum, we found the SOLUTION!
I'm cutting it up...cutting... cutting... and...
Nothing's happening.
The doubles have stopped multiplying, but they're not disappearing or anything.
I don't think cutting up the certificate is what the witch's riddle meant. I think we're STUCK with these doubles.
We're doomed.

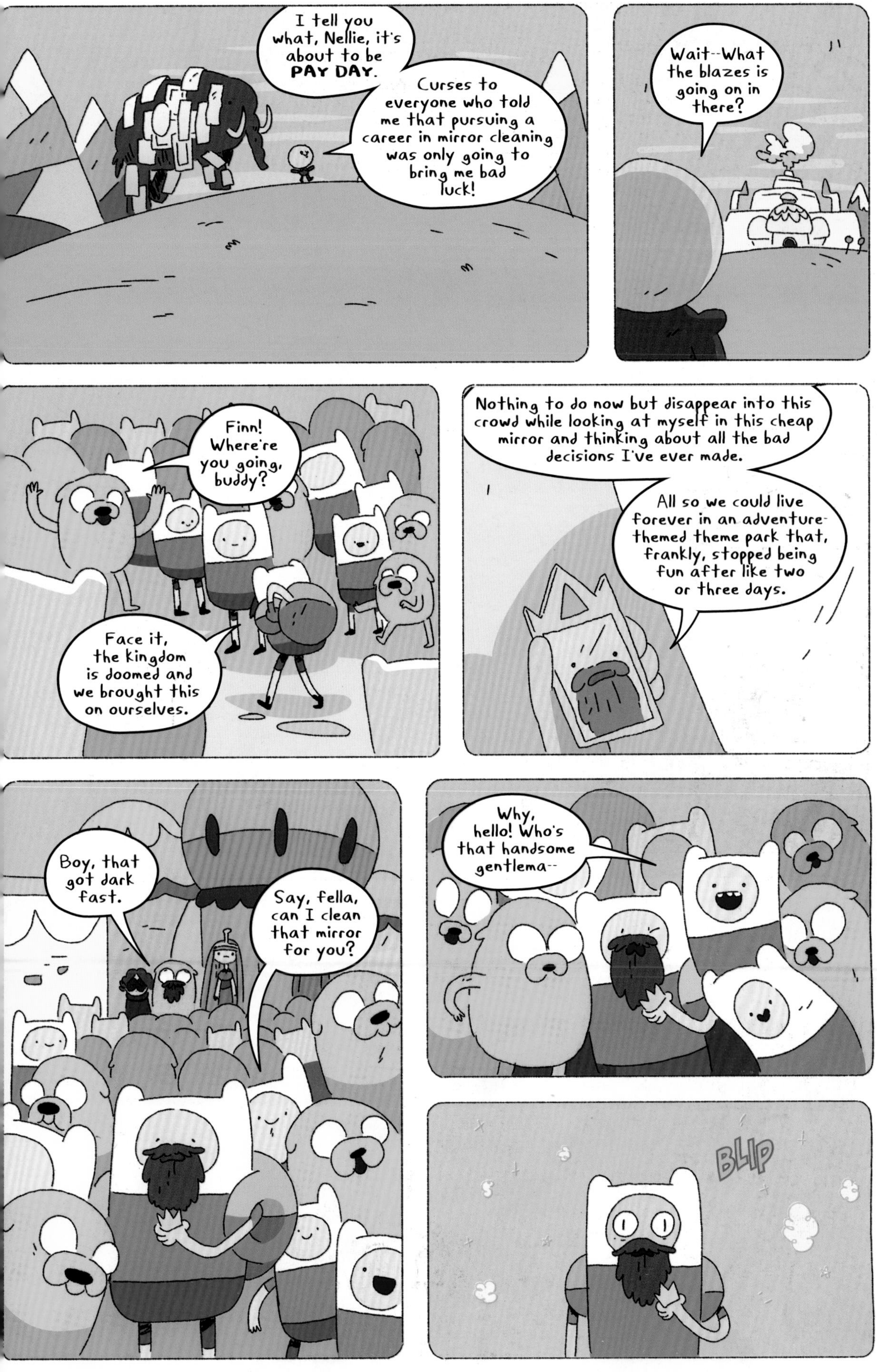
I tell you what, Nellie, it's about to be PAY DAY.
Curses to everyone who told me that pursuing a career in mirror cleaning was only going to bring me bad luck!
Wait--What the blazes is going on in there?
Finn! Where're you going, buddy?
Face it, the kingdom is doomed and we brought this on ourselves.
Nothing to do now but disappear into this crowd while looking at myself in this cheap mirror and thinking about all the bad decisions I've ever made.
All so we could live forever in an adventure-themed theme park that, frankly, stopped being fun after like two or three days.
Boy, that got dark fast.
Say, fella, can I clean that mirror for you?
Why, hello! Who's that handsome gentlema--
BLIP

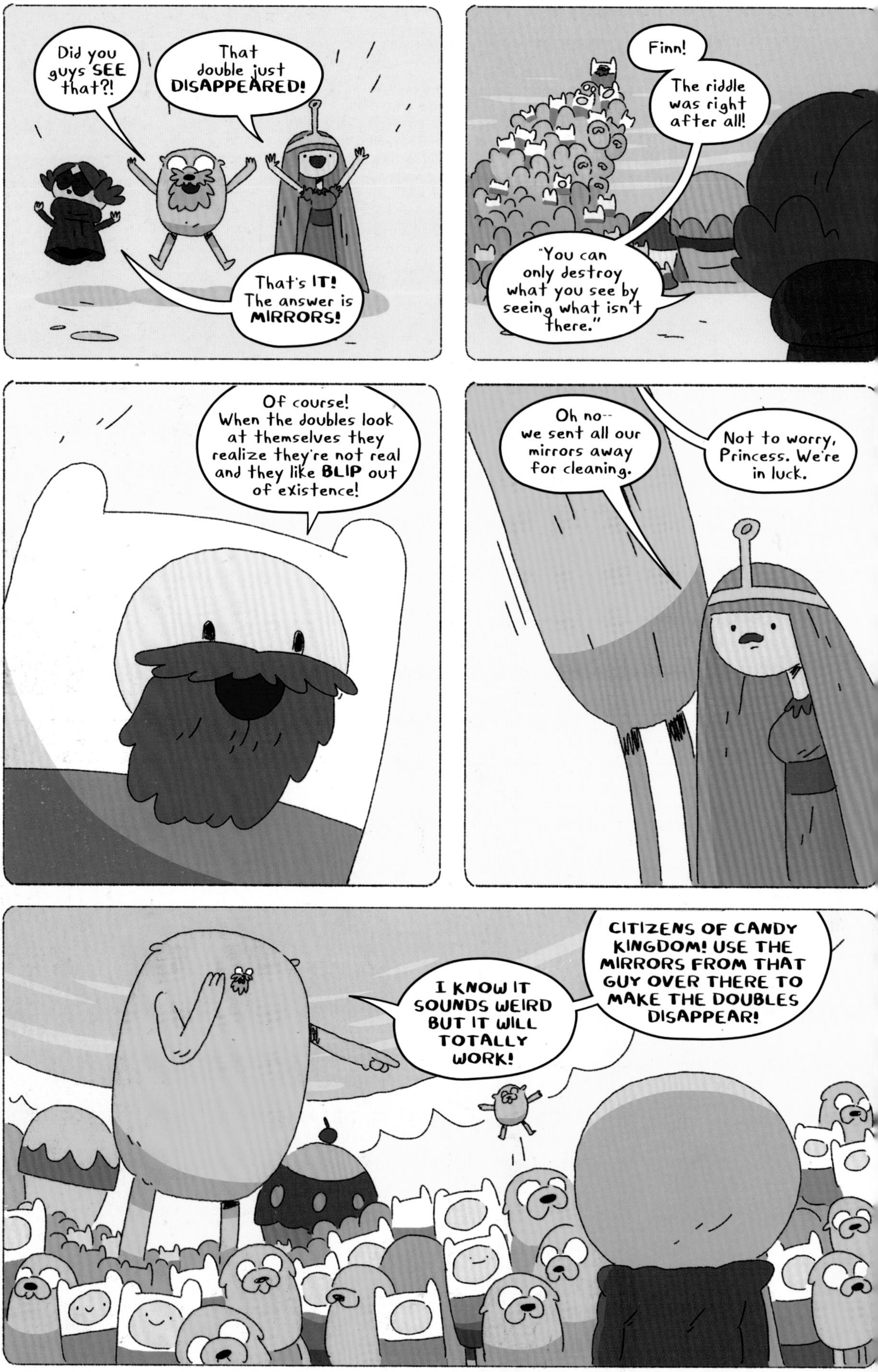

Did you guys SEE that?!
That double just DISAPPEARED!
That's IT! The answer is MIRRORS!
Finn!
The riddle was right after all!
"You can only destroy what you see by seeing what isn't there."
Of course! When the doubles look at themselves they realize they're not real and they like BLIP out of existence!
Oh no-- we sent all our mirrors away for cleaning.
Not to worry, Princess. We're in luck.
CITIZENS OF CANDY KINGDOM! USE THE MIRRORS FROM THAT GUY OVER THERE TO MAKE THE DOUBLES DISAPPEAR!
I KNOW IT SOUNDS WEIRD BUT IT WILL TOTALLY WORK!

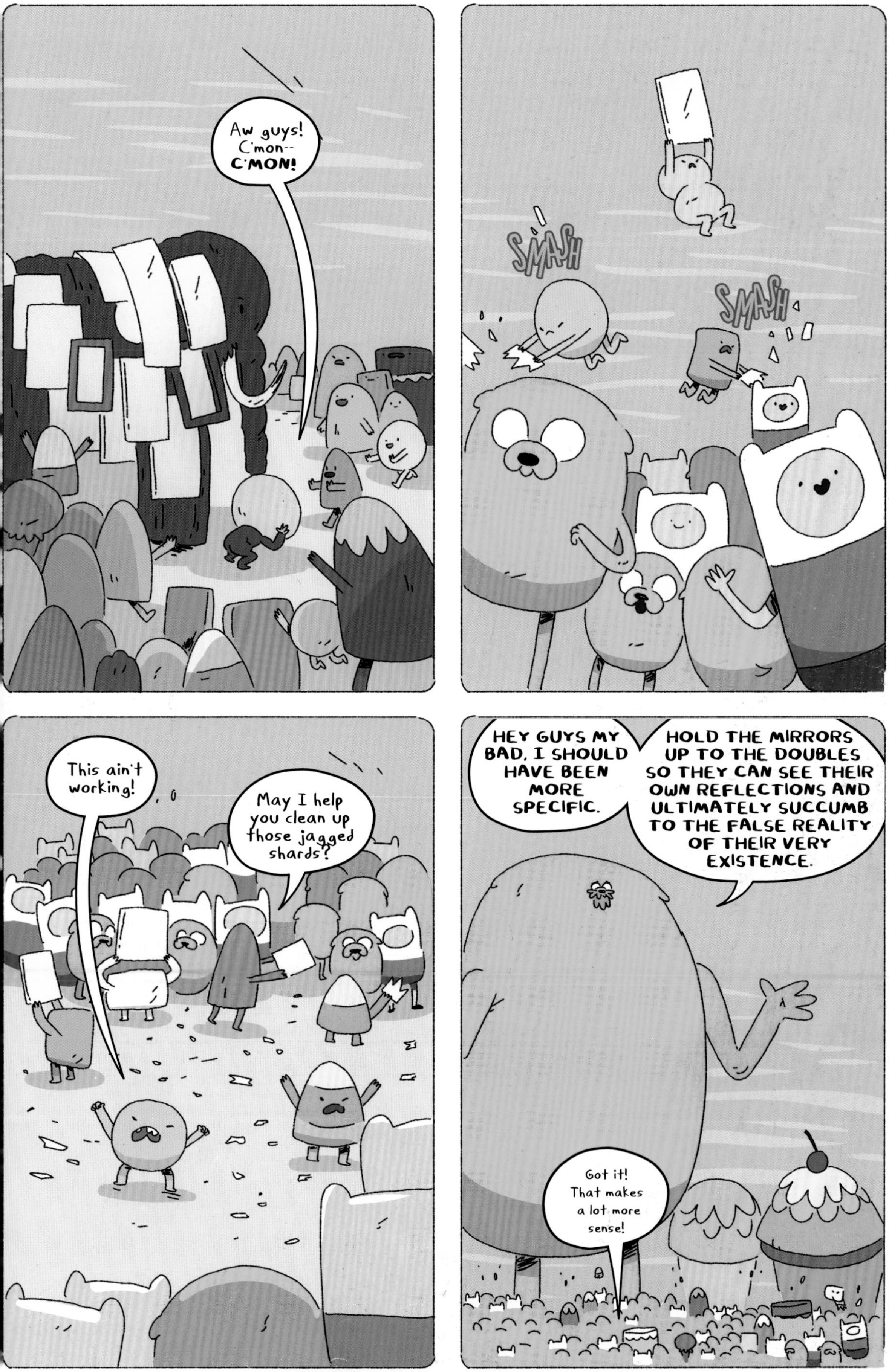

Aw guys! C'mon-- C'MON!
SMASH
SMASH
This ain't working!
May I help you clean up those jagged shards?
HEY GUYS MY BAD, I SHOULD HAVE BEEN MORE SPECIFIC.
HOLD THE MIRRORS UP TO THE DOUBLES SO THEY CAN SEE THEIR OWN REFLECTIONS AND ULTIMATELY SUCCUMB TO THE FALSE REALITY OF THEIR VERY EXISTENCE.
Got it! That makes a lot more sense!

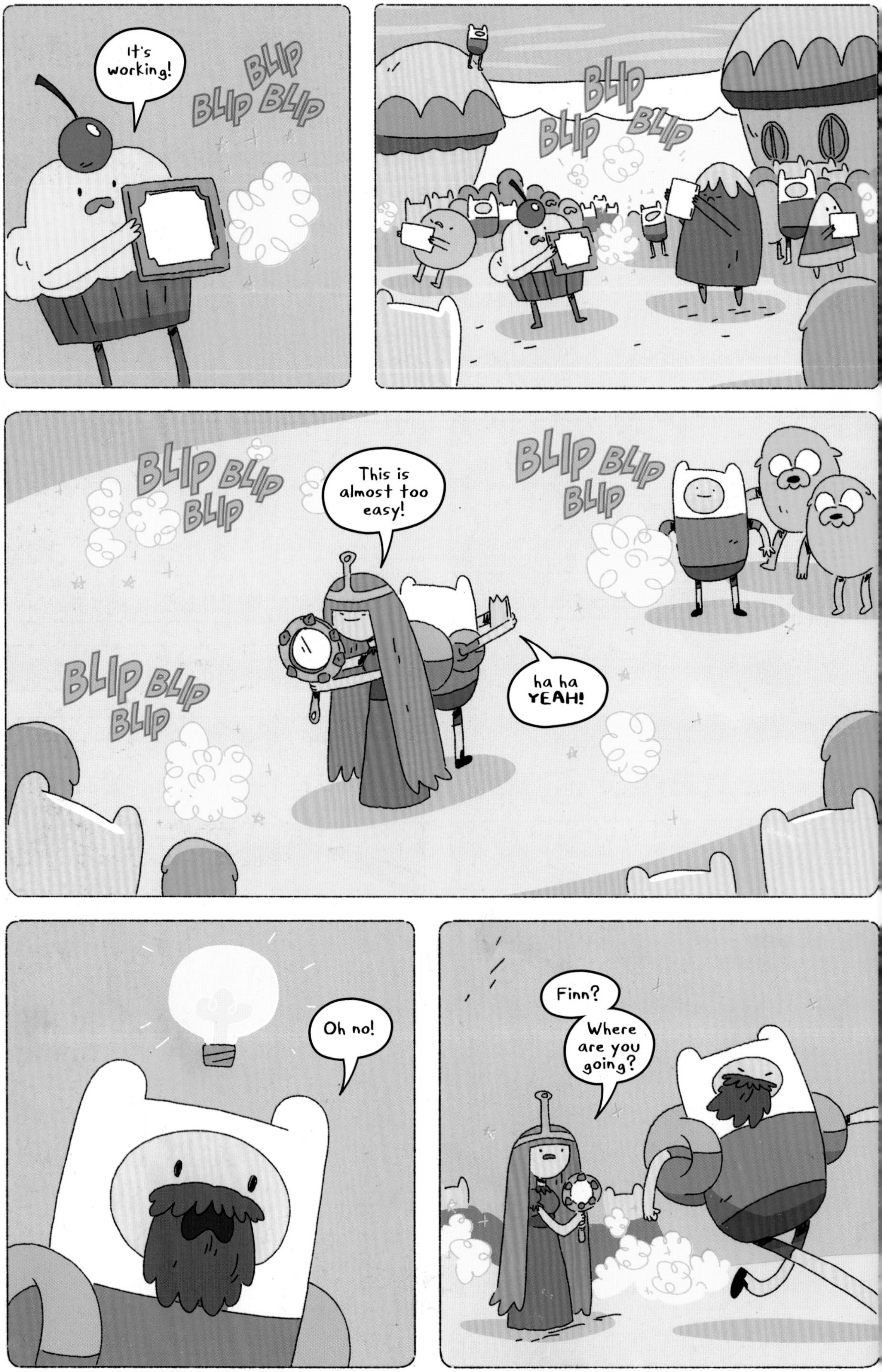

It's working!
BLIP BLIP BLIP
BLIP BLIP BLIP
BLIP BLIP BLIP
This is almost too easy!
BLIP BLIP BLIP
BLIP BLIP BLIP
ha ha YEAH!
Oh no!
Finn?
Where are you going?

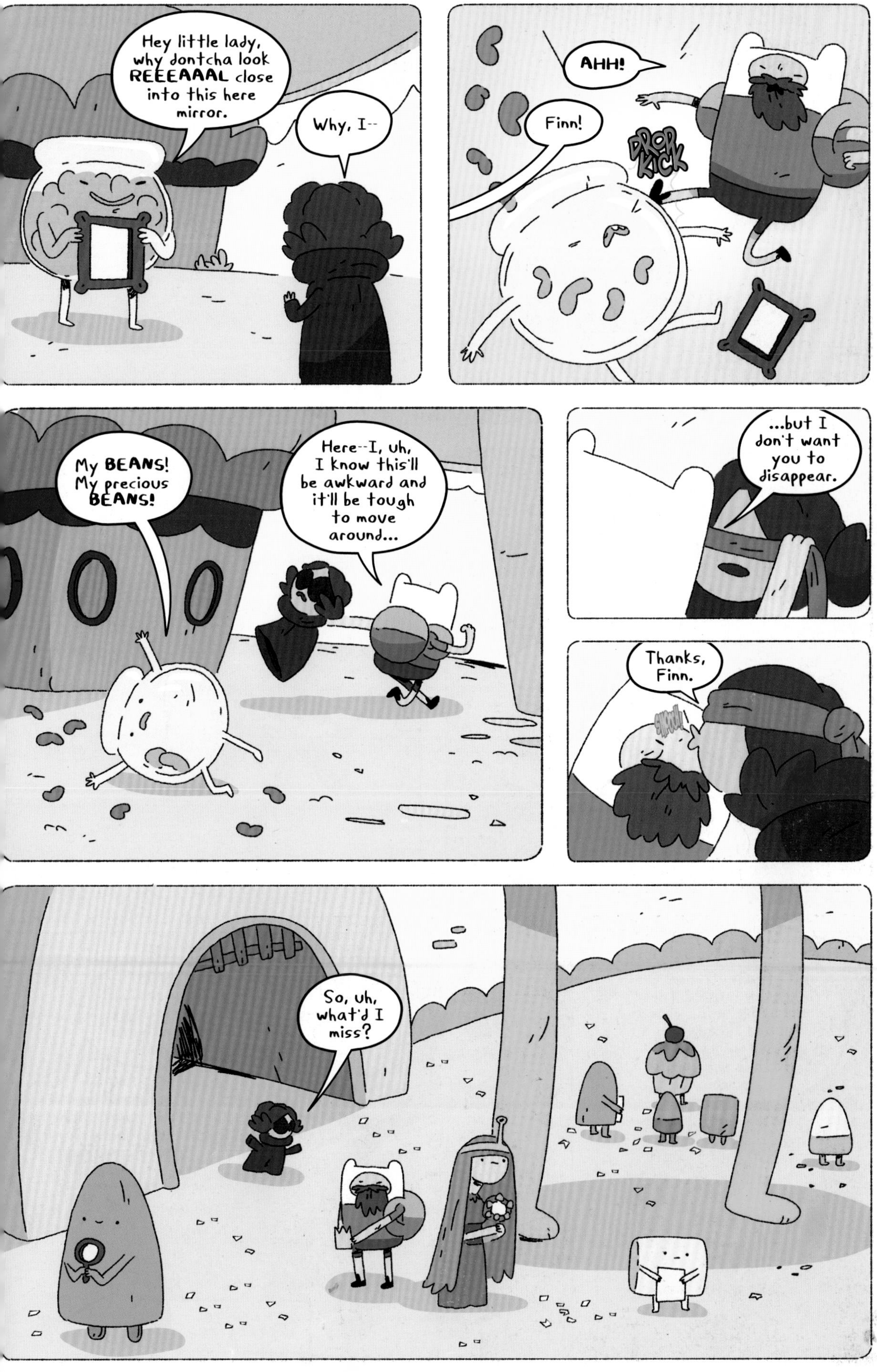
Hey little lady, why dontcha look REEEAAAL close into this here mirror.
Why, I--
AHH!
Finn!
DROP KICK
My BEANS! My precious BEANS!
Here--I, uh, I know this'll be awkward and it'll be tough to move around...
...but I don't want you to disappear.
Thanks, Finn.
So, uh, what'd I miss?

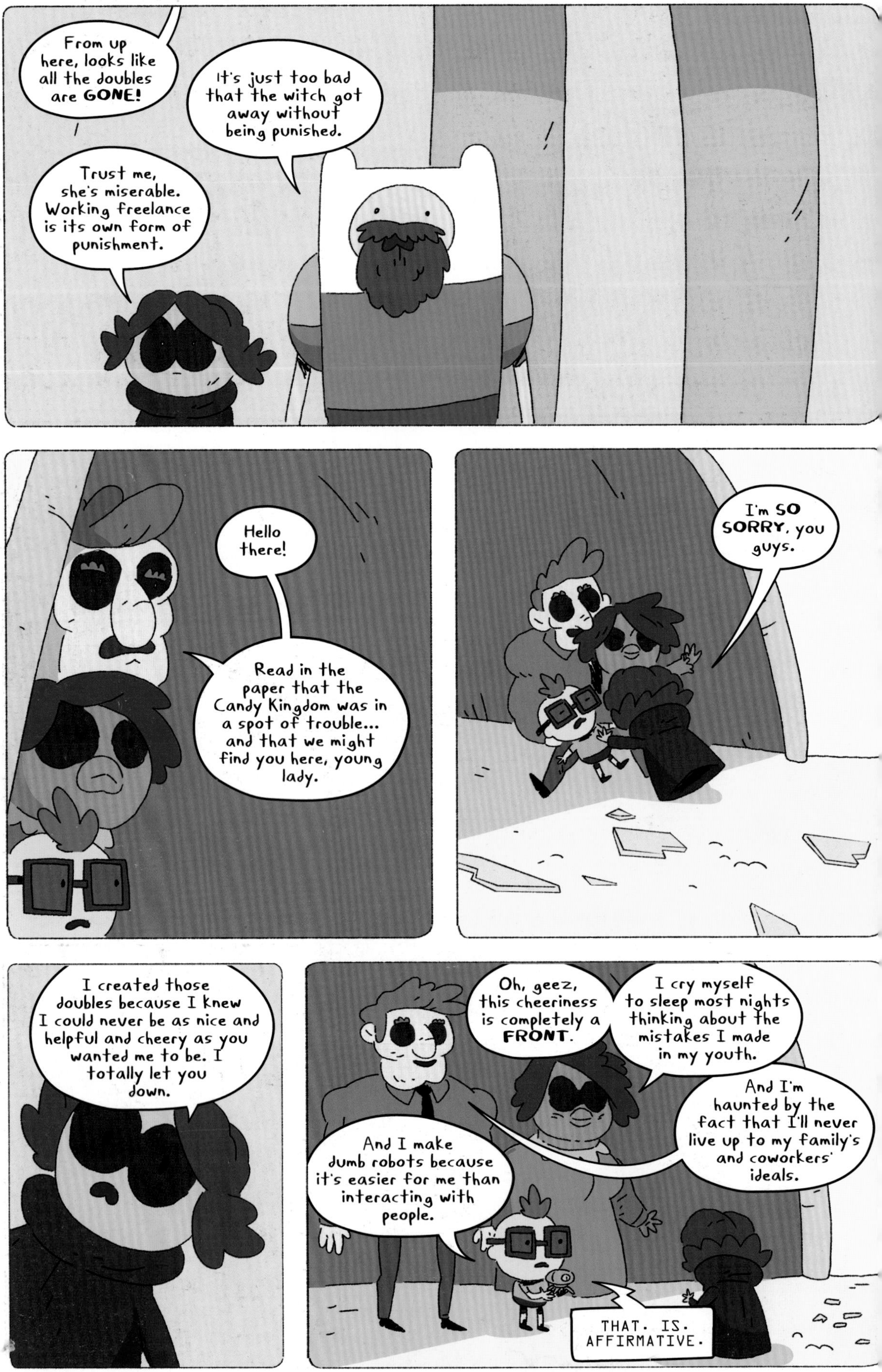
From up here, looks like all the doubles are **GONE!**
It's just too bad that the witch got away without being punished.
Trust me, she's miserable. Working freelance is its own form of punishment.
Hello there!
Read in the paper that the Candy Kingdom was in a spot of trouble... and that we might find you here, young lady.
I'm **SO SORRY**, you guys.
I created those doubles because I knew I could never be as nice and helpful and cheery as you wanted me to be. I totally let you down.
Oh, geez, this cheeriness is completely a **FRONT**.
I cry myself to sleep most nights thinking about the mistakes I made in my youth.
And I'm haunted by the fact that I'll never live up to my family's and coworkers' ideals.
And I make dumb robots because it's easier for me than interacting with people.
THAT. IS. AFFIRMATIVE.

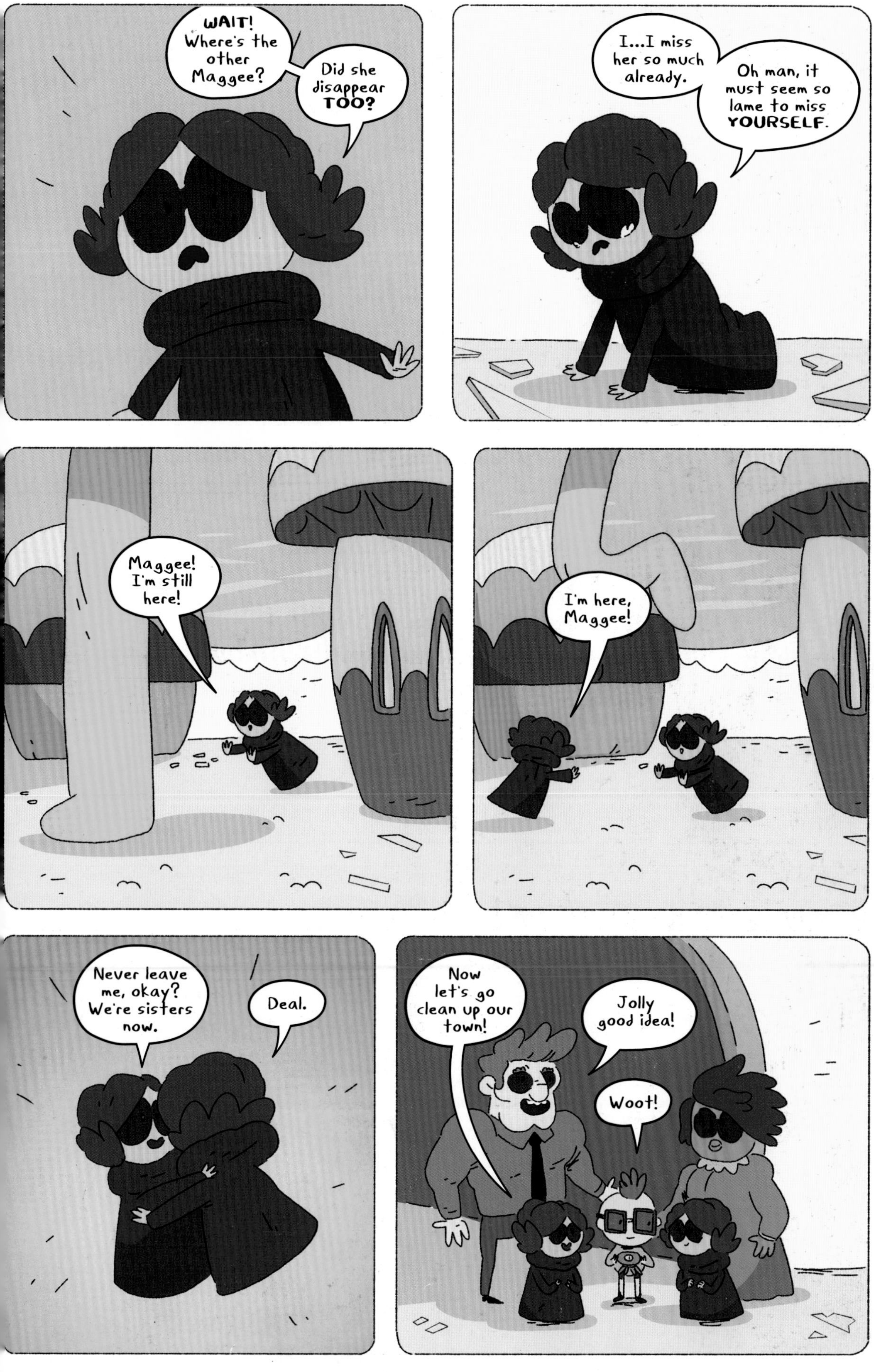
WAIT! Where's the other Maggee?
Did she disappear TOO?
I...I miss her so much already.
Oh man, it must seem so lame to miss YOURSELF.
Maggee! I'm still here!
I'm here, Maggee!
Never leave me, okay? We're sisters now.
Deal.
Now let's go clean up our town!
Jolly good idea!
Woot!

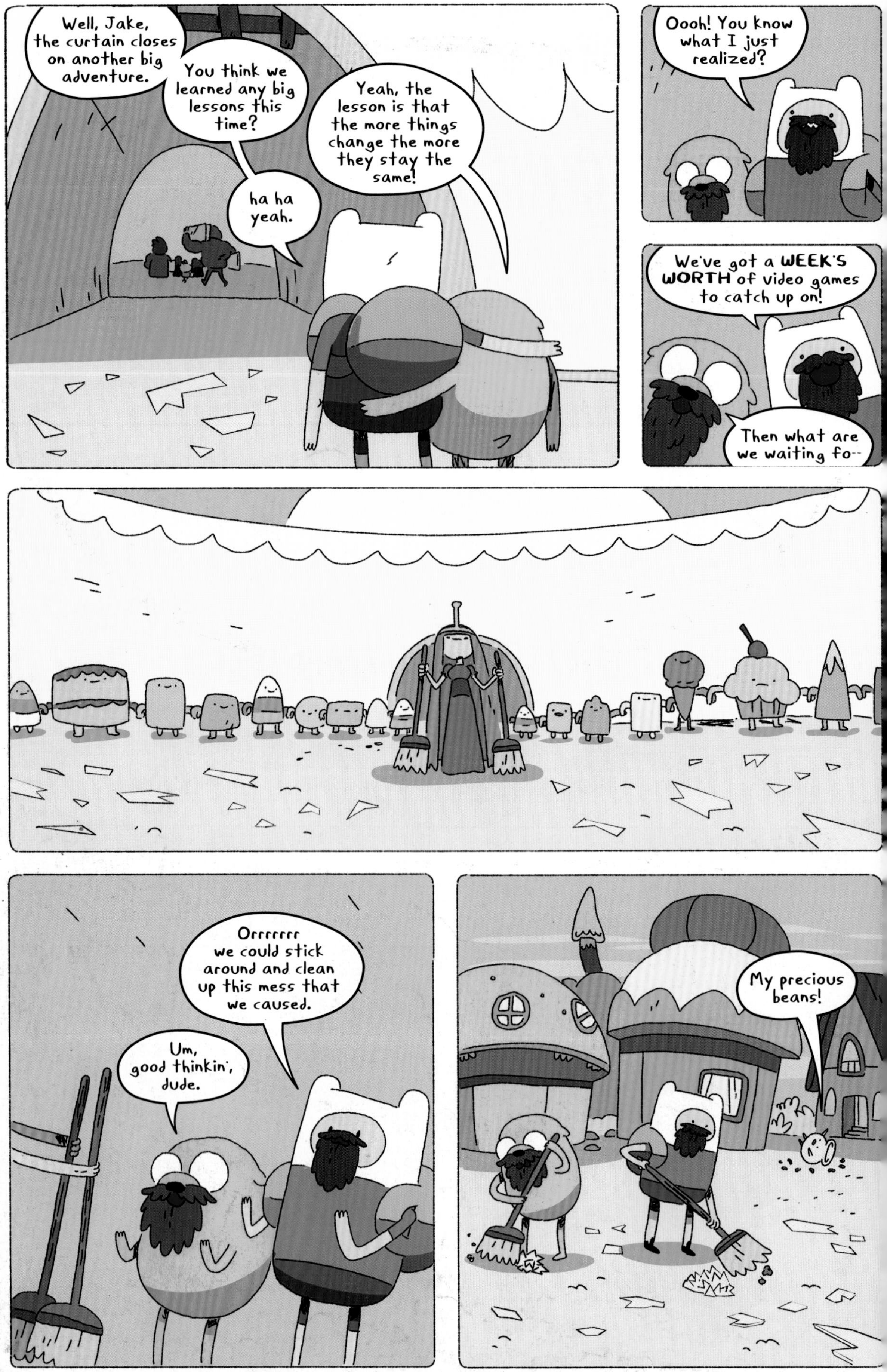

Well, Jake, the curtain closes on another big adventure.
You think we learned any big lessons this time?
Yeah, the lesson is that the more things change the more they stay the same!
ha ha yeah.
Oooh! You know what I just realized?
We've got a **WEEK'S WORTH** of video games to catch up on!
Then what are we waiting fo--
Orrrrrrr we could stick around and clean up this mess that we caused.
Um, good thinkin', dude.
My precious beans!

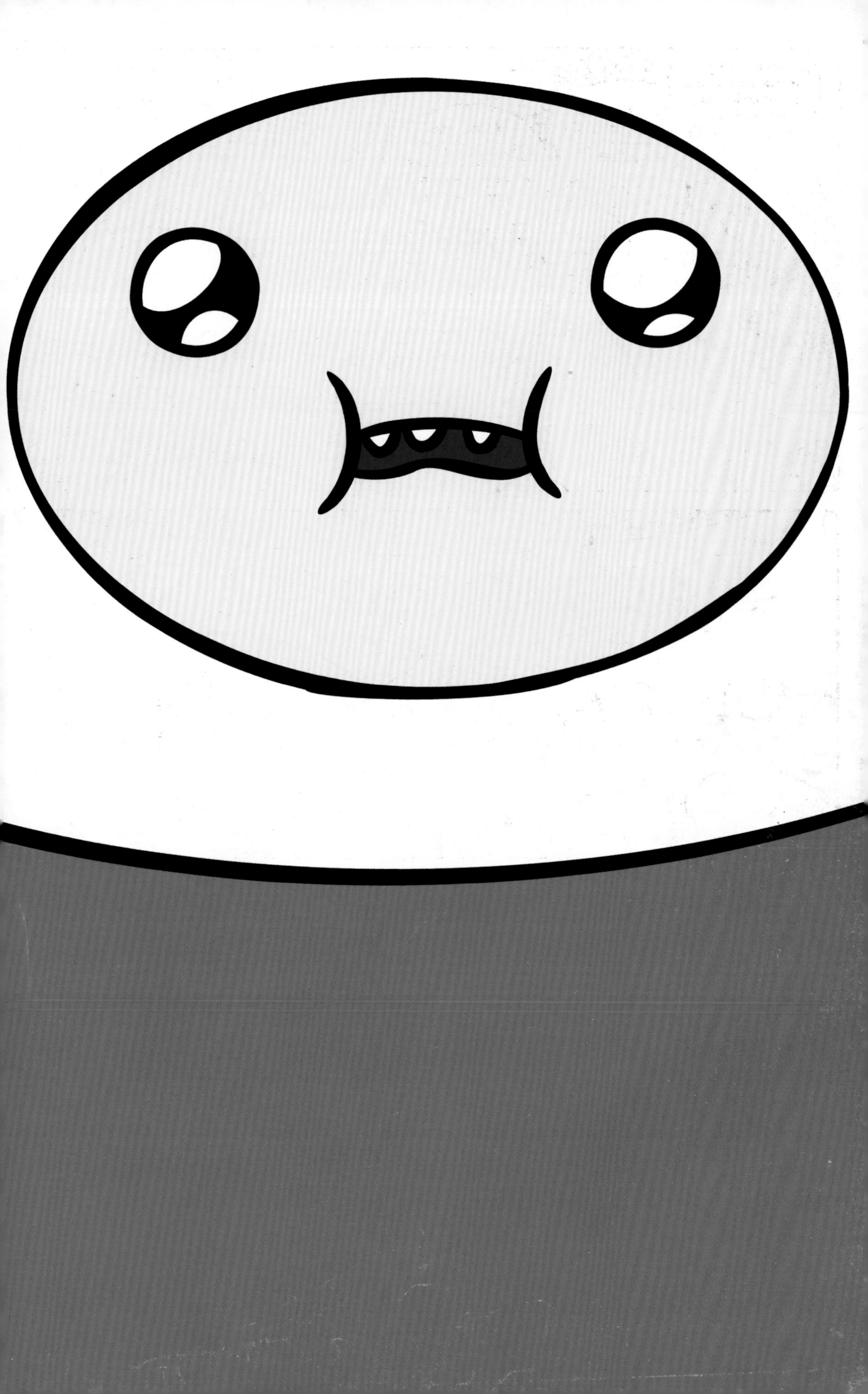

# COVER GALLERY

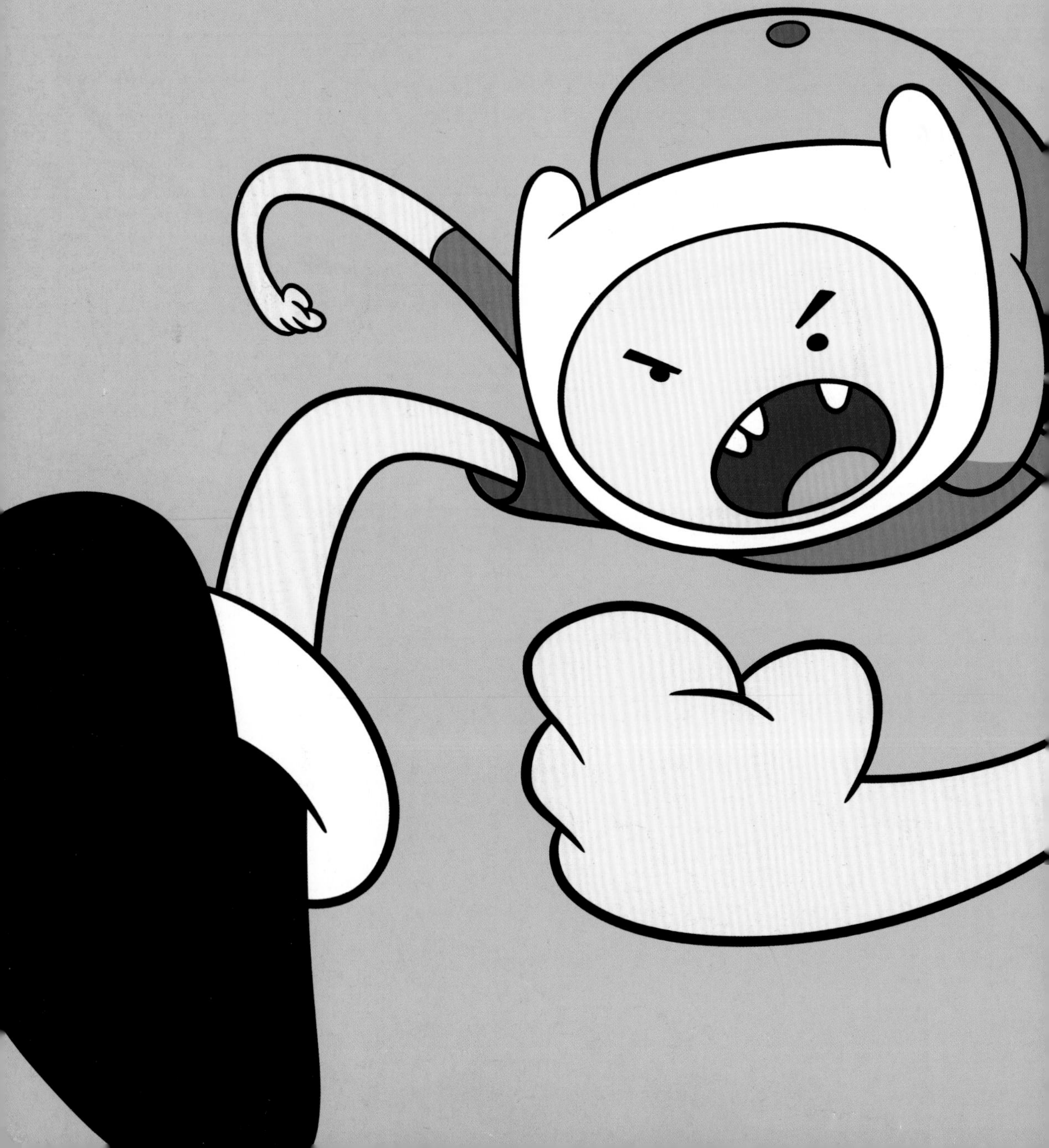

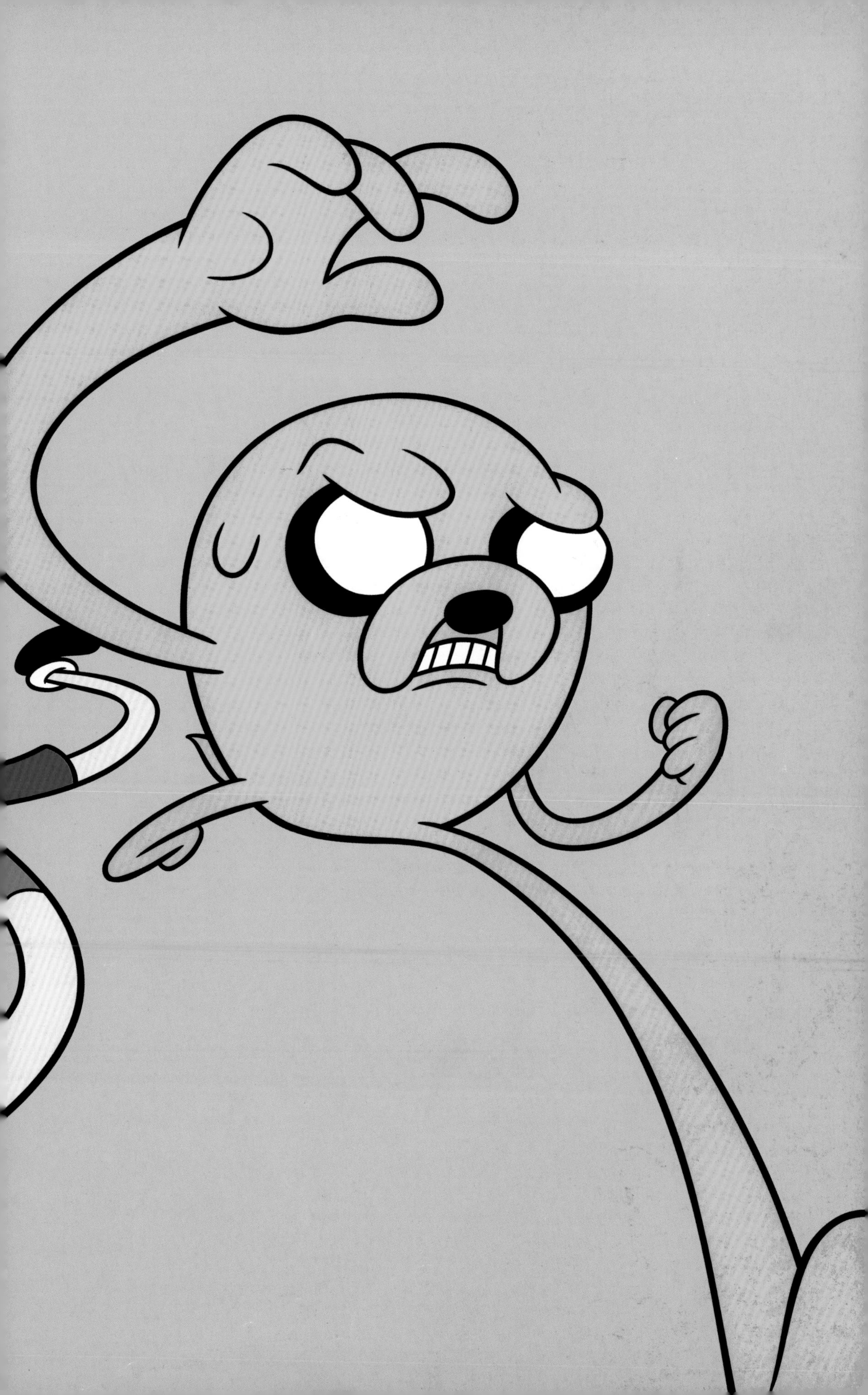

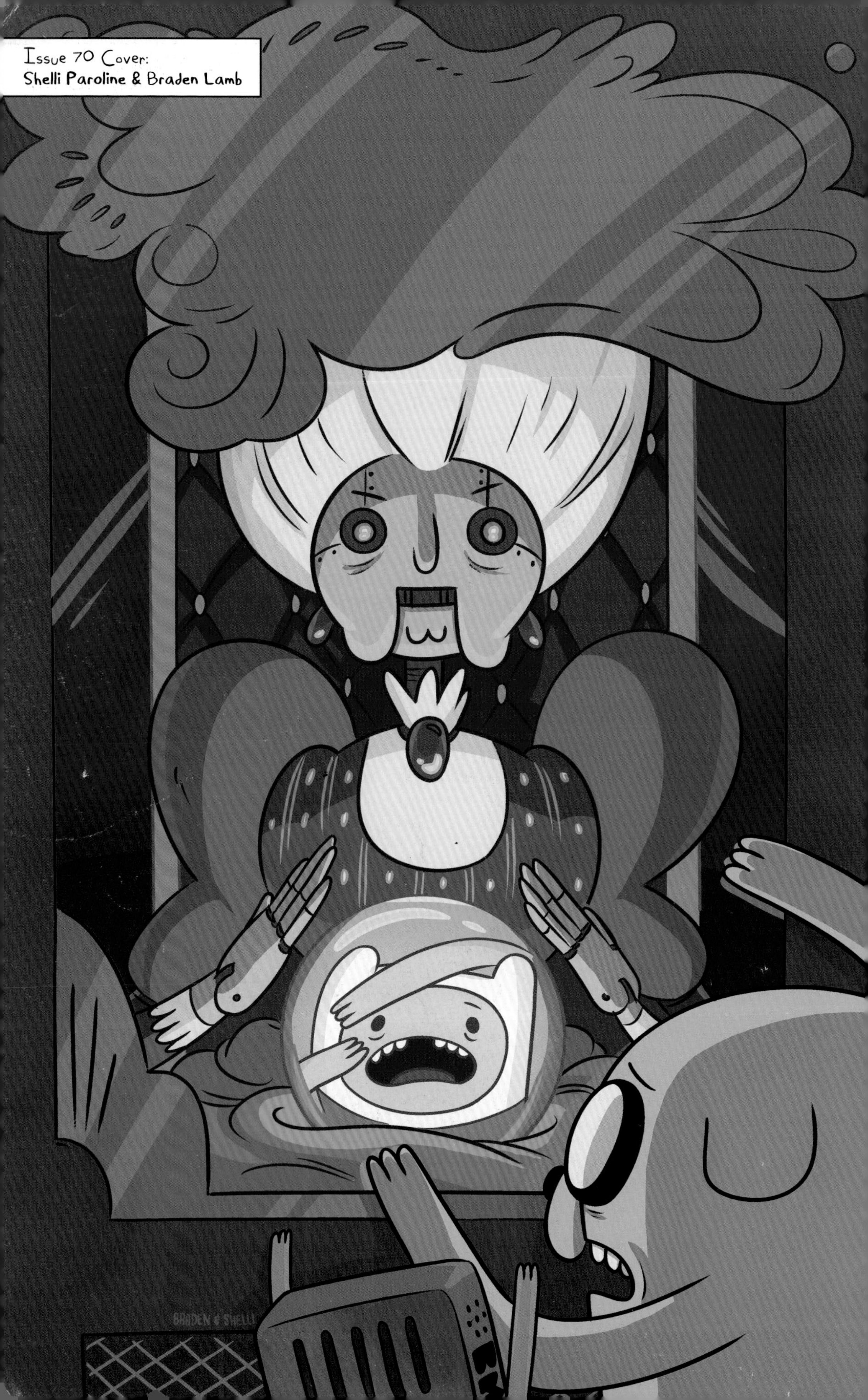
BRADEN & SHELLI

Issue 70 Cover:
Shelli Paroline & Braden Lamb

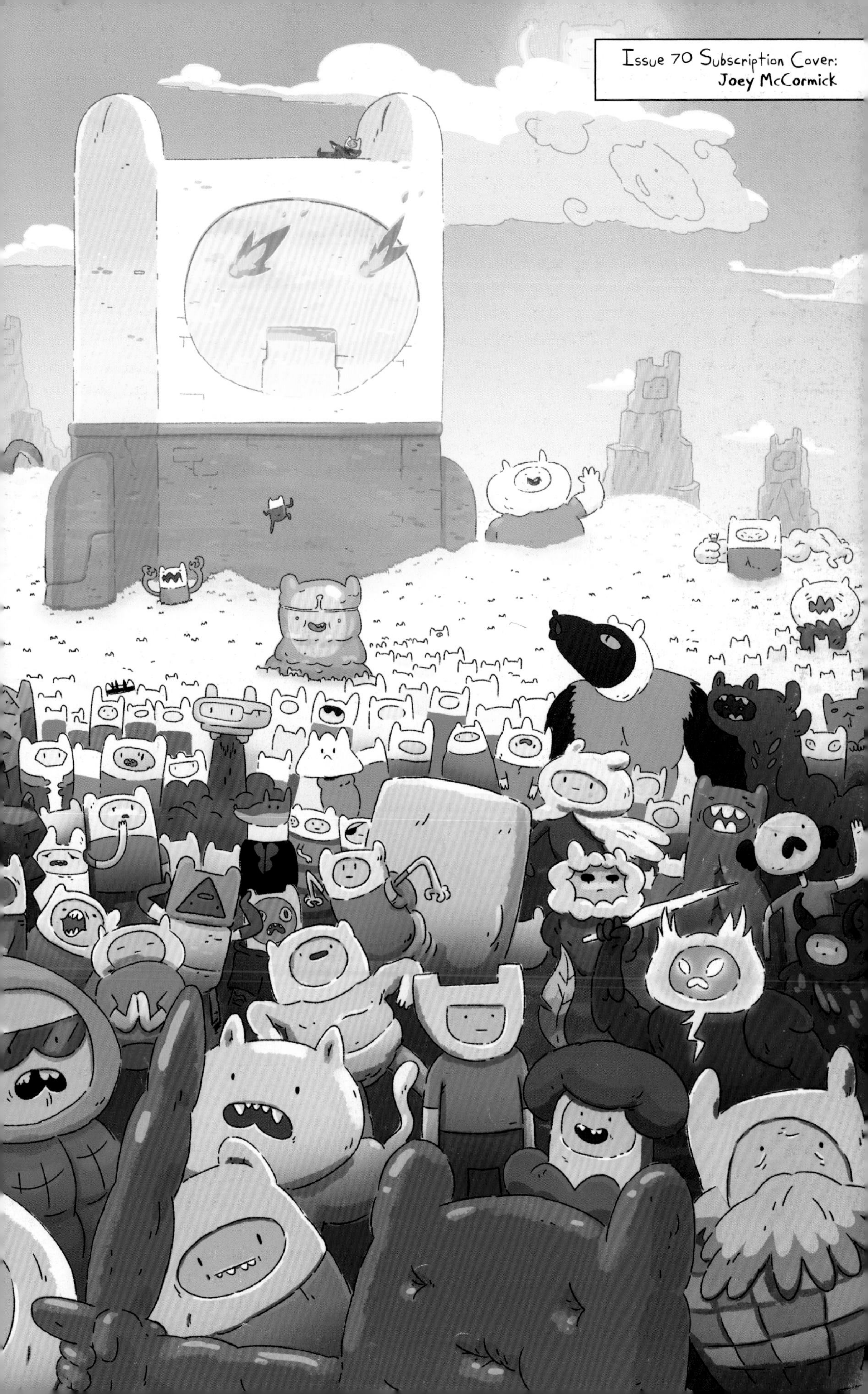

Issue 70 Subscription Cover:
Joey McCormick

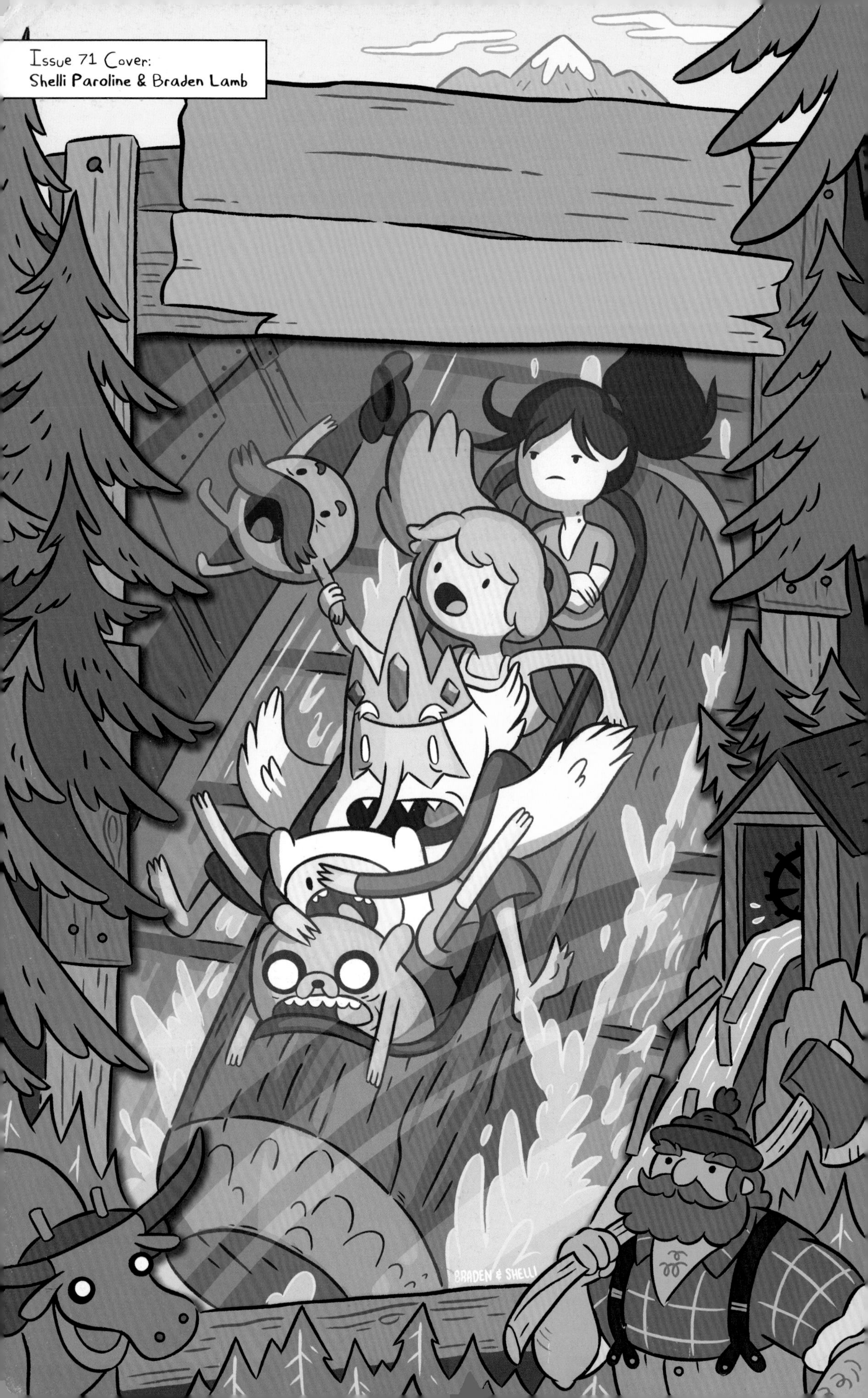
BRADEN & SHELLI

Issue 71 Cover:
Shelli Paroline & Braden Lamb

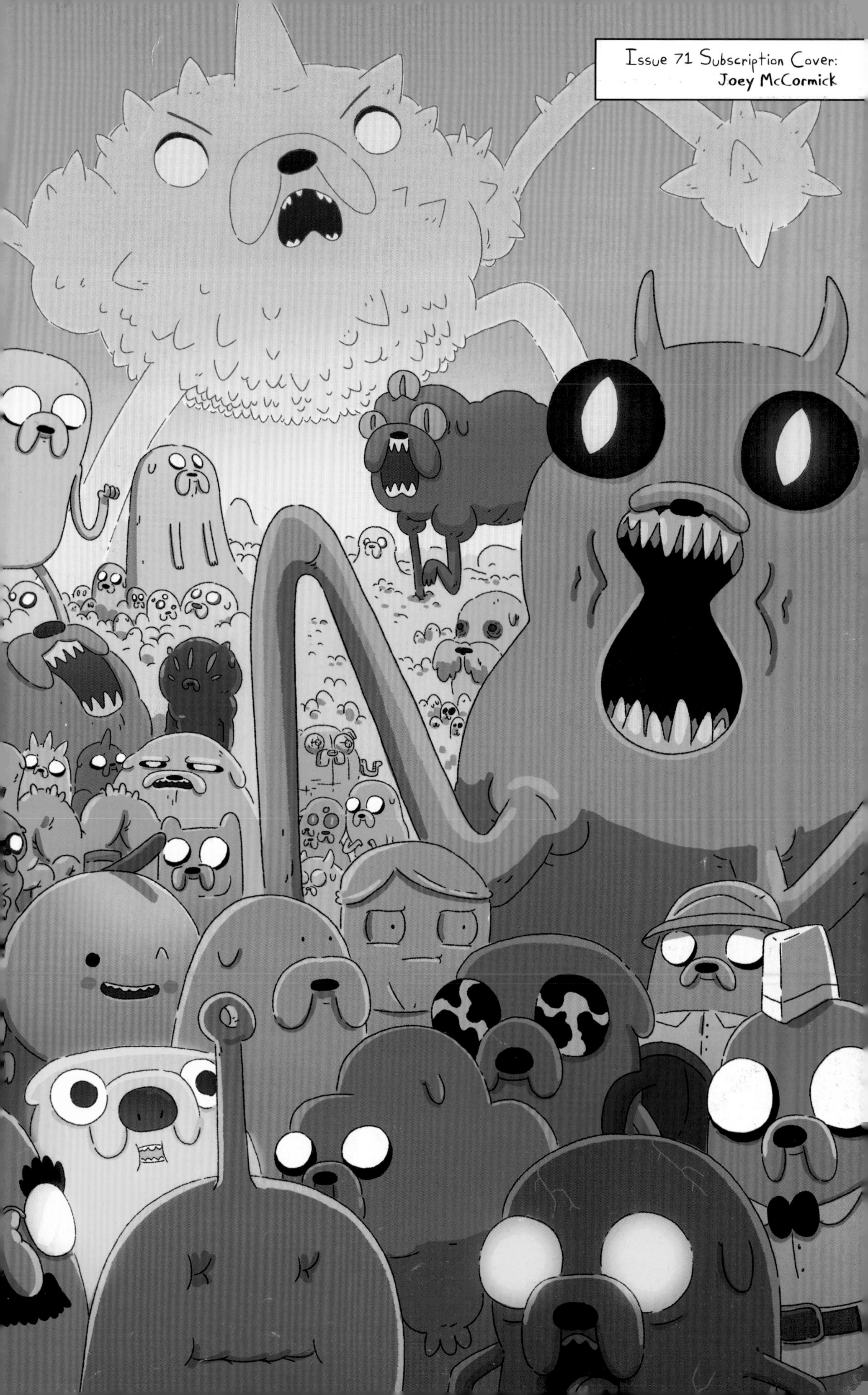
Issue 71 Subscription Cover:
Joey McCormick

Issue 72 Cover:
Shelli Paroline & Braden Lamb

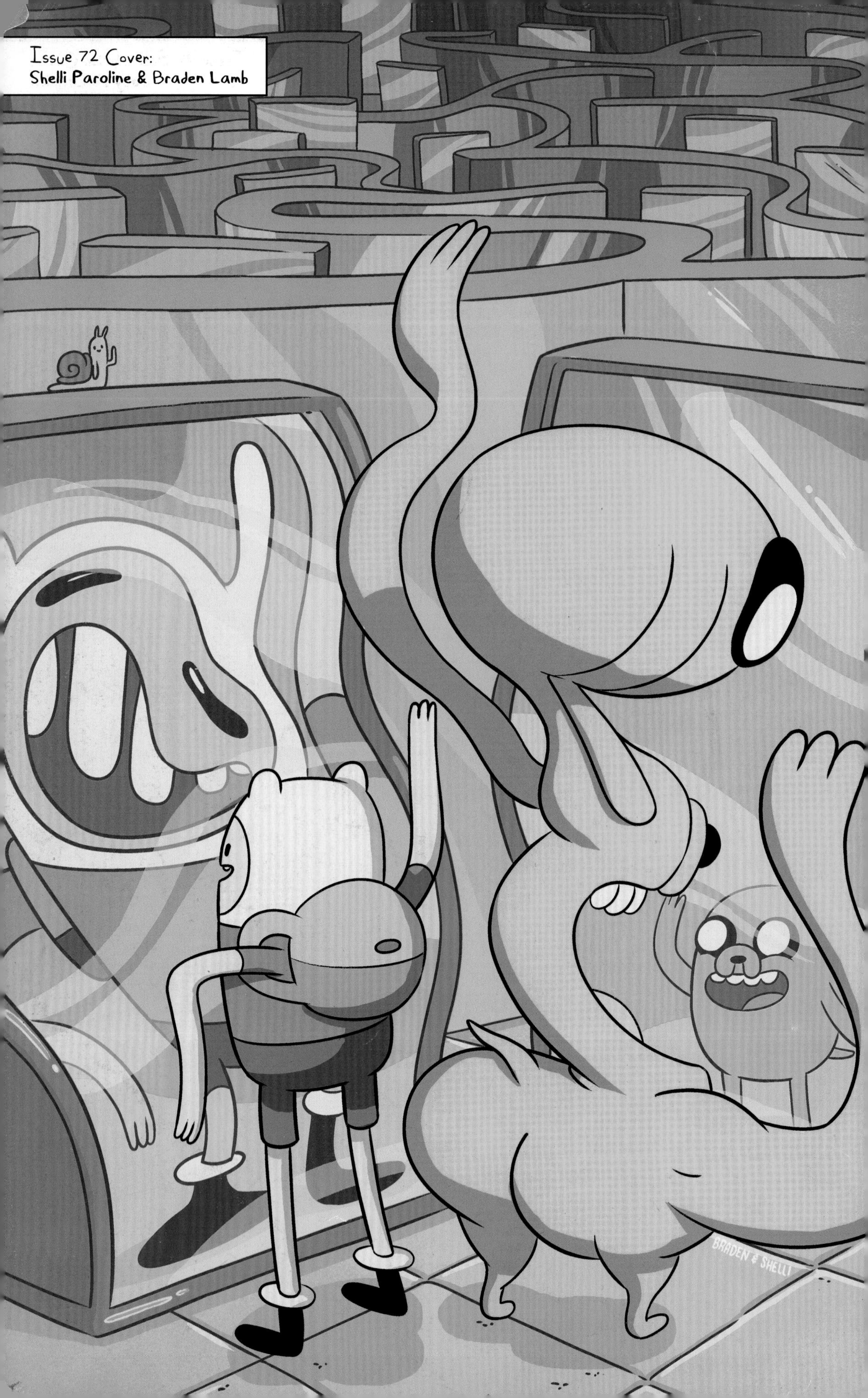
BRADEN & SHELLI

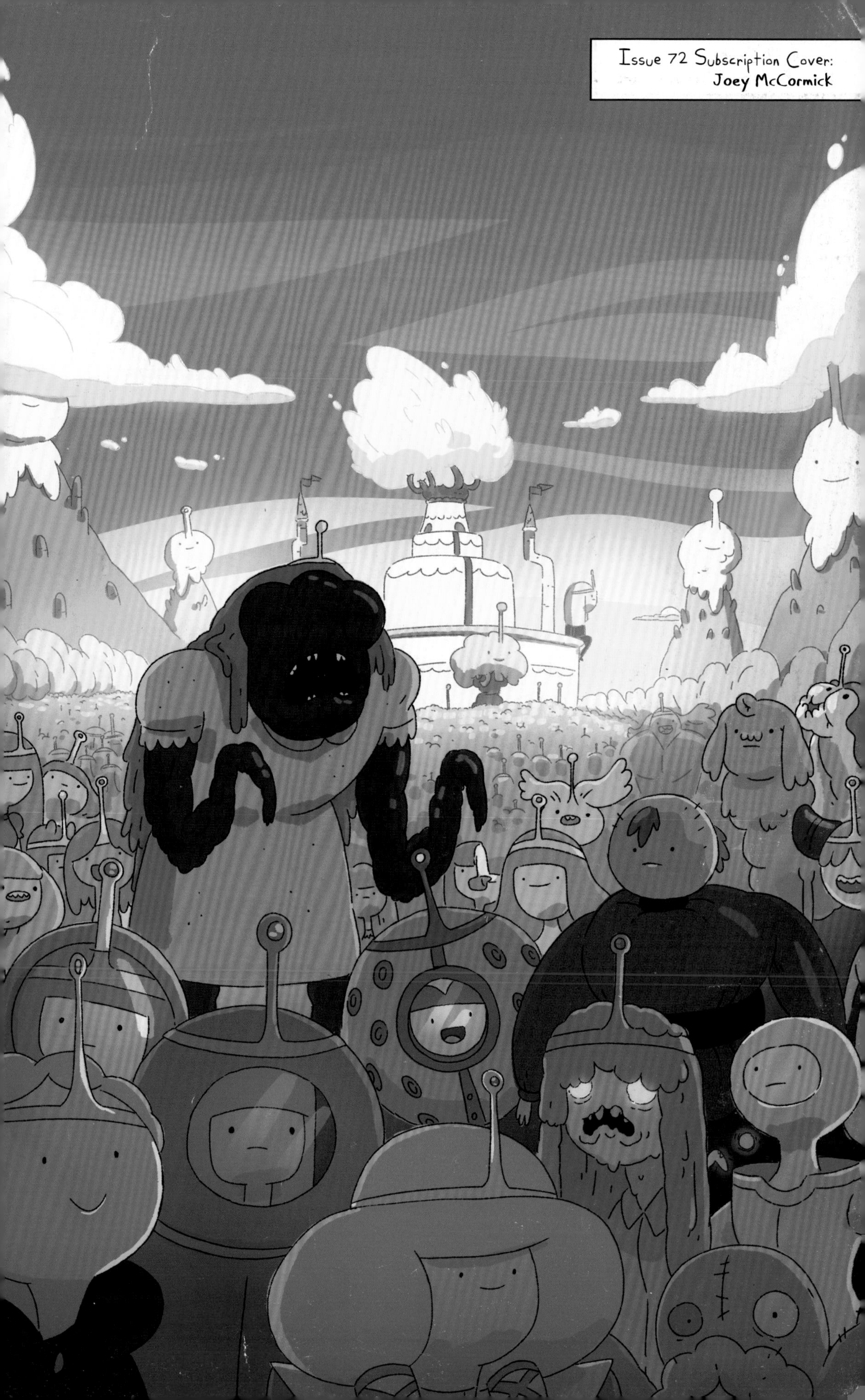

Issue 72 Subscription Cover:
Joey McCormick

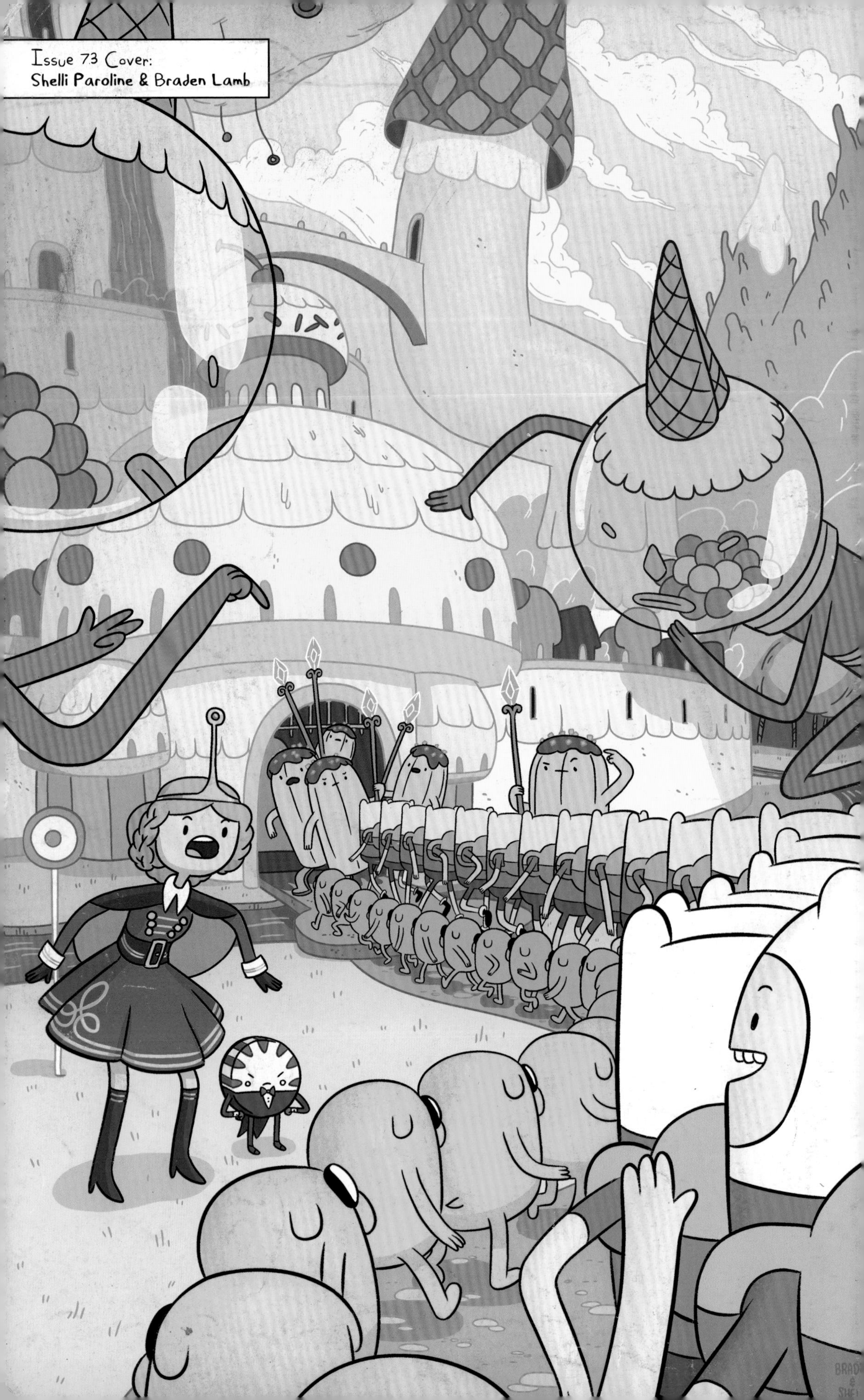

Issue 73 Cover:
Shelli Paroline & Braden Lamb

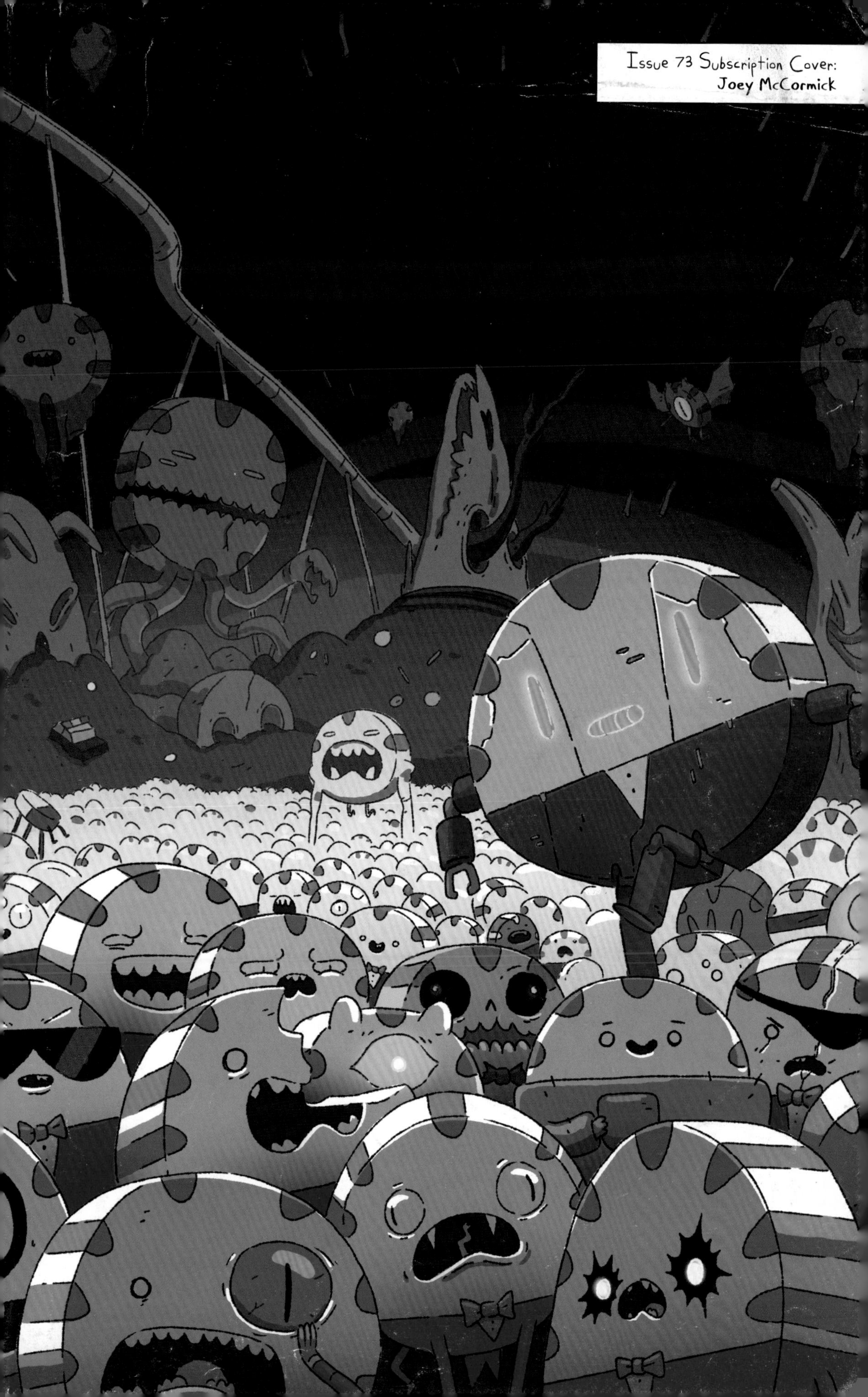

Issue 73 Subscription Cover:
Joey McCormick

# DISCOVER MORE
# ADVENTURE TIME

**Adventure Time: Islands OGN**
ISBN: 978-1-60886-972-5 | $9.99

---

**Adventure Time**
**Sugary Shorts**

**Volume 1**
ISBN: 978-1-60886-361-7 | $19.99

**Volume 2**
ISBN: 978-1-60886-774-5 | $19.99

**Volume 3**
ISBN: 978-1-68415-030-4 | $19.99

**Volume 4**
ISBN: 978-1-68415-122-6 | $19.99

---

**Adventure Time:**
**Marceline & the Scream Queens**
ISBN: 978-1-60886-313-6 | $19.99

**Adventure Time: Fionna & Cake**
ISBN: 978-1-60886-338-9 | $19.99

**Adventure Time: Candy Capers**
ISBN: 978-1-60886-365-5 | $19.99

**Adventure Time: The Flip Side**
ISBN: 978-1-60886-456-0 | $19.99

**Adventure Time:**
**Banana Guard Academy**
ISBN: 978-1-60886-486-7 | $19.99

**Adventure Time:**
**Marceline Gone Adrift**
ISBN: 978-1-60886-770-7 | $19.99

**Adventure Time:**
**Fionna & Cake Card Wars**
ISBN: 978-1-60886-799-8 | $19.99

**Adventure Time: Ice King**
ISBN: 978-1-60886-920-6 | $19.99

**Adventure Time/Regular Show**
ISBN: 978-1-68415-166-0 | $19.99

ADVENTURE TIME
ISLANDS

ADVENTURE TIME
SUGARY SHORTS

ADVENTURE TIME
PRESENTS
MARCELINE
AND THE SCREAM QUEENS

ADVENTURE TIME
with FIONNA & CAKE

ADVENTURE TIME
ICE KING

A CARTOON NETWORK ORIGINAL
ADVENTURE TIME
×
REGULAR SHOW

kaboom!
A BOOM! Studios Imprint

**AVAILABLE AT YOUR LOCAL COMICS SHOP AND BOOKSTORE**

WWW.BOOM-STUDIOS.COM

CARTOON NETWORK.